Ed lives in Essex, England with his greatest inspirations, his wife and daughters.

A lifetime love of the outdoors and six years in the army have left their mark and he spends much of his time itching to be far away from the tarmac of town and surrounded by trees, which might just come across in his writing.

Blessed with an outdoorsy soul mate and two adventurous, nature~loving girls, the opportunity to get out there and do just that is never far away...

Acknowledgements.

I'd like to offer my huge and heartfelt thanks to the following people:
To my wife… for her support and patience while I dreamed up this whole mad thing,
to my daughters… for putting up with all the spoilers as I tested chapters out on my future audience,
and to Chrissie… my faery~loving reader of proofs, for spotting all the wrongs I thought were right!

Love,
Ed.
x x x x

For Squishy, Twinkle
and my very own Flo.

Always.

× × ×

To Lisa,

Thanks for joining Team Lex!
I hope you enjoy it as much as I did!

Ed x

Any similarities to places or persons real or imagined, alive or dead, human or faery is sometimes purely coincidental... and sometimes not.

Just Flow with it.

Chapter List

Prologue ~ The Legend
A Secret Unearthed
The Long Awaited Day
Daisy
Across The Water
Arrival
An Invitation
Borson House
An Offer From Luke Borson
The Wisdom Of A Child
Shanklin
Confirmation
A Message From Freya Redfin
The First Step
A Cavern And A Cave
D.O.W.T.
Time's Up
A Card And Some Presents
Vindication
Quality Time
Goodbye
Introductions
Explanations
Know Your Enemy
Key Evidence
True Colours
Escape
Dinner Plans
Showtime
New Perspective
Click
Shared Advice
Carpe Diem
Sentries
Recon
Tricked
Trapped
Suspicions
Surprising Ally
The Main Event
Sacrifice
Understanding
Words From Beyond
Parting Gift
Epilogue ~ The New Alternative

Prologue - The Legend

*'White grief and bitter loss abound,
By a Broken Soul, Nine Keys are found;
To wake the Aft from crystal ground,
And free the Veil to feed unbound.'*

Excerpt of verse from the legend scroll.
Circa 13,000 BC
(Earth contemporary calendar)
2,241 AH
(Age of Harmony)

The Spark conceived the universe and with the final flourish of an artist signing their name on a finished canvas, life Flowed. For billions of years the beautiful cycle of birth, life and death continued until life became self aware, recognizing the wonders around it.

As life evolved, it became conscious of the Flow within every living thing and worship was born. After millennia of worship and learning, it was understood that the Spark created life, life Flowed and after living things died, the Veil reabsorbed Flow back to the Source to be used again.

In an unassuming corner of this miraculous universe, two worlds shared this knowledge... Lux and Earth. They lived in peace and took moral responsibility for the state of Flow in the universe. It was a time of grand enlightenment and joy.

Then, in 2,241 AH came the Legend.

It foretold that following a time of great loss, the Pit would be opened on Earth by a Broken Soul using Nine Keys. This event would somehow warp the basic nature of the Veil, compelling it not just to absorb *surplus* Flow, but to actively feed on *all* Flow until all that remained of the universe was a lifeless void.

Although it had been laid down in the dreams and visions of the most highly respected spiritual leaders of both Lux and Earth, few believed the threat. In many people's eyes, the Legend's wording was vague at best. In this time of absolute harmony, the masses simply did not accept the idea of a universe without life.

Time marched on and with neither race abusing their connection to the Flow, this happy reality may have continued indefinitely if not for an evolutionary design flaw. Humans were capable of greed.

It manifested over millennia, humanity's soul worn down as a cliff face is worn away by the tide. Following in greed's footsteps, lies, distrust and cruelty increased day by day, creeping inch by inch, infecting and spreading through hearts and minds. These unfamiliar traits chipped away at the friendship the two worlds had shared for so long and travel between Lux and Earth lessened and finally ceased.

This Great Divide dispelled all remaining doubt in the Legend. The harmony that had existed before was gone and everything the Legend warned of seemed all too possible.

Lux's culture faltered, its people living in fear of what might come and humans were left to their own devices for countless generations, believed by many to be beyond help. On the human world, this abandonment only succeeded in making matters worse while man steadily poisoned his heart and his home.

Special places were forgotten, crumbling and fading into landscapes, their purpose only to be guessed at. Humanity, busying itself with wealth and power and the 'mastery' of nature, allowed its absent friends to drift into the realms of folklore and myth.

But no apocalypse came and slowly, fear was replaced by new hope and determination.

It was agreed unanimously that Legend aside, it was Lux's moral duty to help humanity back from the darkness. If the Great Divide was *not* the time of loss the Legend foretold and if they still had time to act, then act they would.

The Department of Off World Travel was founded and passage via the ancient routes between the two worlds began again, not to share cultural and spiritual knowledge this time, but quite simply to heal humanity's soul.

To bring positive change, a new breed of traveller was needed. The ambassadors of the past were replaced by an energetic and happy young generation charged with the task of saving humanity and bettering the universe and they revelled in it.

It was hoped that D.O.W.T.'s plan would work...

It was hoped that humanity's connection to the Flow could be restored...

It was hoped that humans and faeries could share destinies once again.

A Secret Unearthed

The huge oak tree stood at the head of the chine looking out over the choppy sea, a mighty guardian that had stood watch over this stretch of coastline for hundreds of years.

Its branches and nooks had witnessed the births, lives and deaths of countless creatures and it loved each one as a parent loves their children. Brimming with its own life and that of those it sheltered, it had purpose here. It was happy.

In exchange for the chine's pure flowing water and rich, fertilized soil the oak and its fellow trees gave protection and sustenance to the wildlife that called this place home. In the height of summer, the chine was cool and shady and even in the worst of the wind and rain, it was shielded, safe and calm. It was a timeless, bustling bubble of life.

Today though, the oak's very roots ached at the approach of a storm, the way the elderly feel the first chill of winter in their joints. Its leaves and branches shivered in anticipation as ever-worsening gusts of wind blew in from a sea topped with white horses.

Above, the angry clouds boiled in the sky high up where the winds were worst, their dark greys and blacks an omen of what was to come.

As if taking its cue from an almighty thunder clap, the skies opened and the rain tore down in large, heavy droplets, combining with the harsh wind to drive powerful sheets against the coast, lashing the trees and bushes and forcing the last few animals out in the open to scurry for cover, instantly drenched.

Lost leaves became twigs and twigs became branches as the storm pounded the island, leaving even the sheltered chine blasted and sodden.

The animals hid in their burrows and dens, warm and safe in their homes. Though scared, they felt protected from the elements screeching outside and looked forward to the sun of the following day and whatever gifts of food the storm had deposited on their doorstep. Even at its most destructive, nature *always* provided. That was the way of things. It took… but it also gave. They huddled with their young, grateful for their lives here.

The oak sensed the loss of one of its own kind now and then as they were torn from the ground, disconnected and carried away into the dark night to meet their doom and it grieved for them. Not all of them had its strength and could only grip the earth for so long against the weather's onslaught.

A little way off, the cliff edge at the mouth of the chine suddenly dropped out of sight as it collapsed, taking with it grass and wildflowers and a small tree. The oak lost contact with its friend as the smaller tree's roots were ripped away like cut telephone lines. The old tree had mingled roots with the younger since it had germinated here and had felt it growing strong and healthy all its life… and in an instant it was gone.

The waves were now powerful enough to reach the head of the chine where they smashed, churning and frothing, before they retreated in readiness for the next barrage. They crashed in again and again, washing further up the chine as the storm worsened, collapsing the sides as they advanced. Bushes and trees and burrows were lost and the oak lost friend after friend as the storm raged on.

It seemed the old tree would be the only one left standing, the only one strong enough to hold fast against the weather. It was not to be.

There was a deep shudder in the ground and the area around it was suddenly gone, tonnes of earth and rock and life tumbling and crashing into the chine below. The damage to the oak was enormous and instant. As the ground fell away, it ripped more than half of the trees roots with it, leaving the remainder torn and exposed like severed nerves.

It was an injury not even the old giant could bear. It lurched forward and jerked to a halt, angled towards the beach, a terrified owl taking flight from it amid a cloud of spray as it fell. Unable to take the unnatural movement, a mighty bough broke off with a terrible, splintering crack and crashed down into the seething cauldron below. The enormous branch landed in an explosion of water and leaves, the pulverizing waves showing it no mercy as it was dragged out to sea in a mass of foam.

The devastating waves continued their assault, denying the oak what weak grip it had left and finally, inevitably, the old tree fell. It crashed and splintered its way into the bowl formed by the waves at the head of the chine and the power of the swells wasted no time in stripping it of its leaves and branches until it was barely recognizable as the beautiful living thing it had been.

As Flow ebbed from the oak, it felt a new emotion. Fear. Its roots had been in the ground for many years and had reached deep into the Earth. It had found interesting things and strange things… and a secret thing.

From sapling to tree, the oak had kept the secret, hidden it from plant and animal, covering the ways to it with its thick roots, certain that the world was protected. But now, in the stripped head of the chine, was a hole. An entrance.

Animals who had been left homeless by the devastation outside ran in panic into the safety of this new refuge, glad to be out of the bludgeoning wind and rain.

A badger trundled along the tunnel in his customary 'I'll get there in the end' fashion and emerged into the chamber he found at the end. Lightning flashed powerfully outside, its light reaching down the tunnel, catching the crystalline floor of the cavern and offering him glimpses of this new space as he plodded towards its centre. He shook rain from his fur and snuffled on, looking decidedly unimpressed with this temporary replacement for the smashed ruins of his warm sett.

He paused for a moment, confused… and died. No injury, no pain, no fuss, he just stopped being alive. Other animals who had followed him in also began to fall and the floor of the chamber was soon littered with the bodies of several creatures.

As the realization of what was happening set in, the animals who had made it into the cavern but not yet crossed its floor panicked. A small scale stampede ensued as they raced back the way they had come, more willing to face the dangers of the storm than the unknown horror inside.

As the sounds of scrambling paws faded, a jagged fork of lightning flashed outside the tunnel, illuminating the lifeless forms of those who had been taken, but these meager offerings had done only what was necessary to *wake* the strange phenomenon.

Energy swirled deep within the crystal beneath the still warm bodies.

If it was to reach full potential, it would need more. Much more.

The Long Awaited Day

"TC's all wet Mummy!" called Willow from the kitchen.

She was making the family's pet cat his meat and crunch breakfast. TC curled around her legs expectantly, looking up at her with his big, green, slow blinky eyes and handsome whiskers... and wet fur.

Mum, who had just got up, walked into the kitchen. "There's a goood boooy!" she said, bending down to scratch TC behind his ear and feeling how wet he was. "Urgh, he is wet! Enjoy the storm last night, did we?"

Mum held open the cupboard door for Willow to throw the empty cat food sachet in the bin and gave her a good morning kiss.

"I let him in at about half six this morning... mewing at the window he was." Mock-frowning at him, Mum continued, "I swear that cat thinks people don't need sleep."

She knelt down again to stroke their other cat, the indoor-loving and much drier, Jazz.

"Morning, sweet pea," she said, as Jazz mewed loudly at her. "Sort your boyfriend out, will you?"

"He should've been inside in the dry with us monkeys," Dad said, scratching his head and yawning sleepily as he joined them.

"Wife..." he said as he kissed Mum loudly. "Blondie..." he said to Willow, kissing her on the top of her head.

Filling up the coffee percolator with water, he got a filter ready and switched it on.

"Mmm, coffee," said Mum as it started making its usual plopping noises. "Just what I need. That thunder and lightning was terrible. Kept me up far too long." She hugged Dad, laying her head on his chest sleepily.

"Is lightning faeries? I like faeries; they're shiny," announced Lea, walking into the kitchen in search of people.

Mum reached out and stroked her red hair, wishing for what seemed the millionth time that everybody could be blessed with an imagination as vivid as hers.

"Morning, sweetheart. Nice hair," joked Dad, smiling at the shock of just-woken-up bed-hair and bending down to kiss Lea on her rosy, pre-puckered lips.

"Thank you, Daddy," she replied, giving him a big smile before going to Mum for a cuddle.

Mum gave her a hug, then reached for the radio on the windowsill to click it on.

"… ight and the south coast of England the worst hit. Similarities to an equally devastating storm in the sixties have led weather experts to speculate that the Isle of Wight in particular is being afflicted by a fifty year storm cycle, although some are denying the claims due to a lack of reliable historical evidence. The Isle of Wight Tourist Board gives assurances that all travel routes are running smoothly today and there is no cause for concern, although this will do little to aid local residents as the clear-up begins in earnest this morning. This is Peter Orr, for Essex FM."

This was *not* the sort of news report you wanted to hear on the very morning you were going on holiday there.

Mum pulled a face. "Great," she said, unhappily. "I'll give the ferry company and the campsite a ring; make sure we can still go."

The percolator had finished bubbling.

"OK, love, good idea. I'll bring you a coffee," said Dad. He turned quickly to the girls. "Who's hungry then?" he asked loudly and a barrage of 'Me! Me! Me!' echoed around the kitchen.

"We've got a really nice breakfast to set us up for the trip. Can anybody guess what I'm having?"

"Bacon sandwich!" Willow and Lea sang out together, grinning.

"It's like it's a first day of the holiday tradition or something. They know you so well," laughed Mum. "Girls, after we've eaten, you can help me pack the picnic stuff for lunch if you want."

Dad took Mum's coffee over to her while she was on the phone and online hoping for good news, then poured his own and a couple of juices for the girls. While they were holding an in-depth debate over the merits of different cereals, Dad carried the croissants and jam to the table for them, then started on the bacon and eggs for him and Mum. She joined them just as her egg muffin arrived.

"Mmm, thanks, love," she said, reaching for the brown sauce, giving her egg a good squirt and taking a big, hungry bite. She looked up when she realized the chatter had stopped, to the sight of three faces all staring at her expectantly. She finished her mouthful and laughed.

"Sorry! Hungry lady. Well, looks like we're still going on holiday," she told them happily, to whoops from the girls. "There've been lots of landslides on the south coast but the ferries in the north are OK. Ours between Portsmouth and Fishbourne is running. The place is in ruins though; they're clearing downed trees and wreckage *everywhere*. Oh… and a farmer reported a cow went missing in the night."

"Ahh, the old cow missing in the middle of the night scenario. I know it well!" Dad joked, referring to the time in the army when he was so tired driving a lorry on manoeuvres that he'd hallucinated hitting a cow on the A1 in Yorkshire. When he'd got out to check, there had been no cow and no damage to the lorry to show that he'd hit one. He chuckled. "Is he sure it was ever really there?"

Mum knew the story and giggled.

"They interviewed the farmer and he said it was in the field by the cliff just before the storm started."

Willow, a confirmed lover of animals everywhere, frowned. "Don't laugh, that's not funny. That cow is lost. It might be very scared. *I* would be scared if *I* was lost."

Mum shot Dad an 'I've been told off' look and he smiled into his coffee.

"You're right sweetie," he said. "I tell you what. If we find the lost cow while we're away, we'll make sure it gets home. It can be our holiday good deed! Mummy can lasso it like a cowgirl and lead it back to the farmer."

Willow nodded in agreement. The deal was done.

"Can I lasso the cow?" asked Lea, who really rather liked the idea.

"Yes, darling, we'll all take it in turns to lasso the cow," said Dad.

The cattle wrangling was an interesting new development, but the family had been looking forward to their summer holiday for almost a year now. After what seemed to have been the slowest twelve months of their lives, the day had finally come, so they were *very* relieved to hear that they could still go and that a whole year of waiting hadn't been ruined by last night's terrible storm.

The girls were particularly excited and they chattered about what they wanted to do when they arrived and where they would go and who they would meet and what they would like to wear and eat and see.

How they came to be going on holiday to the Isle of Wight in the first place was a bit of a strange story.

They'd won a ferry crossing and a two week stay on a campsite near the southernmost tip of the island. The whole south coast was an unbroken stretch of beach from The Needles at the west tip, to Bembridge in the east. Sections of it were sandcastle friendly but other stretches were made up of either huge pebbles or large, flat plates of bedrock. Its whole length was peppered with chines, steep-sided ravines made by small rivers draining towards the sea.

The campsite they'd be staying on, Cinan Farm, took its name from the old Saxon word for chine, meaning a gap, or yawn. It had a small one called Shepherd's Chine running right through it. It sliced through the lush greenery of the campsite, its steep sides dropping sharply down to a pebbly beach at the base of some relatively high cliffs.

Cinan was a working farm with chickens, ducks and cows and there was a farm shop, a shower block and a little playground with a sandpit.

There was even an amusement park called Blackgang Chine a couple of kilometres down the road. It had the interesting habit of occasionally dropping sections of itself into the sea as the waves reclaimed another sliver of the coastline. The girls were very keen to see *that*. (The park, not so much the dropping into the sea!)

The family's itinerary was pretty full and they had plans for archery, horse riding, bike trails, coastal path hiking, a dinosaur museum, paragliding, boat trips and even a clay pigeon range. It was going to be a busy couple of weeks.

The strange thing was, neither Mum nor Dad could remember what they had done to win the tickets. Probably an online thing, Mum had thought. The letter that accompanied the tickets wasn't very helpful either. It read:

Borson House,
Undercliff Drive,
Isle of Wight,
PO38 9HX.

Mr M. & Mrs K. Raulich,
3 Luchair Crescent,
Southend-On-Sea,
Essex, SS0 0MU.

Dear Mr and Mrs Raulich,

Please accept our congratulations on your good fortune in winning the STAR PRIZE in our 'Island Life' competition!

The enclosed vouchers entitle you to a two-week holiday on the beautiful Isle of Wight, an officially designated Area of Outstanding Natural Beauty and Clear Sky Area.

Please find enclosed your Wightlink Ferries return ticket, valid for a car, driver and up to six passengers using any designated Wightlink Ferries crossing and your Cinan Farm Campsite voucher, courtesy of Borson House.

All arrangements are to be made via the relevant providers, who will advise you of any terms and conditions specific to your booking.

Please note that these tickets are strictly non-transferable and have an expiry date of one year from the date of this letter.

Congratulations once again and we hope your prize proves to be both an adventure and an opportunity to explore an exceptionally beautiful part of the world.

Wishing your family the holiday of a lifetime on our wonderful island,

Yours sincerely,

Mr L. Borson,   for and on behalf of Borson House.

There was no telephone number to ring to confirm the holiday and when they tried to find one, none was listed. Even an internet search only got them an aerial view of a country house and several references to Borson Diamonds, but that was a name synonymous with the rich and famous and unlikely to be giving away camping holidays to the Isle of Wight.

'Oh, very useful, thanks,' Mum had said to the computer screen. 'That'll come in handy if I lose one while I'm cleaning my tiara…'

She'd called the ferry company and the campsite and after reading out the serial numbers, had been assured that the tickets and voucher were genuine and had been paid for by Borson House.

They had typed a thank you letter to 'Mr L. Borson of Borson House,' confirming that they would be using their prize the following summer and had received a letter of acknowledgement that once again wished them a wonderful holiday. An unexpected letter containing a mystery gift. The sort of surprise *no one* minded getting!

Their pre-holiday breakfast was a relaxed affair and with an extra coffee or juice or two, took a good hour. When they were done and the table was cleared, Dad got on with the washing up while Mum and the girls packed the picnic lunch.

Fed and watered, the cats had taken up residence on the patio now the sun had dried it and were sprawled across each other, monitoring the sounds of showering, splashing and tooth brushing that drifted from the house.

TC raised his head briefly to lazily lick a paw, then went back to sunning himself with his girlfriend. Exhausting work, supervising humans.

Mum came out of the bedroom looking gorgeous in a white summer dress with embroidered daisies at the neck and the hem.

Dad wolf whistled. "You look lovely," he said.

Mum looked flattered. "Oh, thanks, honey. Are the brood dressed yet?"

As if on cue, Lea, red hair in pigtails and Willow, blond hair in a pony tail, came bowling out of their bedroom into the hall to show off their outfits and what they had done to each others hair.

"Do you like my hair?" asked Lea, spinning round. "I got pigtails. Willow did it."

"You look lovely sweetie," Dad answered. "Nice hair honey," he said to a smiling Willow, who was waiting patiently to be admired. "Aren't I lucky, going on holiday with you gorgeous lot? Lea… TC does *not* need a hairclip."

TC had come back in to check up on his humans. Lea, who'd knelt to stroke him, looked up cheekily, clip poised for action. Busted.

Daisy

Dad went to the hallway and pulled on his trainers. Picking up a very important set of keys from the bowl, he went outside to the garage and unlocked the doors, swinging them open wide. You could almost hear the

TA DA!

There, looking as ready for a holiday as the family, was Daisy, the Volkswagen camper. Dad had found her about two years ago while cycling home from work one afternoon, looking a very forlorn yellow and white on someone's driveway with a mobile phone number and the message

Bargain – Quick sale needed – Must go

written on a scrap of cardboard box stuck to the inside of her windscreen.

She was a 1968 four-berth bay-window model with a side-opening, pop-up roof section. Rusting, with three flat tyres and no interior, she was a shadow of her former self and in desperate need of some love and attention.

Harvey, the man who'd answered when Dad rang the doorbell, explained that she'd been taking up space in his garage since his dad passed away a few years ago and had to be sold quickly as he and his wife Carol were emigrating to Australia very soon to be closer to their family.

Dad had excitedly called Mum and she'd piled the kids into the car and met him there to have a look at her. They had always wanted to do up a VDub, but even in terrible condition they held their price, so after a long inspection, they knocked on the door again to ask Harvey and Carol the dreaded question...

'How much?'

They seemed genuinely pleased that the old camper was going to a family that wanted to fully renovate her. True to their cardboard sign, they offered them an eye-popping deal they couldn't refuse. They paid a deposit, did a receipt together and went home that night the proud owners of a new (if a bit tatty) holiday home.

Three days later, she was paid up, towed home and parked on their driveway, her four new tyres the first in a very long line of much-needed improvements. In the time since they'd bought her, there wasn't much of her that hadn't been filled, sanded, resprayed, oiled, greased, replaced or repaired somehow.

At some stage in her life, someone had replaced her dashboard with an oak panel and carved a *beautifully* intricate field of daisies into it, which helped them to decide on what wood to use for the missing interior and earned 'Daisy' her name.

They managed to find most of what they needed for the inside on eBay: units, cushions, a folding bed, a cooker, a sink and a fridge. Boot sales had helped with some of the other important bits and pieces.

The big front seat was covered in soft tan leather and in pretty good condition, so they'd colour matched all the new upholstery and curtain material to that and now there were curtains on every window so they could close up completely when they turned in for the night.

There was a double bed for the girls in the pop up roof of the camper with an open hatch and when you poked your head up there, it felt more like a den than a bedroom. On each side, there was a twelve volt socket for gadgets and a clicky pull-cord light so they could read before they went to sleep.

There were a couple of mains sockets in the living area and on the bit of the roof that didn't pop up at the back, there were two boot-sale bargain ex-marine solar panels hinged to a new luggage rack. They charged a powerful leisure battery so they didn't end up flattening the main battery at night.

There was even a DVD player for long journeys or rainy days.

They'd done a fantastic job. With her new turquoise bodywork, matching striped pop up roof and chrome trim, she looked very slick indeed. The turquoise paint job had been Mum's idea and was a tad more holiday friendly than Dad's ex-army influenced suggestion of olive green. The new turquoise and white-striped canvas for the pop up roof had taken a while to find, but was definitely worth the wait... she was a stunner.

So it was with a feeling of great pride that Dad started Daisy and pulled her out of the garage, through the gates and on to the road. He switched off the engine and turned on the radio, then climbed into the back and unlocked the sliding side door.

Mum, who had heard the familiar sound of a VDub engine, had come outside and was watching from the front garden. They loaded the last few things together: the girls favourite cuddlies, the picnic for the journey and a backpack, then stepped back and surveyed Daisy.

Done. All packed up with enough camping equipment, toys, clothes, food and drink for a very comfortable fortnight of glamping. She'd been on a few day trips and camping weekends, but this was to be her first proper holiday since they'd finished her.

"You love it, don't you," stated Mum.

"Yeah, I do," Dad said, "'bout time the old girl got to do what she was made for again. Imagine being a camper and not campering."

All the hard work bringing Daisy back to her former glory had made Mum and Dad wonder about her history. Where had her previous owners been in her and what sights had they seen on their travels? Someone had obviously loved her enough to carve that beautiful daisy scene for her dashboard and probably still talked about the camper they used to have.

So, to mark Daisy's reincarnation Mum had bought a journal to tell the story of her adventures. Her time as a builder's van with Harvey's dad, her years resting in his garage and their first few short trips were already in it. They'd left the first ten pages blank, just in case they ever met a previous owner and had the chance to learn something about her past. It was impossible to imagine they would ever sell her, but if they did, they'd pass on Daisy's diary to her new owner to carry on the story.

"That's it then; all packed. All we need now is a couple of kids and we're set. Got any?" joked Dad.

"I think there might be two inside that like camping... will they do?"

"Do you mean us, Mum?" said Willow, who had come out to join them, holding Lea's hand.

Even the furry friends had come along for a look, which was no real surprise as they followed the children about like shadows much of the time anyway.

"Yeah, unless you want to stay here and look after TC and Jazz with Clive. You know it'll be boys' nights in watching David Attenborough though... wanna stay?"

Willow shook her head, smiling. She liked Mum and Dad's friend Clive, who was cat sitting for them while they were away, but miss a camping holiday? Not likely.

Lea saw the opportunity for a pretend drama. "I don't wanna do a boys' night!" she wailed, then giggled.

"Oh, alright then, we'll take these two!" said Dad and swept the giggling one into his arms, blowing a raspberry on her neck amid lots of squealing and wriggling. "Let's go!"

TC padded over to the front gate and looked expectantly down the street first one way, then the other, as though he had understood the names 'Clive' and 'David Attenborough.'

Dad belted the two very excited children into their seats in the camper while Mum went back to lock up the bungalow. With a note left for Clive, who had picked up the front door keys the night before and a couple of interested felines looking on from the gate, Mum joined Dad at the open camper door and gave him a hug.

Lea poked Willow and pointed at them and they both chirped, "Ooo la la!" together.

Dad blew a big raspberry at them, reducing them to giggles and slid the side door closed with Mum laughing in his ear.

"Excited?" she asked.

"Yeah… and relieved. It's been a long time coming. I can hardly believe it's today. I had a really horrible dream last night as well. Faeries trapped in jam jars… and I couldn't undo the lids to let 'em out."

Mum frowned, "Faeries in jam jars? Been eating cheese before bed again?"

Dad laughed. "Yeah! Loads of 'em there were, like little fireflies. What with that and the storm, I didn't sleep too well after that."

"Ahh, you need a holiday," she teased.

They gave the cats a last fuss.

"See you soon furries," said Dad, giving them both a good scratch behind the ears, "look after Clive for us."

TC blinked slowly at him in reply.

"Look at him," said Mum, "I *swear* he understands every word. You can see it in his eyes."

'*Almost every word,*' thought TC.

They climbed in, shut the doors and Mum turned to the girls. "Ready?"

They nodded enthusiastically.

"Hokey dokey then!"

She put on her sunglasses, started Daisy and they pulled away from the bungalow to the cheery, bubbling sound of her engine, laughing and chatting as sunlight flashed and glinted on shiny chrome bumpers. They were off!

Across The Water

Four and a half hours, one minor traffic delay, a couple of driver swaps and lots of singing later…

They pulled in to the ferry port with forty five minutes to spare and after being guided to the head of a numbered lane ready for driving onto the ferry, Dad jumped out of the camper and headed for the restaurant building for posh coffees.

As she and her little helpers unpacked the cold bag that held the picnic, Mum marvelled at the benefits of having a camper with a dining table.

When Dad came back, lunch was waiting and Mum and the girls were engrossed in a game of ferry port I-spy: ferry, caravan, water, cars and flag had already been covered and he'd arrived just in time for another 'C.'

"Coffee!" he said brightly, as he leant in the open side door, putting the coffees down amid the cheese and ham sandwiches, bottled water, cherry tomatoes, crisps and grapes.

"Nice," said Mum, "like your style!"

The game was temporarily abandoned for lunch and they tucked in gratefully, chatting about the crossing. While they were eating they watched the comings and goings of the busy port. There were lots of smiley faces here today. It was August, the height of the school summer holidays and the loading lanes were soon full.

As the last of the vehicles driving off the ferry trundled past, fluorescent-vest-clad staff took up positions at the front of the queues and started waving vehicles on board.

Leaving the ladies in comfort at the dining table, Dad jumped into the front seat, started Daisy and drove slowly forward, heading for the lady that was waving them over. They reached the metal lip that bridged the gap between the quayside and the ferry and bumped over it with a

CLANK CLANK

on to the vehicle deck. Another crew member guided them into position and after pointing out the stairwell to the passenger area, went back to directing drivers into place.

They went upstairs and found the viewing deck, a big room with a drinks bar, enclosed by floor to ceiling windows. The girls ran down the length of it and found a table. They managed a full thirty seconds of taking in their new surroundings before the inevitable, 'Can we go outside?'

Smiling at their excitement, Mum and Dad followed them out onto the warm deck, grateful for the cool coastal breeze that tempered the summer heat.

When the last of the vehicles and foot passengers were aboard, vibrations shivered through the metal decking as the tailgate came up and the low rumble of the ferry's engines kicked up a notch to a loud growl. Their transport eased itself away from the quayside and out to sea.

They watched the mainland recede for a while, then turned their attention to their destination. Now facing south, the blazing fireball of the sun sparkled dazzlingly on the water as they looked across the Solent.

By the time they reached open water halfway between the mainland and the island, the cool breeze had turned decidedly cold, but they weren't concerned with that. It was the spectacle before them that had their attention.

Where they lived in Southend, if the conditions were right you could look out over the Thames estuary upon a crystal-clear Kent. It was like that here today, but *vastly* more impressive. The island was in startlingly sharp focus and both it and every sailboat between here and there seemed to jump out at them in the finest detail, as though magnified somehow. It was incredible and bizarre in equal measure.

Camera wielding tourists were lined up along the bow rails, snapping away happily to capture the peculiar effect. As Dad joined them, Mum called up to one of the crew on the bridge, who was also taking pictures. "Nice to see you still enjoy the view!"

He smiled down to her and pointed at the island. "That's quite special even for us. I've *never* seen it *that* clear and I've been across... well, once or twice now," he joked.

Willow and Lea were filling their time well. Someone had dug out the remains of a bag of leftover lunch cheese puffs from their backpack and the two of them were busy flicking them into the air from their palms for the cawing seagulls that followed the ferry. The girls giggled and pointed as the large birds swooped and squabbled with each other.

Willow suddenly froze, gasping mid-giggle. "DOLPHINS!" she shouted with a huge smile.

Everyone on deck rushed over to her side and peered over excitedly, to be treated to the sight of four sleek, shiny fins breaking the surface and submerging at intervals as they kept pace with the ferry.

"Wow!" said Mum, "we've got an escort to the other side!"

They watched the members of the playful pod crisscrossing each other and darting in and out of the ferry's wake until they broke away a little way off from Fishbourne Harbour. As the ferry slowed and docked, the tannoy crackled to life.

"Would ALL vehicle passengers please make their way to the vehicle deck. ALL vehicle passengers to the vehicle deck. Thank you."

After making their way through their fellow travellers to the lower level, the four of them climbed back into Daisy and she purred into life. When it was their turn, they drove off the ferry and headed out of the harbour, wondering what adventures the island had in store for them.

Just for the time being, ignorance was most definitely bliss.

Arrival

They drove to the campsite along hot, windless, sun-dappled country lanes. The trees on either side met in the middle and created a tunnel of green for them to drive through, the sun through the leaves sparkling on the windows as they went. The occasional gap in the trees at a farm entrance or crossroads lit up the inside of the camper in a flash of full sunlight, then dropped back to a soft glittering as they re-entered the canopy.

Every now and then they came across evidence of the storm the night before, but considering its severity, the islanders had done a remarkable job of clearing roads and disposing of wreckage. Fields and gardens buzzed with the sound of chainsaw-wielding workmen turning downed trees into piles of logs and they saw broken sheds and fence panels stacked onto lorries, waiting to be taken away. Plumes of smoke from several bonfires coiled up into the sky, signaling other spaces cleared of storm debris and the many patches of sawdust by the roadside were a sure sign that work had already gone on there. Despite all of this, the journey went without a hitch and they pulled through Cinan Farm's main gate at around four o'clock.

After checking in at the farm shop with the owners, Jan and John, and being warned to 'mind the cliff edge... might be a bit loose,' they drove through the tents and campers in the main field heading for the smaller, narrow west field.

It was closer to the cliffs and had a fantastic view of the sea, so Dad parked Daisy along the western edge, leaving a bit of space between her side door and the rough hedge that bordered the field.

Willow and Lea jumped out and ran off to explore their temporary new home and Mum and Dad tagged along for a bit to check out the cliffs and the chine to make sure they were safe. After a while they left the girls to it and went back to the camper to start setting up.

They'd owned a trailer tent and camping equipment before they'd bought Daisy and selling the trailer and some of the gear had helped with the renovation costs. There were certain items that they kept though; a portaloo to avoid those middle of the night in the rain treks to the toilet block, a proper petrol lantern like they remembered from their childhood camping trips and a table and chairs.

Although she was well equipped, there was no denying that Daisy was small inside. This was fine for weekends away, but to give them a bit more space on longer trips they'd got themselves a four sided gazebo tent to use as a dining room. Dad started to unpack and unfold it while Mum lifted up the solar panels, locked them into place facing the bright sun and put on some music.

They stretched out Daisy's striped awning onto its poles and pegged the guy lines out, then finished setting up the gazebo, moving it slightly so it met the edge of the awning. After they'd pegged it down, they rolled up the side wall that faced the camper so the two doors were facing each other with the awning covering the gap between. Very cozy.

While Dad hung the lantern from a chain inside the tent and put out the table and chairs, Mum rounded up the girls and took them off on a quick trip to the farm shop for some eggs.

As their voices faded across the field, Dad put the kettle on for drinks and sat in Daisy's side door, listening to the hissing of the gas stove and the chirruping of the grasshoppers.

If their holiday was going to be *this* relaxing, two weeks on the Isle of Wight was going to be a breeze…

An Invitation

Willow stood happily next to Lea, who had taken responsibility for the safe passage of the twelve freshly laid eggs they had just bought.

Negotiations with Jan regarding the girls coming back after tea for a spot of chicken feeding had concluded successfully and they were just about to go back to Dad when John pulled up outside the shop cum farm office in his Land Rover and joined them inside.

"Hello, folks, glad I caught you," he said, leaning over the counter and feeling about for something. "Aha, gotcha! This came for you early yesterday morning. Some fella from Borson House brought it in person. Asked if we could see that you got it the day you arrived. That's the people you won the tickets from, isn't it?"

"Uh huh," said Mum intrigued, tearing open the envelope and pulling out the letter inside, "and sending us mystery holiday post too!"

She unfolded the letter and held it up to read it. "Dear Mr and Mrs Raulich... could you please return tickets... sent in error... envelope enclosed," she said.

Jan looked genuinely horrified.

"Nooo! That's awful!" she declared, shocked.

Mum laughed. "No, only kidding! Dear Mr and Mrs Raulich... further to our previous letter... I would be delighted to have the pleasure of your company... dinner at Borson House... this Sunday evening at 7pm. L. Borson. Wow, that's tomorrow night! The prize that just keeps on giving!"

John was still chuckling at his wife's reaction. "Got you a good 'un!" he said, poking her gently in the arm. "Will you go?" he asked Mum.

"Dinner at a country house? Definitely. Hubster'll love it and the girls will probably feel like the royal family's asked us to tea."

The girls nodded in agreement.

John jerked his head in the direction of what Mum assumed was Borson House.

"It's un'eard of… no one *ever* gets an invite there. They even get tradesmen in from over the water when work needs doing. I think the last time locals were there regularly was the early seventies. Got less and less until the fella went almost full recluse. You still see his staff around the island now and then, but hardly ever him."

"Should be an interesting night then; we'll let you know how it goes. Thanks for the eggs!"

They said goodbye and made their way back to camp, stopping off for a quick swing in the play park on the way.

By the time they got back to Dad, he'd finished a coffee and was lying on a blanket on the grass, propped up on a camper seat cushion with his hands behind his head, looking out to sea as the sun crept lower. A second satisfying whistle was just escaping the kettle as they arrived.

"Settled in then?" Mum asked, turning the gas off and before he had the chance to reply, the kids ditched what they were carrying and bundled him, arms and legs flailing wildly in all directions as he was pinned down and tickled.

When the squealing and wriggling had subsided, Mum flopped down on the blanket with the three of them. She handed Dad the letter.

"Look what came for us!" she said, happily. "It was left by someone from Borson House."

Dad took the letter and read it through, then looked up at Mum. "Tomorrow night? That's handy," he joked, "I'm off work tomorrow!"

"First day was going to be a mellow one anyway, wasn't it? A lay in… a bit of exploring down the beach… barbeque lunch… and now dinner at a country manor!"

"Sounds good to me," said Dad. He did like to let the inner caveman out and cook over an open flame now and then. His definition of now and then was every time he had the chance and he'd even been known to have a barbeque under an open garage door in the rain. Pretty much *any* day was a potential barbeque day.

"I might do a bit more of this too," he said, patting the blanket.

They had a late tea in the gazebo and spent a good deal of it waving and saying hello to people as they walked past on the way to the cliffs and back. Some had children, some had dogs and to the girls' delight, one couple even walked past with a pot-bellied pig on a pink diamante lead! You had to be on holiday when people were walking pigs on pink diamante leads, surely?

After the plates were cleared away, they set off in the direction of the farm shop together to commence

OPERATION CHICKEN

and help Jan feed her feathery flock. When they arrived, Jan showed the girls how to fill their feed buckets using a scoop from a big drum of grain. She led them into the enclosure where the birds were and they bustled over, clucking and scratching expectantly, obviously aware of what time of day it was.

Lea decided on a mobile approach and wandered around spreading handfuls of grain, followed by a small but very dedicated group of chickens.

Willow opted for a stationary technique and sat on an overturned milk crate like Old Mother Hen, knee high and five deep in her new family as they pecked at the feed she dropped for them.

Mum and Dad stood chuckling with Jan at the sight of the two of them with their new friends and when the buckets were empty, they thanked her and wandered slowly back to Daisy, talking about the following day.

It was almost dark by the time they got back, and there was just enough time for a hot chocolate before bed. Dad boiled the kettle and made the chocolates, (with mini marshmallows, of course) while Mum read the girls a chapter or two from their books.

They sat in the gazebo with their drinks, watching the stars blink into life one by one as the darkness deepened. Out in the country with none of the light pollution of a big town, the view of the cosmos was incredible. Even the brightness from the not-quite-full moon did little to dull the stars that stretched across the sky in the unmistakable band of the Milky Way. Area of Outstanding Natural Beauty and Clear Sky Area indeed!

After a spot of oohing and aahing at the view above them, the girls were sent off to get ready for bed. Lea finished brushing her teeth and leaving Willow brushing hers, she climbed upstairs into the roof.

"I can see lights on the sea," she said, pointing out of the window in the raised roof. Dad popped his head up to have a look.

"Probably fishing boats, pickle… or faeries, they travel in packs out in the country," he joked.

"Teams, Daddy," said Willow, standing on the seat next to him and climbing up into the roof.

"Sorry, sweetheart?"

"Well," she said with the air of a lecturer teaching a student, "I dream about faeries quite a lot and they're *always* in teams. They're very good at working together, you know."

"Please forgive my ignorance, Miss Raulich. Thanks for putting me straight."

Willow giggled, enjoying the moment. "It's my pleasure, Daddy. I know grown ups don't know much about this sort of thing!"

He gave her and Lea a kiss and swapped places with Mum. After she'd snuggled them in and made sure they had their cuddlies, she dropped back down into the camper.

"Nighty night, girlies," she said, "sleep tight. Don't let the bed bugs bite!"

"Or the vampyre faeries!" said Dad.

"They're vegetarians, Dad," Willow replied, exasperated. "You don't really think they'd *bite* people, do you?"

Borson House

The family spent the next day on the campsite in yet another day of glorious sunshine. Their lazy breakfast and barbeque lunch was followed by a walk on the beach and a decent amount of lounging about as they relaxed into being on holiday.

That evening, following the directions enclosed with the letter they pulled out of the campsite and drove east along Military Road. Heading south when they reached Niton, they turned left along Undercliff Drive, through more of those wonderful green tunnels of overhanging trees.

After about a kilometre and a half in a particularly shady tunnel, they turned into a driveway flanked on each side by a low stone wall. It sloped gently downwards away from the road, disappearing into thick trees.

Forty metres further in there were two large stone gate posts with a large wrought iron arch linking them that proudly announced that this was

~ BORSON HOUSE ~

Dad drove Daisy down a straight slope and round a tight right hand bend to where the driveway encircled a grass island in front of the house. The camper rolled to a halt between the island and the main entrance, nose to nose with a beautiful old pure white Jaguar Mk 2, with a blood red leather interior. It was all Dad could do not to start drooling.

In the centre of the grass was a fountain. A ring of gently arcing water jets surrounded a strange metal sculpture of a male faery trying to take flight, but being pulled back by... were they *ropes?*

"Well I don't like *that*," said Lea pointedly as the family clambered out. "He should be free."

Mum took her hand. "It's just art, baby; it's not necessarily about trapping things. It might be about breaking free of things."

Borson House stood proudly against the backdrop of a gorgeous orangey-red sunset, a mini country house built less for its number of rooms and more for its wonderful setting.

Its stonework gave it an air of solidity and strength and it felt just right where it sat, looking out over the sea like a sentinel. The tile-roofed towers that sprouted from each side of the building gave it a vaguely castle-like appearance, more fairytale than military, and its windows seemed to watch expectantly as the family crunched across the gravel driveway to the large carved wooden front doors.

Mum pulled an ornate wrought iron bell pull, smiling at Dad at the sound of the ringing bells inside the house.

"I swear," joked Dad, "if some creepy butler type answers the door and says, 'the master will see you now,' we're going home!"

Mum laughed and with that, the door opened and there stood the butler. No creepy hand wringing or 'goood eeevening' in a Transylvanian accent, just a very smart gentleman probably in his late forties, impeccably dressed in a butler's tailcoat and gesturing them inside with an outstretched palm.

"Welcome, one and all. My name is Neery. If you would please follow me to the drawing room and make yourselves comfortable, I will inform Mr Borson that you have arrived. He is *extremely* keen to meet you."

Neery led the family across the entrance hall past an impressive wooden staircase and showed them into a beautifully appointed room, before leaving to fetch their host. While Mum and Dad took in the paintings and sculptures to the deep tick, tick, tick of a rather splendid grandfather clock, the girls sat in plush winged armchairs chatting about the benefits of such comfortable and 'ginormous' seating. Their discussion was cut short by Mr Borson's arrival and greeting from the doorway… and by his odd appearance.

"Well, well, well, if it isn't the Raulich family! I am *so* pleased you could come. I am Luke Borson. Welcome to my home."

The very tall, pale, stick-thin man strode over to Dad with one skeletal hand outstretched.

"Mr Raulich, a pleasure to meet you."

"Likewise, Mr Borson," replied Dad, smiling at the gusto with which their host was shaking his hand.

"Luke, please, no formalities here, my dear boy!"

Dad's smile grew wider, pleasantly surprised to hear someone call him 'my dear boy.' He didn't think anyone still spoke like that!

Luke turned to Mum, his smile broadening and stretching his skin even more tightly over his boney face. "And the delightful Mrs Raulich. An exquisite pleasure to meet you. Truly the brightest gem upon our fair island!" He kissed the back of her hand.

"Hello, Luke," Mum replied, touched by his old-world chivalry. "Katy and Mike, please. These are our daughters, Willow and Lea."

Luke folded his elongated frame like a concertina and knelt down with his hands on his knees.

"Hello, children. May I enquire as to who is who?"

"I'm Lea," said Lea, looking at Luke seriously.

"And I'm Willow," continued Willow. "We're on holiday. Is this your castle? Are you a king?"

"I am very pleased to meet you both. I'm sure you will have a lovely time here," Luke said with mock solemnity, shaking their hands. He smiled broadly. "This is my castle but I am, alas, not a king… not yet!"

Lea, still holding Luke's hand, asked, "Why is the faery tied up? Don't you like faeries?"

"That is a very good question. Why indeed? Let us just say that the previous owner of Borson House had some very interesting theories on faeries. Some people believe that faeries are our equals and should be treated as we would wish to be treated. Others believe that like many animals, faeries should be 'farmed' for the things they can provide us with: wool from sheep, milk from cows, eggs from chickens, that sort of thing."

Lea was gobsmacked. "What can faeries give us?" she asked in a hushed voice.

Luke crooked his finger twice and leant forward as if confiding in a trusted friend.

"Answers," he whispered, eyes shining. "They can teach us about nature and the wondrous universe we live in." He stood, returning to full height and spread his arms wide. "*If* you believe in that sort of thing!"

"We do!" exclaimed Willow, pointing her finger rapidly back and forth between herself and her sister. This was their favourite subject, but her face soon turned solemn again. "But they should definitely *not* be tied up. Mummy says that things that can fly shouldn't be put in cages. If *I* could fly and someone put *me* in a cage I would be *sooo* angry!"

Laughing, Luke turned to Mum and Dad.

"Extraordinary children! So bright and so forward. You must be very proud."

Dad nodded, chest swelling with pride almost visibly. "Very. Whatever we did seems to have paid off," he joked.

Luke gestured towards the rear of the house.

"So Katy, Willow, Lea, Mike… now that we are on first name terms, shall we adjourn to the patio for drinks before dinner?"

He led the way back through the hall and on into a morning room at the back of the house where Neery asked them what they would like.

After he'd taken their orders and left, Dad, always a fan of firsts said, "I can honestly say that's the first time I've been asked what I'd like to drink by a butler on a country estate."

Luke laughed loudly. "Ha ha! Forgive my opulence… his buttling is a mere fringe benefit. His other talents I'd be lost without, I'm afraid. Marc Neery. Ex-military chap, special forces. He handles my home security, maintains the vehicles, acts as a courier for my business interests… his services are unquantifiable."

They made their way out onto a patio overlooking a beautiful garden that sloped gently down towards the sea some distance away. Completing the whole vista for them was the sun, putting on a magnificent show as it sank lower in the blue of a cloudless sky.

The girls ran down the stone steps to the lawn to play and the three adults watched the sunset in comfortable silence until Neery arrived with their drinks on a tray and went over the evening's menu. After thanking him for their drinks and calling the girls back for theirs, Mum sighed deeply.

"Wow," she said, awestruck, "that is quite the sight. I can see why this house was built here. It feels like sunset at Avebury or Stonehenge. Very special. Protected almost."

Luke looked over quickly. "Yes, this place does have a certain aura to it, doesn't it? Gratifying that you should compare it to sites of such grandeur."

"We've spent a lot of time in Wiltshire and Somerset. We're quite interested in stone age sites, you see," Mum replied. "They do have a certain feel to them."

Luke nodded. "The whole island has a long history of ancient occupation. Tens of thousands of years, in fact, predating much of the knowledge currently considered accurate by so called *experts*. Ancient pre-history is something of a passion of mine. I have a personal conviction that the most important of discoveries is yet to be found right here on the island. What a pleasant surprise that you share an interest in such things. I can see this evening will be interesting!"

The girls were rounded up from the garden and three snails and a ladybird had to be returned to their families before hands could be washed back inside the house ready for dinner.

When they came back out onto the patio, Luke led everyone down the steps and through the garden, passing beautiful sculptures, scented shrubs and seating areas… a garden you could truly lose yourself in.

As they passed a small octagonal summer house, Dad saw that it was filled with huge glass globes, the kind his aunt and his mum had kept miniature gardens in when he was little. The sight of them made him feel instantly uneasy but he couldn't quite put his finger on why. Mum saw them too.

"Ooo, what a waste. They'd look lovely on that great big patio. Someone should fill those," she said, already imagining where they'd look best.

Luke came over to the summer house and peered in with a chuckle. "Yes, I have been working on that. I only have need of a certain number though. These are spares, in case of breakages."

They walked on, with Dad glancing back at the summer house a couple of times until it was out of sight.

Eventually, they came to a section of lawn on which sat the most amazing dining table and chairs set for dinner under a large khaki canvas canopy. The canopy was supported by thick polished tree branches and the structure was staked out with tough ropes that held it taut. The dining chairs looked like they had each been carved from a single piece of wood and the circular table top appeared to be made the same way.

Seeing their delight at all this, Luke told them of a huge storm one summer evening that had claimed a beautiful oak tree that had been on the land for hundreds of years.

A local artisan that worked for his parents and several carpenters had immediately been put to work saving as much of the old oak as possible. The dining suite they were to eat at and many of the carved sculptures and outbuildings scattered around the gardens had come from the tree. The huge front doors of the house and several pieces of furniture inside were made from it too. Any left over wood had been chopped, stacked and seasoned and had kept the estate hearths burning for several winters.

As Luke himself said, "Almost anywhere you'd care to look on the grounds holds a memory of the old oak."

Mum was captivated. The setting was about as close to perfection as she could imagine and she only hoped that Luke knew how lucky he was. She said as much and he agreed wholeheartedly.

The girls climbed onto their seats and Dad saw Mum to her chair, although the solid piece of oak was too heavy to actually pull out for her. As Dad and Luke took their seats Luke took a moment to introduce his housekeeper, the similarly named Mrs Raullings, who greeted them with a warm smile and a "Good evening, it's lovely to meet you all!"

She began serving dinner from a hostess trolley while Neery poured wine for the adults and juices for Willow and Lea. They chatted about Borson House and ancient sites they had visited, but conversation soon trailed off as they devoured the amazing meal Mrs Raullings had prepared.

The catch of the day seafood starter was followed by melt in the mouth pork medallions with fresh vegetables and an incredible gravy. Dessert was a rich warm chocolate cake served with creamy homemade vanilla ice cream. As they ate, Mrs Raullings stood in the background, delighting in their noises of appreciation and the looks on their faces as they tucked in.

When they were finished and mouths were wiped, Mum and Dad leant back in their chairs, feeling as though they had just feasted in honour of something far more prestigious than the winning of some holiday tickets. As they drank their after dinner coffees, listening to the girls playing in amongst the garden's trees and flowerbeds, they felt very spoilt and very grateful.

"Thank you so much for inviting us here tonight, Luke," Mum said. "I don't think I've ever had such a wonderful meal in such lovely surroundings."

"You are most welcome, my dear. Mrs Raullings is quite the culinary genius."

Dad raised his glass. "Yes, thank you, Mrs Raullings, it was delicious."

"You're all very welcome; the pleasure was all mine… and it's Prisy, if that's alright by you, Mr Borson?"

"Yes, I'm sure that would be perfectly acceptable, Mrs Raullings," said Luke. "Would you be so kind as to fetch me my ebony box from the study, please?"

She nodded, but before heading for the house, she cleared the empty dessert plates and lit the candles scattered around the table to fend off the approaching dusk and bring a sparkle to the glassware.

Luke clasped his hands together, fingers intertwined and smiled across the table.

"Now for my confession," he stated quite unexpectedly, "followed swiftly by my apology and an explanation of my ulterior motive for bringing you to the island and inviting you here this evening. A motive that could be extremely beneficial to us all."

An Offer From Luke Borson

Wow.

Mum and Dad looked at each other for a moment before Dad said, "Go on."

Luke sighed as if releasing a burden he'd been carrying, lowering his hands to the table.

"The competition was a lie. Borson House is *not* a charity and there was *no* star prize. I simply sent you the tickets with a view to bringing you here to the island so I could meet with you in person and make my proposal."

Mum and Dad's ears were still ringing with the words *confession* and *ulterior motive*. They didn't like being lied to and they didn't like being tricked. Their hackles were up.

"You should have spoken to us, not tricked us into coming," said Mum calmly. She was a gentle soul, but Dad heard a frosty timbre in her voice that was reserved for her rare annoyed moments.

'*Watch out, Luke,*' he thought. '*Make that explanation a good 'un!*'

Luke sensed the tone too and raised his hands in contrition.

"I am truly sorry for lying to you. I would have preferred another way but my proposal requires your presence on the island. Please don't be concerned; I intend no harm to your family and my trickery can only benefit you if you will only let me explain?"

Mum softened a little. A *little*.

"OK," she said, "go ahead."

"Borson House is my family home. My great grandfather, Lionel Borson, made his name in the diamond mining industry and my family has been rather wealthy ever since. His son, Robert, my grandfather, developed a deep love of the Isle of Wight after several family holidays here and built Borson House as a summer home in what he considered to be the most beautiful place on Earth."

Luke smiled and waved a hand toward the beach.

"A true romantic, who apparently knew a good spot when he found one. He was also something of a globetrotter and was renowned for his swaggering boast that in spite of all the places he'd visited, the most beautiful sunsets on Earth were to be found looking south from his own patio."

Mum and Dad nodded in agreement.

"He was an imaginative man with a passion for mythology. My father, Oscar, inherited his desire to uncover the mysteries of the past and became an historian, but fell out of favour with mainstream intellectual society. Mythology itself is a recognized discipline, but he had some colourful theories that he insisted were true and he was ridiculed and made a laughing stock by his peers. He withdrew from professional circles and dedicated his life to spending time with my mother, Elizabeth, and I."

He smiled, seeing them together in his mind's eye.

"They bred horses together and made quite the name for themselves both here and on the mainland, but he never lost his interest in ancient history and amassed an impressive collection for his private museum and library. Unfortunately, the things he sought most avidly eluded him until the day he died. He had found documentary evidence that there were nine artifacts, Keys actually, hidden somewhere here on the island. I'd always been fascinated by his work and found I had his passion for it, but following their deaths when I was eleven, I have to admit it became something of an obsession."

"I'm sorry, Luke, did you say 'their deaths?'" asked Mum. "You lost them both?"

"Yes, I'm afraid so, just a very few months after the storm I mentioned, in a cave here on the grounds. This whole island is a Swiss cheese of underground features and my father was trying to reach a new discovery when he got into trouble. My mother went to his aid and was killed trying to save him. I was with them."

The girls had rejoined them and were listening to the story absolutely transfixed. Luke had lost his Mum and Dad at the same time. Looking across the table at theirs, they couldn't begin to imagine what that must have been like.

Mum caught their look and took a deep breath. "I'm so sorry Luke, no child should have to go through that."

He gave a jaded smile. "Thank you. Though strangely, the pain of losing them gave me a focus and empowered me to continue his search. I had come to an impasse until just over a year and a half ago, but if you pardon the pun, I now believe that you may be the key to finding the Keys."

He paused. "I have made it my life's work to find these artifacts and realise my father's dream. To compile and catalogue the largest collection of faery lore in the world."

Faery lore. Okaaay...

It seemed a strange obsession for a man of his age, wealth and influence. Faeries were an interesting fantasy to entertain your kids with, but it seemed an odd lifestyle choice for an adult. But each to their own. At least he had a hobby.

Prisy returned, carrying a small tray on which sat a small, black, carved wooden box. She placed it in front of Luke and he lifted the box from the tray, placing it on the table in front of him, drumming his fingers gently on its lid.

"What makes you think *we* can help you?" asked Dad.

"Let me just say that I put a lot of faith in instinct and my instinct just now is telling me that you are the guiding light I have been waiting for. I dreamed of you."

"Excuse me? You *dreamed* of us?" Dad repeated.

"I feel like a fool when I speak the words aloud," said Luke, shaking his head. "Believe me, it was my dream and it sounds preposterous even to me. I dreamed of who you were and where you lived over and over again for months on end. I can't impress upon you enough the effort of will it took to suspend my disbelief and send Neery on a little field trip to your home town. He is a fine employee, but I think even *his* ability to follow orders may have been tested somewhat. Can you even begin to imagine his incredulity when he reported back that you were real? Can you imagine *mine?*"

Luke looked a little sheepish, but both Mum and Dad thought it had the look and feel of a well-rehearsed part that was being played, a picture of self-mockery that was being painted to... what? Lower their guards? Soften the blow of being lied to and tricked into coming here? It wasn't working on them. He knew exactly what he believed and he knew exactly what he'd done to get them here. And he certainly didn't sound like he felt like a fool when he 'spoke the words aloud.'

"Well, I don't think you're a fool. I think you believe what you're saying; I just don't think we're who you're looking for," Mum said with her usual diplomacy, "but I'll be blunt... it bothers me a lot that we were brought here under false pretences."

"You are very kind my dear. In my rather weak defence, I felt that to telephone or visit making an offer was almost a guarantee of failure. I could hardly tell you that I *dreamed* that your lovely family could help me in the completion of my life's work, now could I?" Luke smiled knowingly. "What would you have made of me? What do you make of me *now*, I wonder?"

His bony digits opened the small box and reached inside.

"I cannot make amends for my dishonesty," he said, plucking something from the box and sliding it slowly across the table towards Mum, "but I do have the means at my disposal to say sorry in a more tangible way than some."

He drew his hand back, leaving behind a rather large and very beautiful cut diamond.

"A small token of my gratitude for your tolerance and patience in the face of an old man's eccentricity. Real, I assure you," he said, smiling as four faces leant towards the diamond for a closer look.

"For us?" asked Mum, furrowing her brow, puzzled.

"Yes," said Luke emphatically. "A gift in recompense for my trickery and for your time here tonight. Two carats, round cut. With a market value of around ten thousand pounds, if you are curious."

Mum and Dad's jaws dropped. They sat back in their chairs while Luke stirred the contents of the ebony box with his forefinger, making a sound like pebbles on a beach.

His tone changed to one of a man familiar with high-value commodity trading. The 'eccentric old man' apparently still understood something of the origins of his family's wealth.

"So to business then… I need your help and I have a very simple proposition for you. I believe that you are in a position to help me find the Keys and I am in a position to make your lives very comfortable should you do so. All you need do is go about your holiday business and nothing more."

He reached into an inside pocket and passed Dad a business card that held nothing more than the name 'L. Borson' and a mobile telephone number.

"If during your stay on the island you hear news of the artifacts, I would very much like you to contact me. If the information you supply leads me to them, the contents of this box belongs to you."

Luke picked up the box and holding it over the tray it had been brought out on, he tipped out a sparkling waterfall of mineral wealth.

His demeanor lightened again.

"I believe that we should seize life's opportunities when they present themselves. *I* can't explain the dream and yet here you sit. You are very probably thinking your host is one diamond short of a tiara and yet here *you* are, ten thousand pounds wealthier! I only hope you can suspend your disbelief like I did and humour me long enough to strike a deal."

Mum and Dad looked questioningly at each other. It was a no brainer. The single diamond alone was worth way more than what he was asking of them. The pursuit of wealth certainly wasn't a driving force in the Rauliches' family life, but there was no denying that it would make things easier.

"The diamond's an extraordinary gift, Luke, thank you," said Mum, looking over at Dad again. "I think we're both in agreement over the rest. We'll keep our eyes and ears open but I'll be honest… I just don't think anything will come of it."

"Then simply don't worry yourselves about it for another second," Luke replied comfortingly. "You either find them and receive your reward, or you don't and I go back to my search. Open minds are all I ask for… and eyes and ears, of course! Let fate do the rest. If it's meant to be, you'll know soon enough," he continued, gesturing at the diamonds.

Luke stood up, his pale face glowing almost healthily in the candlelight.

"So we have an understanding, then?" he asked hopefully.

"I think we do," said Dad, holding his hand out. Luke shook it vigorously and did the same with Mum and the girls.

"Marvelous!" Luke exclaimed, "I do love a good gentlemen's… and ladies' of course… agreement!"

The rest of the evening was very enjoyable, but it was obvious that Luke had done all the sharing he planned to do on the subject of the deal they'd struck. Neery refreshed their drinks and they stayed a couple of hours longer, Luke calling upon his vast knowledge of mythology to delight them with tales of the fae in the flickering candlelight.

As he spoke, his voice low and comfortable, they were transported to a realm of love and reward and of trickery and betrayal. He was quite the story teller. It wasn't lost on Mum and Dad that these may not be the only stories Luke had told that night.

When their last drinks were finished, he led them back through the gardens to the house. The grounds were lovely enough in the daylight, but now night had fallen, many of the sculptures, buildings and trees were illuminated in one form or another and the glowing islands of light made it a truly magical place in the darkness.

You passed a shrub and the face of a woven willow deer peered out at you. Casting your eyes into the branches of an uplit tree, an owl sat staring back with huge eyes. Catching a glimpse of something under a shrub, you crouched down to find a carved wooden badger hiding beneath. Everywhere you looked there was a new discovery and the girls pointed out each one before excitedly hunting for the next.

They reached the hallway of the house where Luke said his goodbyes.

"An absolute delight, my friends. I have so little time for pleasure and your company tonight has been a wonderful distraction!" he said, shaking four hands again in succession.

"Thanks for inviting us, Luke, it was a lovely evening. A bit surreal... but lovely!" said Mum, laughing.

Luke chuckled. "Yes, I can imagine! I am honoured I could be your host."

He bent towards the girls, pulling the lower lid of one eye down with a forefinger and cupping an ear with his other hand.

"Remember, young ladies, eyes and ears open! It was a pleasure to make your acquaintance. Thank you for coming."

The girls thanked him in return and he stood and pointed out Neery standing nearby.

"Mr Neery will see you out and furnish you with proof of ownership of your new acquisition and the details of some reputable jewellers on the island... for your peace of mind, you understand."

Luke inclined his head respectfully.

"Katy, Willow, Lea, Mike... I bid you good evening," and with that, he strode away down a side hall on his impossibly long legs and was gone.

Neery showed them to the door and handed them two envelopes, explaining which one was the ownership letter and that the other held a list of contact details they might find useful.

"Thank you," said Dad, shaking Neery's hand.

"Best of luck, sir, I hope your stay is fruitful."

Dad paused, not sure whether he should ask his question, but under the circumstances, unable to help himself.

"I've got to ask... is Luke serious about this? It's not exactly the sort of thing that happens every day," he asked quietly.

"Completely, sir. When it comes to the collection, Mr Borson is... tenacious. He also has the advantage of an immense family fortune. There are not many things of worth in his particular area of interest that he hasn't already secured. Hopefully your agreement tonight will bring him some closure."

He opened the door wide for them and pointed to the envelope containing the contact details.

"May I suggest that your first port of call is one of confirmation? I find that nothing banishes doubt quite like an independent second opinion," he said with a meaningful look.

"We will, thank you, Mr Neery."

They said goodbye and piled themselves happily back into Daisy, pulling out of the driveway back onto the dark road and leaving Borson House behind them.

Neery closed the door gently and turned to face Luke, who had returned when he heard them leaving.

"Very convincing, Mr Neery. Well done."

The Wisdom Of A Child

Daisy crawled her way along the country lanes back to the farm under a clear sky and a glowing moon, following the twin fans of her headlights as they lit up the grass verges and the road ahead.

Considering how late it was, the girls had managed a very respectable four minutes before falling asleep, leaving Mum and Dad to chat about their far from average night out as they drove. Given a diamond, promised more if they helped to find some old relics and told that all they had to do to accomplish this was enjoy their holiday. A strange night indeed.

There was a saying: 'If it sounds too good to be true, it probably is,' but here they were on a free holiday, with a diamond worth ten grand in their pocket and until a jeweller proved it otherwise, they'd just have to give Luke the benefit of the doubt.

They got back to the campsite at around twelve. After Dad had returned Daisy to her spot, they gently woke the girls to brush their teeth and get into their bed clothes, then Dad lifted them up into the roof. Mum popped her head up to join him to say goodnight.

"Can you read us a story?" Lea asked sleepily.

"Nice try, sausage, not a chance. It's past midnight," said Dad.

"OK…" she replied, putting on her best disappointed voice.

"You need your rest, honey," said Mum. "We're going to Shanklin tomorrow to explore the chine. It's like a big garden with a waterfall, but in a big hole in the ground."

"Luke has the best garden *ever!*" said Willow, "I absolutely loved it there! I'd like a garden like that one day."

"Didn't like the statue though… it made me sad," Lea told them, demonstrating that it really had made an impression on her.

Dad stroked her hair.

"Art does that sometimes, darlin'. It can make you happy or sad or calm or angry… it's supposed to make you feel something. That's sometimes what the artist wants, to make different people feel different things."

"I don't get it."

Dad looked at Mum for help.

"What don't you get, sweetheart?" she asked.

"So they don't mean for it to be happy or sad, just whatever you want?"

"I think so, yeah. They must have something in mind when they create it, but it's up to the person looking at it to decide how it makes *them* feel."

"So it's just for whoever looks at it to decide?"

"Yeah."

Lea looked thoughtful for a moment. "Well, if they want you to make up your own mind, why did they make the faery look like it's crying?"

For that question, they had no answer.

Shanklin

The beautiful little village of Shanklin could hold an amazing number of people considering its size. Every last inch of pavement was filled with relaxed, happy, meandering tourists and the vehicles moved at a snail's pace to avoid the ones who frequently spilled out onto the road.

That sort of thing often infuriated drivers, but here in Shanklin the slower pace seemed to produce a calming effect and you could almost see the blood pressure lowering and the stress fading away. Furrowed city brows and serious expressions were replaced with worriless foreheads and smiles.

Must be something in the water. Or the sunlight. Or the air. Or maybe the earth. Whatever magic this little village was weaving, it worked. It made you glad to be alive.

After slipping Daisy through the crowded streets, they pulled into the very obviously full main car park. They slid alongside one of the ticket machines for a bit until Mum saw someone pulling out of a space, then she gunned Daisy's engine and quickly appropriated it! A good one too… in the shade. Important stuff, as anyone who's got into a car that's been baking in the sun all day knows only too well.

Everybody climbed out and Dad grabbed the backpack with the camera and other valuables.

"Stay close, girls, lots of cars in and out," he said, holding out both of his hands to take theirs while Mum got a parking ticket from the machine, stuck it in the window and locked Daisy.

They walked between the flower beds that separated the car park from the road and joined the throng of people snaking along the pavement. Heading down the sloping High Street, they didn't have to go very far before they found what they were looking for. The familiar brown tourist information sign said

~ CHINE & HERITAGE CENTRE ~

and they followed the direction of the arrow, heading between the Pencil Cottage Tea Shop and the Crab Pub into a cool, shady little lane that led downhill, getting thinner as it went.

After about a hundred metres, they came to a stone trough on the right that spouted water and made a little stream that flowed across the lane before vanishing under a slatted fence. The girls instantly lost their shoes and splashed in the deeper part by the trough for a bit until Mum exclaimed, "Oh, this is it!" and they looked round to see a small wooden hut and a gate set back slightly from the lane with the words

~ SHANKLIN CHINE ~

arched across them.

Shoes back on and entrance fees paid, they descended the first flight of wooden stairs into a different world of ferns and mosses. Looking for all the world like some prehistoric forest scene, it felt as though a dinosaur could appear from behind a tree or a rock at any moment.

As a whole, the chine looked as if a giant had taken a swing at the coastline with an equally giant axe, leaving a ragged cleft that led down to the beach and the sea. They looked back at the steep sides looming over them and saw that the stream that disappeared under the fence in the lane actually flowed over the edge as a waterfall. The water made landfall on a bed of sand and pebbles at the base of the fall and then continued on down the chine as a gentle stream.

It was astounding to think that all this had been carved out of the landscape by nothing more than water. And time… lots and lots of time. Mum and Dad were fascinated by geology so while they wandered slowly down the path chatting, the girls left them and shot off ahead to explore.

There was plenty for them to find. Not only did the chine have pathways that headed downward, there were also tracks that led up to outbuildings and seating areas, carved animals, gnomes, pixies on toadstools, models of miniature buildings… there were even little doorways that led into the base of tree trunks.

"What's behind that?" asked Lea, pointing to one as Mum and Dad caught up with them.

"Faery land!" said Mum. "It's a faery door; try the handle."

Lea leant over the fence that bordered the pathway and gave the tiny door handle a tug. It didn't budge.

"What a rip," said Dad, pretending to be disappointed. "I was hoping for a little stairway with lanterns."

The children debated this for a while. Between them, they decided that to keep it out of the way of prying eyes, an entrance to the faery realm would need to be somewhere *much* more remote than a busy tourist spot. *This* door must just be a decoy intended to trick people.

They walked on, coming to a beautiful little stone bridge over the stream. It was covered in moss and lichen and had young ferns sprouting from its base, making it just about the prettiest thing in the chine. Mum and Dad looked over the edge, downstream and towards the coast, while the girls tried to see what was underneath it. No trolls, but a fair few snails.

It was such a lovely spot that they decided to stay a while for a snack and a drink. There was a bench nearby, a little way up a slope on a small plateau and they made their way up to it. The girls, who rarely sat still, grabbed their snacks and drinks and carried on with their exploring. Dad cracked open the flask and he and Mum had a coffee, the peace and quiet of their elevated position broken only by the girl's laughter and the babbling of the stream below them.

They waved at a few other visitors that passed by on their way down the chine and it seemed that, like a box at the theatre, they'd managed to grab the best seats in the house.

Mum spotted a robin watching them from a bush no more than a couple of metres from where they sat. She threw a few tidbits for him and he flitted to the ground to collect a piece of this new bounty before going back to his bush again to study and eat it. He did this a few times until he'd finished everything. Mum put down another piece of cookie for him on the arm of the bench and judging by the casual way he perched there and ate it, he seemed to sense he was safe and on to a winner. Very confident and forthright little birds, robins.

When they set off again, they'd gained themselves a feathery escort. The little robin stayed with them all the way down to the bottom, past the set of stocks that the girls (and Mum) had to have their photos taken in and past the remains of P.L.U.T.O. the PipeLine Under The Ocean that had carried petrol to France during World War II.

Passing through the turnstile exit, they made their way up Everton Lane back towards the High Street with the newly named 'Dave' still following. He stayed with them all the way through Tower Cottage Gardens and then sat on the last fence post as they rejoined the lane, singing to them like he was saying goodbye.

They bade farewell to their tiny new friend as they left and the next time they looked back, he had gone. On the hunt for more cookie crumbs, no doubt.

Confirmation

They reached the High Street again and the pressing question at the back of Mum's and Dad's minds resurfaced. Even their happy children, the beauty of the chine and the glorious weather couldn't quite make them forget they had a valuable diamond in Mum's purse that needed authenticating.

After asking for some directions in a gift shop, a couple of hundred yards later they found themselves down a side lane facing the shop front of H. Stone the jeweller. The girls leant on the glass, shielding their eyes from the sun with two hands cupped around their faces while they admired the sparkly stuff displayed there.

A smiley chap with a full head of the whitest hair they'd ever seen greeted them when they went inside and introduced himself as the proprietor, Harold Stone. Barely ten minutes later, they were standing on the pavement outside the shop again, looking at each other in shock.

According to Mr Stone, Luke Borson was as good as his word. The Borson diamond family were mind-bogglingly wealthy and that, coupled with Harold's appraisal of the diamond and Luke's proof of ownership letter, meant that amazingly, unbelievably, the deal was genuine.

Mr Stone had even gone so far as to make them an offer for the diamond fairly close to its actual value, but they'd said no thank you, not wanting to make any hasty decisions.

Their shock meant that a bit of a sit down was required, so they found themselves a table in the gardens of the Holliers Hotel off the High Street. Mum and Dad watched the girls playing on the swings in the small but very new play area while they waited for the waitress to come back with their drinks.

"So," said Mum quietly, "this is officially the weirdest holiday we've ever had."

Dad smiled. "I always remember having been out of pocket after a holiday, not better off!"

"I just don't know what to make of it," Mum went on, "but I *am* still miffed at being tricked into coming here, that much I *do* know."

"Yeah, me too. Feels like a proper mystery though, doesn't it? It's like being in the middle of an Enid Blyton book or a Hardy Boys' adventure," he chuckled. "Even if we don't end up fighting pirates or poachers, it's still been pretty cool. And this is only day two!"

Mum rested her chin on her hand, dreamily remembering how much she'd loved losing herself in adventure books as a child.

"If it gives Luke some comfort to think we can help, I s'pose it can't hurt to play along. It'd be mad if we did actually find something though, wouldn't it?"

Dad nodded enthusiastically. "Uh huh. That whole dream thing's bizarre too, what d'ya make of that?"

"The world's a strange place," Mum laughed, "I'm not even going to *try* and make any sense out of that one. Let's just be grateful our new diamond pretty much covers what we spent on Daisy…" She tailed off. "Now that *is* a coincidence."

"A very handy one. Liking this holiday more and more!" Dad smiled. "I tell you what... if we find Luke's Keys and he hands over a box of diamonds, we'll get a matching trailer for Daisy with a couple of motorbikes on it to scoot about on day trips. How's that sound?"

Mum grinned from ear to ear. She'd been keen to get a motorbike for years.

"Deal."

The waitress arrived with their cold drinks and Mum called the girls over. They chatted as they thirstily finished them, then got their things together and went back to exploring the town, wandering about in that floppy, relaxed way that people on holiday do when they have plenty of time and nowhere to be.

They drifted in and out of shops, picking up some fudge and other presents for family and friends back home and by the time they had seen most of the High Street and the side roads that led away from it, it was lunchtime.

Although they had a camper full of food parked nearby, the weather was so lovely they decided to treat themselves to an al fresco lunch at the Crab Pub, sitting outside and people watching as the world, in slow motion it seemed, floated by.

A Message From Freya Redfin

The after-lunch plan was to drop their purchases off at the camper and head back downhill to try to find a beach or a promenade to walk along, maybe even have an ice cream, but that all changed as they reached the car park where they'd left Daisy.

Across the road was a tiny shop they hadn't noticed before, nestling between Old Village Gifts and Grange Gifts like an after-thought. But *what* an after-thought.

It looked as though once upon a time, there had been two buildings with a slightly wider than average alleyway between them. Someone had obviously been unable to handle the thought of so much wasted space and had filled the gap by cramming in another property. It was without doubt the skinniest building the family had ever seen.

The imaginative owner of

~ Freya's Faery Forum ~

had certainly made good use of the tiny frontage. The whole façade had been painted to resemble an old, high stone wall, heavily overgrown with ivy. Real ivy spilled from planters hung between the ground floor and the first floor and the shop's leaf shaped sign was mounted on a chunky wrought iron bracket that projected through the growth, suspending the board on a pair of chains above the pavement. It swung calmly, almost beckoningly back and forth in the warm breeze that moved along the High Street.

A glimpse of an old weathered wooden door with iron fittings behind the hanging greenery hinted at an entrance to a secret walled garden and promised magic and discovery if you dared to venture inside.

On either side of the door there were tall planters that had been hewn from whole sections of tree trunk, their tops and the stumps of their side branches hollowed out into pots and filled with grasses and wildflowers. The trunks themselves were carved with a meadow design, scattered generously with buzzing insects and hiding the occasional furry face. A field mouse on a stalk, a hedgehog sniffing at an earthworm that broke the surface next to him, a fox cub peering out of its den.

The whole shop front was a frozen moment of classic British countryside grafted on to a busy street.

In wonder, they approached the entrance and Dad held the ivy aside for Mum and the girls. Mum opened the door and they walked in to the gentle tinkling of a shop bell, the sheet of ivy falling back into place behind them as the tourists bustled past outside.

It was cooler and quite a lot darker inside. The ivy did a superb job of keeping the sun at bay and it took a moment or two for their eyes to adjust. As they made their way further in, accompanied to the sound of gentle Celtic music, they realized they had entered a room full of treasures.

In little nooks in the walls, on shelves with carved edges and displayed on logs, were faeries. Faeries of every description. On their own, with others, with animals, tending plants, doing jobs, eating, playing, just about anything you could imagine.

These were no factory made, machine produced clones though. Each had its own personality and no two were alike, all beautifully sculpted from wood and painstakingly hand painted.

Mum and Dad marvelled at them while the girls went down each row excitedly, singling out the cuter ones, of which there were quite a few.

Mum had a bee in her bonnet about sculpture. The faces had to be right, in particular the eyes. A figurine could be perfectly formed, but if the artist hadn't got the face right, it just didn't work. The faces on *these* carvings were most definitely right. Gentle, calm eyes that seemed innocent and wise all at once and soft mouths that curved permanently at the corners in contentment.

They were pulled back from this immersion in their remarkable surroundings by the gentlest of coughs behind them and turned to see who it was. Behind the counter stood an elderly lady with crackling blue eyes. They looked out from a rosy face that yelled health at you from under a mop of dyed red hair.

"Hello, lovelies!" she chimed, giving them all a dazzler that showed she very likely had all her own teeth. "I'm Freya."

"Hello yourself! I'm Katy. My husband Mike… and the squeaky ones are Willow and Lea," said Mum, introducing everyone.

"Hello everybody," replied Freya warmly. "Make yourselves at home, look around, feel free to ask questions and above all, enjoy."

"This place is incredible, did you do all this?" asked Mum.

Freya smiled modestly. "Yes I did, but I've had lots of practice."

"I think it's safe to say you've got the hang of it… these are beautiful," Mum went on, waving her hand around the walls and displays.

"Ah, stop it… you're making me blush," Freya joked, a sparkle of quiet pride in her eyes, "but thank you. I do love what I do. There's nothing quite like seeing what you saw in the wood slowly revealing itself to the rest of the world."

"Does the wood know what it's got inside?" asked a fascinated Willow.

Freya laced her fingers together, placed her chin on them and leant on her elbows towards Willow over the counter.

"What an interesting question. I like to think so," she answered. "I think a piece of wood has infinite possibilities hidden in there, but maybe only one really special thing that it could become best of all."

Lea liked that idea. "Just like people."

The old lady laughed, delighted. "Yes! The trick is to be able to see the one special thing. All the wood needs is a little nudge to help bring it out." Freya smiled and winked at the girls. "Just like people."

The girls grinned hugely and Willow wrapped an arm around her sister's shoulder.

"Faeries are our absolute favourite… they're kind and gentle and they love animals, just like we do," she stated, as though she knew several personally.

"I *thought* I could see some faery traits in you both," Freya replied, looking thoughtful. "Seeing as how you're such lovely young ladies, how would you like a treasure hunt?"

The girls thought that was a smashing idea, so Freya pointed out into the shop.

"If it's alright with your mum and dad, if you can find my favourite one out of *all* these, you can pick one each as a prize. A present from one faery fan to another. It'd make me very happy to know that they're watching over you and making you smile."

"Are you sure Freya?" asked Mum, moved by her generosity. "You put so much effort into them."

"Quite sure dear, they're a couple of sweethearts and it's my pleasure." She winked conspiratorially. "Not just *anyone* that visits The Forum gets this treatment you know!"

Freya crooked a finger at the girls and they came closer.

"I'll give you a little clue to start you off. There're some faeries in here with prices on and some without that aren't for sale… the ones that I carve to keep."

Willow's brow furrowed. "You wouldn't sell your favourite…"

Lea's eyes widened. "So it's one of the ones without a price!" she finished explosively.

"Exactly!" said Freya. "Ready? Steady? GO!"

They burst into action and the search for Freya's favourite began in earnest. While the hunt was in progress, Mum and Dad had a look for their usual holiday keepsake and after umming and aahing over three or four different ones, they agreed on the one of a faery holding the face of a hedgehog in her hands. The faery looked as though she was speaking to the hedgehog and the slightly tilted face of the hedgehog made it look as though it was listening intently to the faery. Lifelike wasn't the word. Like Mum said… you *had* to get the faces right.

She sat their choice on the counter and Freya started wrapping it just as two little girls came back from the depths of the shop looking very pleased with themselves.

"We've found it!" they squawked together, crumbling into giggles as they '*jinxed*' and '*double jinxed*' each other.

"That was quick, well done! Show me," said Freya, coming around the counter.

The girls led her straight to a female faery sitting cross legged with her back against a tree, holding a baby. She had her head over the little one, her dark, wavy hair cascading down around her face while she whispered some secret thing to the child. The baby had that happy, surprised look on it's face, the one babies get when you play 'Aaaaaahh.... BOO!' It made you want to be just that tiny bit closer so you could hear what the baby was hearing. The piece of wood exuded love and looking at it, you were certain the baby was her own.

"Yes," said Freya, reaching out and lightly brushing a speck of something from the top of the mother's head. "That's the one. What made you pick this one then?"

"I thought..." began Lea, but was halted by Willow's elbow.

"We!" added Willow.

"*We* thought," continued Lea, "that 'cause you're so nice to children, it would be one with children in it... then we found this one and it's so lovely, it *had* to be the one." She nodded at the end as if confirming their own logic.

"Works for me. I think you've earnt those faeries... why don't you go and choose one each?" Freya offered. "Remember though... don't pick my keepers, they have to stay here with me."

Saying "Thank you!" in harmony, the girls rushed off to choose their prizes and Freya finished her wrapping. Dad looked in the backpack and pulled a face.

"Damn, no wallet. I'll just nip back to Daisy and get it," he said, kissing Mum. "Won't be a sec."

He started towards the shop door.

The old lady looked interested. "Daisy?"

"She's our VDub camper," Dad explained. "This is our first proper holiday in her."

"Oh, that's lovely. I spent a few years in the sixties and seventies living in one of those. I called her Daisy too, after my favourite flower. Wonderful, wonderful times," Freya said, looking dreamy as she reminisced.

"They're my favourite too!" Mum exclaimed. "She probably would have got named Daisy, even without the carving."

Freya's head snapped around as if she'd had an electric shock. "Carving?"

"Yeah, she has the most amazing carving of wild daisies on her dashboard, a real expert job," said Dad.

Freya sat down quickly on the stool behind the counter.

"Well I never… it's always the things you least expect that take your breath away the most. I think I carved those daisies," she said.

"No!" said Mum, eyes wide.

"I think so. Would you mind if I had a look to be sure? You see, if it is my Daisy, I think I'm supposed to give you a message of sorts…" She tailed off, shaking her head in amazement and disbelief.

Dad laughed. "What is it with this place? People keep wanting to give us stuff... first holidays and diamonds, then faeries, now messages."

Freya looked questioningly at him and he and Mum explained about their dodgy holiday prize, the invitation to dinner at Borson House with Luke, his very generous and very strange offer regarding the Keys and the fact that he had arranged all of this on the basis that he had dreamed about them!

Freya listened intently without saying a word and when they had finished, the old lady stood and silently beckoned for Mum and Dad to follow her. She led them into the kitchen and dining room behind the shop and went to a cupboard. Taking out what looked like a chunky photo album tied with a ribbon, she placed it on the round table in the middle of the room.

"I think we're in the thick of a genuine mystery here. You see, I worked at Borson House. It was that job that paid for Daisy actually. But more to the point... I *also* had a recurring dream."

She rested her hand on the album.

"Luke Borson's parents had seen my work around the island and wanted to hire me to do some bits and pieces on their estate. It's not always steady money being an artist and they paid pretty well, so I took them up on it. I lived on the grounds in one of the outbuildings until I'd saved up enough to buy Daisy, then lived in her. There was a *massive* storm one night, as bad as the one we've just had. It was that night I dreamed about this place for the first time. Fifty years ago."

She untied the ribbon and paged through a series of pencil drawings and sketches, spreading a few of them out on the table. They were mostly of a steep hillside with a deep, bowl-like depression in it ringed by trees, like a giant ice cream scoop had taken a huge dollop from the landscape.

"I dreamed that one day I would meet a family I'd never met, but shared a home with. I'm guessing that must be you and Daisy. I dreamed that I had to find this place on the island and show them the way there," Freya said, tapping one of the drawings. "It seemed so real and so important at the time that I sketched some of these the moment I woke. I had the same dream for weeks after that and spent all my free time drawing it and searching for it. It was only when I actually *found* it that the dreams stopped. Eventually, this and a little stretch of the beach below it came up for sale and I snapped it up."

She leafed through a few more pages until she came to some drawings of a beach and a collapsed cliff with the hill and the depression in the background. The wreckage of a battered dinghy lay at the base of the cliff face, casting a dark shadow against it.

She laid out a final set of sketches. At first glance, they looked like the inside of a geode, with a crystalline inner layer and a single large crystal growing up from the bottom in the centre. It wasn't a geode though. The top was open, with clouds in the sky overhead. It was a cave. A really, really big cave. A cave about forty metres high with a centre crystal roughly ten metres long and two metres thick.

Freya watched their faces as they took in the pencil sketches.

"I always assumed the drawings meant there was something wonderful hidden there, but I've explored it *a lot* over the years and never found anything unusual about it. I'd almost convinced myself I was doolally for buying the meadow in the first place… but now here *you* are."

Freya pointed to a large canvas oil painting hung on the wall behind them next to the door they'd come in through.

"Look."

It was the finished article, the thing that all the pencil drawings had been for and it left you in no doubt as to scale. There were several birds circling in the sunlight that streamed in through the massive opening in the roof and way down on the floor of the cavern, a small figure was looking up at the sunlight from the mouth of a tunnel. The crystals seemed to shimmer with iridescence, like oil on water. It was beautiful.

"Never found *that* while I was exploring!" Freya joked, all of them sharing the same thought… '*What a shame.*'

She looked suddenly enlightened.

"But maybe *I* was never supposed to. Maybe that's why the dream said to show *you* the way."

They offered to take her to Daisy straight away. When they went back through to the shop, the girls were sitting on a rug by a display of smaller carvings, playing with their new faeries. Lea had chosen a little girl stroking the ears of a baby deer and Willow's faery was another girl with a family of snails lined up along her arm in size order.

As Mum and Dad rounded them up, Freya reached under the counter for a bunch of keys and turning the little carved sign in the window to 'Closed,' she locked the shop door as they left.

They chatted as they walked to the car park, Freya telling them how Luke had been orphaned by his parents' tragic deaths not long after the storm. The incident had never been fully explained. Apparently, the poor lad had seen them collapse and there had been some speculation about cave gas, but beyond that it was a mystery.

From that point on, the young Luke had been raised by a governess and educated by tutors arranged by the family's solicitors. Without the love of his doting parents though, he'd become withdrawn and distant, far from the happy child he'd once been.

At the solicitor's request, Freya had stayed on at Borson House to honour the list of changes and improvements laid down by Oscar and Elizabeth prior to their deaths. She created some beautiful pieces from the remains of the old oak and left with a generous bonus.

On reaching adulthood, Luke had taken over the running of the estate himself and now maintained the Borson diamond fortune by trading, rather than mining the precious stones.

Years ago, he'd sought her out in her capacity as a local artist to ask her advice on commissioning a metal statue for his estate. She'd put him in touch with a friend of hers on the mainland who was well known for his rather extraordinary creations. He'd taken the commission... but hated every second of it. A crying, bound faery was just a tad too weird.

When Freya had opened the Forum, Luke had visited once or twice, intrigued by her sculptures, but had disappeared from public view since then.

The five of them reached Daisy and Freya went straight to the passenger side. Her hand went to her mouth as she peered in the window. Mum unlocked the door and opened it for her.

"Oh, Daisy, it is you, you beautiful old girl!" Freya said delightedly, climbing in and stroking the carved dashboard, her fingertips lovingly tracing the lines of the leaves, stems and petals that she had put there so long ago.

Dad got in the side door and lit the stove to put the kettle on. They chatted for ages, oblivious to the fact that they were sat in a plain old car park, enjoying each others' company and admiring the renovated Daisy while they drank tea and listened to the girls playing with Freya's gifts.

She told them all about the freedom of having Daisy as a home. Her doubt-filled weeks searching for a place she'd only seen in a dream. Her amazement at finding it. How when the meadow went on the market, the farmer couldn't sell it to her quickly enough as it was on too steep a hill to farm. How she had spent much of her time there, sleeping under the stars in her own private paradise.

Inevitably though, bellies began to rumble. It was decided that they would go exploring in the morning after a good night's sleep and come back late the following afternoon to meet Freya at her friend's tea room to report on the day's events.

Flanked by Willow and Lea, Freya was escorted safely back to her shop and Dad, now with wallet, tried to pay for their new hedgehog.

"Pfff…" said Freya simply, waving the money away as she wrote down some directions. She put them with a few of the drawings from the album and handed them to Mum, who pulled something out of her bag.

"We thought you might like to see this, Freya," Mum said softly, handing her Daisy's diary. "We made a diary for her. There're some blank pages at the front… you know, just in case we ever met anyone that owned her. She's got some important history missing… you can fill in the gaps if you'd like."

Freya took the book, kissing Mum on the cheek. "Thank you, sweetheart, I'd *love* to… and good luck tomorrow."

Mum squeezed her hand gently.

"We'll come and see you as soon as we're done there."

The girls gave her hugs and Freya watched them as they left the shop and disappeared from view through the hanging ivy, feeling like fifty years had just melted away.

'*What a pair of crackers those kids are*,' she thought to herself. She'd have given them faeries whichever one they'd decided was her favourite. She didn't even *have* a favourite. There were the ones she sold… and the ones she kept. What she hadn't told the family was the thing that decided whether one of her works was a seller or a keeper.

Most of the time, she had an idea, saw it in the wood and carved it. Her keepers were entirely different. The inspiration for them came from the same source as her cavern drawings… her dreams.

Back in her youth, after one of those dreams she'd run for her tools and carve feverishly through the night, but more recently her years had caught up with her.

Nowadays, she'd wake full of excitement and sketch the image frantically in her dream diary before drifting back into a deep, peaceful sleep. She woke the next day completely refreshed and so keen to start that apart from a quick cup of tea, she missed breakfast and only stopped again mid-afternoon when hunger started to outweigh inspiration.

She didn't question it too much… just said a quiet little thank you to wherever the images came from and did her utmost to recreate them the next day.

Although it was true she had no particular favourite, there was *one* that stood out from the others. She was always intensely single-minded while she was carving, as she revelled in the thing she was creating.

What really intrigued her was the fact that the girls had picked the only one she'd ever made where she'd spent the whole time sobbing her heart out.

The First Step

The girls didn't put down their new faeries until they got back to the campsite and then only to decorate a suitably faery-like spot on the field with wildflowers and begin construction on a lean to shelter and a picket fence made from twigs and long grass. After a few of their other toys had been added to the scene, it started to look like some kind of faery-related nativity.

Mum came over to have a look and smiled at the picket fence.

"Nice work. Just like the one Daddy built me at home. And the shelter's great!"

The very practical Willow looked up from their building site.

"I know they love the outdoors, but even faeries need a bit of cover while they're camping."

After dinner and showers, Mum and Dad spent an hour getting two very excited children to bed. Dad had to play the sensible card and tell them that, chances were, if Freya had spent years looking and hadn't found anything, there was a good chance they wouldn't either. Mum shot him a sad face as he did so. Sometimes it sucked being a grown up; they hated having to temper their excitement, but better pre-warned now than bitterly disappointed later.

When the girls finally settled, Mum and Dad spent the evening studying the sketches and their map over a rum coffee or two, secretly just as keen to start the search as they were. Sleep didn't come easily that night. They'd seen and heard a lot of odd things that needed processing.

When they woke the next day, the kids were still doing somersaults at the thought of discovering a secret crystal cavern. They rushed breakfast and got ready in record time, jamming their bags full of handy items, food and plenty of water. If yesterday's weather was anything to go by and they were going to be scrambling about on a sunny hillside, they were going to be grateful for a few litres of *that*.

"Don't forget Mummy's rope, Daddy," said Willow reproachfully, tugging at his tee shirt.

Dad looked at her, almost laughing. Random.

"Why does Mummy need a rope, sweetie?"

"Because you said she could lasso the cow if we find it… you said we all could!"

Dad knelt down in front of Willow, reminded of her superhuman memory, especially where animals were concerned.

"Oh, yeah… I forgot about that! Good job you're supervising. I've got a big hank of paracord, how about that?" he asked.

"That sounds perfect," she replied, happy to have helped.

Feeling a bit skeptical that their paracord washing line would end up doubling as a cow's halter, Dad stuffed it into his day sack anyway and they set off, bumping out of the campsite with Mum holding the directions and sketches that Freya had given them.

Shanklin and the Faery Forum were east of their campsite, but the directions sent them west along Military Road for a few kilometres instead. They chatted about a fossil-hunting expedition on the beach as they passed the Dinosaur Museum, then drove on with the sea sparkling and glinting to their left. Eventually, there on the right on a hillside meadow was their destination.

Dad pulled into a lay by just past the hollow and switched off the engine. It was very peaceful there. The family stayed hushed for a moment as they enjoyed the quiet.

Mum, who had been comparing a sketch to the real thing, finally broke the silence.

"She can *really* draw... this is so detailed," she said, studying one that included sheep grazing at the edge of the bowl-like hollow.

She held it up for Dad to see the two together and he looked between the paper and the hillside for a bit, then raised his eyebrows and nodded.

"Yeah, very good. I know it's been an amazing couple of days, but how d'ya think she knew the sheep'd be stood exactly like that?" he asked, pointing up the hill.

Mum did a double take... then a triple take. He was right. Left to right along the lip of the closest edge, just outside the line of the encircling trees, were one, two, three, four, five, six distinct groups of sheep. They weren't doing anything out of the ordinary, just grazing it appeared, but it was the number of sheep in each group that was interesting.

They looked back and forth between the sketch and the scene on the hillside. Left to right, there were three groups of nine, a group of seven, a pair and then another group of nine. Like a snapshot of this exact moment, but drawn fifty years ago... *from a dream!*

This didn't feel half as strange as it would have forty eight hours ago. The human mind has a huge capacity for dealing with the strange and unusual and the last forty eight hours had been both. So taking it all in their stride, they simply grabbed their bags, locked up and walked back to a stile that took them into the field.

As they set off from the bottom of the hill, the hollow had the appearance of a slim oval, but as they waded up through the long grass and wildflowers of the meadow, it grew wider until suddenly they were at the tree line... through the tree line... and it opened out into a wide, circular expanse with steep, sloping sides that were covered in a thick blanket of undergrowth, grasses and flowers. It was absolutely beautiful… a secret garden hidden in plain sight.

"Wow," was all Mum could manage.

"Yeah," Dad replied in quiet awe.

The kids however, had no trouble expressing themselves.

"OH MY GOODNESS! OH MY GOODNESS!" squealed Lea, almost levitating with excitement as she looked for a way down.

"WHOA, WHOA, WHOA! Slow down, missus!" exclaimed Willow indignantly, making Mum and Dad laugh out loud. "I'm the oldest; I should go first!"

Dad looked around for a clear route and finding a badger trail, took a step over the edge into the hollow.

"How about your Dad leads the way down the steep mystery path into the big hole?" he said, smiling at their adventurous spirits. "And watch out for badger poo!" he continued, pointing at something curly at his feet, grinning as the girls pulled '*yuck*' faces.

They picked their way slowly down, pausing now and then to decide on a new direction to get them to the bottom with the minimum of obstacles, of which there were plenty.

Here and there small ponds had formed, creating isolated mini-habitats and occasionally, an exposed rock jutted from the ground. These stony, sun-baked islands seemed to be the preferred basking spot for the hollow's large population of common lizards. Disturbed from their sunbathing, they skittered away as the four approached and Dad told them how, as a boy, he used to go out early in the morning while they were still a bit slow and catch them before they'd had a chance to warm their cold blood in the sun. You were lucky if you even *saw* a common lizard these days. From the looks of it, they'd all somehow crossed the Solent to relocate to the Isle of Wight.

With the journey seemingly shortened by their excitement, they were suddenly at the bottom. They stood amid the buzz of a million insects with the sun beating down on them, staring back up at the tree-lined rim way above them.

The girls found a nearby mini-pond and were delighted to find it contained not only a large contingent of pond skaters, but frogs too. While they studied bugs, picked flowers and chatted, their parents pondered their next step.

"Where should we start?" asked Dad.

"Haven't a clue… but I don't think it even matters anymore. I can't shake the feeling that we've been guided here all along and whatever we *do* do is what we're *meant* to do," replied Mum. "Luke's dream, the fake holiday, his offer, Freya's dream, her drawings, her directions here… I'm not saying I get any of it, but we're *way* past coincidence now."

"Yeah, it's weird alright. How about we take a walk round in a spiral to the top and look out for openings?" Dad suggested, making a spiral pattern with his forefinger. An organized search pattern brought some reality back to what was going on and gave him something to focus on. That would do for now. It *was* all very odd, but he still wasn't totally convinced that precognition had anything to do with it.

Leaving the girls searching the base of the hollow with instructions to be careful around the pond, they headed slowly uphill together, searching for anything odd as they went. It was a big space and heavily overgrown and after an hour and a half, they reached the top tired, hot and thirsty with no discovery to show for it.

Dad wet a bandana with some of his water and passed it to Mum so she could cool herself down. As she patted her face and neck with the cool cloth, he used his fingers to give another high-pitched whistle to the girls down below to check in again. They waved and he and Mum waved back.

After a long drink, they set off in different directions around the circumference of the bowl weaving in and out of the trees that bordered it, but met at the other side still with nothing to report. A little disheartened, they plodded their way back down to Willow and Lea to give them the disappointing news.

By now, the girls had made themselves at home under the shade of a small tree, with drinks and snacks and Freya's drawings spread out on a picnic blanket. After hearing Mum and Dad had found nothing, Lea didn't even look up from the spider in her bug catcher as she reached out and held up one of the sketches.

"Maybe it's the cave on the beach."

"What cave, baby?" asked Mum, taking the paper from her.

"The one behind the boat."

Mum and Dad stared at the picture. Of course! The shadow on the cliff face wasn't a shadow... it was a *hole!*

Marveling at the clarity of a child's view of the world, they quickly helped the girls pack their things away and hustled up the hill again, full of enthusiasm.

They broke through the trees at the top and were greeted by a cool breeze that swept across the meadow. After the heat of the sun trap they'd just been in, it was a real treat. They stood savouring the change in temperature for a moment, heads tilted upward like a dog with its head out of a car window, then ran down the hill laughing, bounding through the tall grass until they reached the bottom.

The road was still quiet, so they jumped over the stile and crossed over the road to a wooden post topped with a public footpath sign that showed the way to the beach.

They squeezed down an overgrown track that obviously wasn't popular with pedestrians, probably due to the fact that it was on a quiet stretch of road with nothing else around. As the track sloped steadily down, the ground on either side of it rose steadily up, until they were walking down a high-sided gulley towards the now-visible sea.

After about two hundred metres, they finally emerged onto a wide beach, revealing a high cliff behind them, soaring steeply back up to road height where Daisy was parked. It was deserted and storm debris lay everywhere. There were far too many well-used public areas that needed attention to worry about a remote spot like this just yet.

"No surprises there, then," said Mum, pointing to the smashed boat they more than half-expected to see against the base of the cliff.

From this distance, the shadow it appeared to cast looked like just that, a shadow, but as they walked closer it gained detail and became the opening they'd been hoping for.

Although waves and rain at the tail end of the storm had washed much of the collapsed cliff away, the area around the boat and tunnel was still a mess. The hull was covered in mud and sand and they all got more than their fair share of dirt as they took hold of it and dragged it out of the way.

Dad examined the sides of the opening.

"Looks like most of this mess is just sediment that was hiding the rock face," he said, slapping the rock. "Solid bedrock. A tunnel through this stuff should be pretty safe, but I'll have a quick look inside 'fore we all go down there."

He put on a head torch and loaded up with some of their extra water before hugging Mum and the girls.

"Please be careful," said Mum, worriedly.

"Straight in, see what's what and back out. Thirty minutes tops. Don't worry, I won't do anything stupid," he replied soothingly.

Smiling at them, he adjusted the torch, pointing it down at the ground in front of him.

"I love you guys; I'll see you soon," he said and disappeared into the dark with the girls' 'Love you too' ringing in his ears.

A Cavern And A Cow

Dad's guess of thirty minutes was a distressing under estimation. It was with intense relief that they saw the light from his torch approaching from down the tunnel nearly fifty minutes later. He stepped out into the sunlight, blinking, dusty and smiling and was greeted by hugs and kisses.

"I know, I know, I'm sorry," he said, holding his hands up. He pulled his mobile phone from his pocket. "I did try to call you after half an hour, but *shocker...* there's no signal down there."

He sat on a boulder by the tunnel entrance and took a swig from a water bottle.

"What did you find?" Mum asked excitedly.

"The tunnel's safe enough, it just runs a *really* long way. You've got to see it to believe it! It's *there!*"

Willow and Lea cheered, jumping up and down and waving their hands in the air.

Mum was thrilled. "Like the picture?"

"Erm... not *quite* the same, but still pretty mind-blowing. You'll see. Get your bags, guys, you're gonna *love* this!"

They put on their head torches, threw their packs on and followed Dad back into the gloom of the passage, treading carefully as they made their way along the rough, pebble-strewn floor.

Mum took up position at the back of the group so they had the children between them, their torches creating an oasis of light on the rock walls as they moved forward. She ran her fingertips along the sides of the tunnel. They were strangely smooth and rippled and they reminded her of caves they'd visited in Cheddar Gorge and the National Showcaves in Wales, where the networks of tunnels linking the caverns had been carved out by flowing water. It made sense. If the chines along the coastline were water formed, why not this?

The girls bombarded Dad with questions and although he was bursting to tell them everything, he refused point blank. He wanted to see their faces when they saw what waited for them at the end of the tunnel.

The way ahead was mainly quite level, with a couple of slight inclines up and down. They were heading through the cliff, under the road and toward the hillside where the depression was, so logically, the further along they got, the deeper underground they were.

Towards the end, there was a final sweeping bend before they broke out of the tunnel into a place they could barely believe. When Dad saw the three sets of dinner-plate sized eyes in the torchlight, he was glad he'd kept his mouth shut.

They were standing in an immense and slightly squashed underground bubble whose sides arched up to a flattened ceiling. As the sketches had promised, the inside of the cavern was completely covered in a layer of crystal like a geode and there were plateaus, protruding formations and even a spring which burst out from high up in the curved wall and cascaded down as a waterfall into a deep pool.

Freya's depiction of an open roof with sunlight streaming in was sadly inaccurate though.

In the flesh, the ceiling was solid, encrusted with crystal like the rest. And then of course, there was the piece de la resistance, the crystal in the middle of the cavern which thrust up at an angle towards the ceiling, leaning roughly southwards towards the tunnel and the beach.

Making their way over to it, they wandered around it in awe, touching its smooth surface as it towered above them, taller even than the huge trilithons at Stonehenge.

Their torches weren't powerful enough to illuminate the whole space, but after a while they noticed an interesting effect... the longer they were near the main crystal, the brighter it seemed to get, as though it were absorbing the light. It was soon bright enough to see by and they turned off their head torches.

Mum suddenly stopped in her tracks.

"We have to get Freya! She has to see this. She needs to know she was right all along."

Dad nodded. "As soon as we're done here, we'll go and get her. Let's finish looking around first." He paused. "You know... we're probably the first people that've been here for... oh, *thousands* of years. Maybe more. Maybe even *ever*."

Mum and Dad smiled, both thinking the same thing. They did like their holiday snaps.

Mum and the girls stood with their backs against the crystal while Dad balanced the camera on a small rock and set the timer to ten seconds.

"Ready?"

He pressed the shutter button and the timer flashed and beeped as he ran for the space they'd left for him. As he took his place beside them, he could feel the cool crystal beneath his finger tips.

"Everyone say SECRET CAVERNS!" said Mum and they did, laughing as the flash went off.

They hushed at the sound of an electrical crackle from behind them. The crystal had spent its entire existence in the darkness of the sealed cavern, isolated from the world above. It had never known the touch of a living thing until today. They were about to discover how it would react to the simultaneous touch of *four*.

The glow it had taken on intensified quickly until it was almost painful to look at and they retreated all the way back to the tunnel entrance. There was a loud

CRACK!

as an intense spark of energy arced between the tip of the giant crystal and the roof. The family recoiled in shock at the power of it, as though they had found themselves too close to a lightning strike.

The large crystal darkened as all of its energy was transferred to the roof, where it crackled outward through the skin of the cavern, down the walls and across the floor, lighting the crystal as it passed through it until the whole cavern was a bright globe of light.

The glow began to pulse, getting faster and faster until it reached the flickering speed of a strobe, accompanied by a deep throbbing sound that rose in pitch until it reached a high, humming, musical tone. The family rubbed their eyes in disbelief as its frequency generated colourful kaleidoscope like patterns in front of their eyes.

When the tone was at its peak, there was a deep

BVVV!

sound as the light drained from the ceiling and walls and was reabsorbed back into the main crystal again, the glare so fierce it obscured the crystal's shape entirely.

With a final, tooth rattling

DVVV!

that they felt in their chests, it sent its blinding brightness upwards in a single, concussive blast of raw power.

The effect this time was *very* different.

The roof simply vaporized, leaving behind a billion dust particles that glinted and sparkled in the sunlight that now suddenly poured in through the hole.

The family had been watching transfixed from the relative safety of the tunnel. A sudden rush of wind roared up behind them as the wind over the top of the new hole created a chimney effect, drawing air up the tunnel from the beach and sucking away the dust that filled the air. They huddled together as the initial rush of wind settled down to a steady flow, then crept back out into a scene that had been transformed into the painting in the Faery Forum.

Mum managed to find her voice first.

"What just happened?"

"Not sure…" Dad replied nervously, putting his hands up in surrender, "but that's it for me. Don't understand it, can't explain any of it, but I'm a believer. It might be time for us to go and have that little chat with Freya now."

Willow peeked nervously between Mum and Dad at the now sunlit cavern. "Are we in trouble, Mum?"

Mum smiled. "I don't think so sweetheart… I think we might've just fulfilled an old lady's dream though."

Dad sighed as they surveyed the changes.

"Either that… or we just broke her best crystal," he said numbly. He was in the habit of breaking glasses while he did the washing up, but this was way worse.

Mum took Dad's hand.

"You and glass, hey… don't worry love, I'm sure she'll prefer it the way she painted it!"

After making their way back down the long tunnel, the Rauliches emerged from the far end to be greeted by a rather large brown and white cow that was licking salt from the walls of the rocky entrance. She barely batted a massive fluttery eyelid when the four of them came stumbling out into the sunlight.

"The lost cow!" stated Willow excitedly, then more matter of factly, "I'm *so* glad we brought the rope."

Unable to control themselves, Mum and Dad burst out laughing. The cow just stared at them with its big gentle eyes, licked its lips the way cows do and blinked slowly.

Mum was right. Weirdest… holiday… *ever!*

D.O.W.T.

Buff walked under the beautiful wooden arch that marked the entrance to the gardens of D.O.W.T., smiling at the irony of the words carved amongst the flowers and leaves.

Despite having worked for the Department of Off World Travel for some time, she still felt the same rush of pride and excitement she'd always felt whenever she thought about the part she played as a volunteer. She considered the motto chiseled expertly into the arch, which she'd learnt as a child and now upheld every day of her life...

Where there is D. O. W. T. there is hope.

Still smiling, she walked the flagstone paths of the gorgeous, lush gardens. Even here in Lux, blanketed as it was in growing things, where nature was revered and the power of the Flow was openly accepted, the gardens never ceased to amaze. Things grew everywhere that a foot didn't fall and a bum didn't rest and the place was so beautiful it left you wishing you'd sprouted from a seed.

It was early evening and the light was taking on a different character now the heat of the day had passed. There are some flowers that seem to glow in certain levels of light and nowhere could that be seen more readily than here. Buff loved the gardens.

She made her way along the winding pathways slowly, savouring the journey and brushing her hands over the top of the plants as she went, enjoying the mingling of her Flow and theirs as she walked.

The sounds of humming and buzzing filled the air as a billion insects went about the business of feeding and pollinating and the air was warm and heavy with the smells of the flowers that called to them.

After a while, she emerged onto a vast band of short, well-tended grass that stretched left and right. You could say it was a lawn, but it was a lawn like none you'd seen before. This was the Lea, a place of absolute wonder. This was where the magic happened, where the purpose of D.O.W.T. was realized and where Buff and many young faeries like her hoped to better the universe.

Spaced out in the grass at regular intervals were daisies. Days eyes to be precise, twice the height of the tallest faery, with stems as thick as a forearm and petals stretching an arms length across, tip to tip.

They were a very special plant indeed. They made the most lovely humming sound as the sun rose and set and many people visited the gardens just to hear their song and commune with them. It only lasted for a few seconds, as those first rays touched their petals in the morning and as the sun dipped below the horizon at sunset, but it was very special.

Just to be close to one, singing or not, was pretty extraordinary due to their size and reputation, a bit like the feeling you get when you stand next to a giant old tree.

Faery Facts.

When the Spark created the universe, one of its finest achievements was plant life. They evolved quickly, reproduced rapidly and adapted to every environment imaginable.

To use daisies as an example, they've been around in one form or another for approximately 42,000,000 years. Yeah... you didn't misread it... forty two MILLION years.

This means that in between being eaten and almost wiped out by one of the many extinction events that have befallen both Lux and Earth, they've had plenty of time to come up with a long-term survival strategy. They did this by diversifying.

There are currently approximately 23,000 species of daisy on the two worlds, of which the days eye is just one. Depending on the species, they can produce anywhere between 1,000 and 26,000 seeds per plant because while most flower heads have just one set of reproductive organs, daisies have an intricate collection of hundreds, ensuring thousands of seeds and the guaranteed survival of the species.

Daisies... an evolutionary success story.

The most amazing thing about days eyes though, was that they could travel, or at least facilitate travel. Only to the one destination, granted, but that destination was very impressive. Given the right stimuli, they became a doorway between Lux and Earth.

It all started because as a sentient plant, days eyes felt a certain affinity with faeries due to their empathetic natures and joy of life. Faeries had a deep understanding of plants and were only too happy to discover one that shared their outlook. So began a friendship whose main drive was to explore what it was to be alive and to search for life elsewhere.

Their openhearted desire to share the wonder of existence with others led to the accidental discovery of a doorway to another world. It soon became apparent that this other world, Earth, also had a thriving population of days eyes and was home to beings who had a deep respect for nature and strong spiritual beliefs.

Unfortunately, humans had never evolved the physical attributes needed to experience Flow as faeries did and all attempts by Earth's days eyes to communicate with them had failed.

After careful consideration, faeries and days eyes agreed to share the wonders of the Flow with their new friends, believing it to be the reason they were led to their world in the first place. Humans were a passionate species and they embraced their new awareness with genuine gratitude and joy. The Age of Harmony had begun.

The first travellers to Earth were pioneers of the highest level, their bravery comparable with modern day astronauts or test pilots. After the initial discovery and some very rough test trips, it was soon discovered that days eyes opened a smoother, more stable doorway if a precise set of ingredients and procedures were used.

Different variations were trialled, but most just caused doorway wobble and travel sickness. Arriving at their destination dizzy and throwing up in the grass isn't a priority for the average traveller, so after the perfect combination was hit upon, it was adhered to strictly.

Faery Facts.

Since the Great Divide, humans had created countless myths and legends about faeries from what was in reality their own forgotten ancient history. Some of these stories were pure fiction and some contained a grain of truth. There were relatively few that were 100% correct.

For example, it's widely believed that faeries collect children's teeth as they sleep. While they don't send out *dedicated* squadrons of dentistry~obsessed collection agents, it is *partly* true.

Teeth are incredibly strong and make awesome knife blades and jewellery, so if the chance to snaffle one presents itself, they'll take it. Next time you put a coin under your child's pillow, take their tooth and later on it isn't where you thought you put it... ask yourself why.

What's *lesser* known is that they do collect the raw materials for lux to Earth travel from human children, in bulk. Hair, ideally red, is a valuable commodity and you know that little tear that forms in the corner of their eye while they sleep?

Gold dust.

It turned out that the secret was to only use ingredients that came *from* the intended destination to travel *to* it and keeping to this golden rule made days eye travel a very comfortable experience. If you kept to the rules, you arrived as fresh as a daisy. Sorry, days eye.

The how-to of days eye travel was actually quite simple:

First, you cabled some healthy lengths of red hair into a ring around the exposed root system of a mature days eye. Great at conducting Flow, red hair, better than any other colour. The ring had to be large enough for four faeries to stand inside.

The cabling itself involved some very elaborate splicing and knot work to link it to the roots. The precise patterns in the root systems of plants in a given area were as individual as fingerprints. Once you'd memorized the 'addresses' and mastered the knots that replicated them, you could open a *very* geographically accurate doorway.

The precision of the knot work also had a large impact on the comfort of the journey, so it paid to have someone who knew what they were doing in charge of *that*.

Next, a liberal sprinkling of fresh water dosed with a teardrop or two was needed along the cables, before they were buried again to 'earth them out.' The tear solution helped conduct Flow better and nothing seemed to do more to alleviate a wobbly doorway than the various pure chemical compounds released in a child's tears.

Finally, once a group was assembled inside the ring, Flow was channeled into the stem of the days eye, setting off a chain reaction.

The pulse of Flow shot up into the flower head and down into the root system of the plant and crackled its way through them, flashing a bubble of Flow into existence around the whole arrangement. The bubble flexed and shivered, sending ripples across its surface for a second, then it 'popped,' giving this form of travel its name and taking the group with it to whatever destination had been knotted in.

Faery Facts.

Language is a funny old chestnut.
Popped in, popping out, just pop to… you could Flow your whole life and not even consider why you say some of the things you do.

Even the name days eye had more to it than met the, erm… eye.
On modern~day Earth, humans believed that it was a precursor to the word daisy, due to the fact that their petals opened in the morning and closed at night, just like an eye.
The name actually had a far older history than that and was originally a shortening of a faery expression first heard in the early days of lux and Earth's friendship.
'Through today's eye into a shared tomorrow.'
From above, when a travel bubble formed it looked very much *like* an eye with its yellow pupil, white petal iris and sparkling Flow bubble cornea. 'From above' was a perspective faeries understood very well and so the name stuck.

From inside the bubble, you could still see the place you were leaving behind through the shimmering sheet of Flow. As it popped, the barrier vaporized and your ears popped too as the double pressure of the air you'd taken with you and the air where you appeared equalized. You were suddenly stood on Earth under the days eye whose root system most closely matched the knot work you'd done.

Simple, init? Sat nav, nature style. Just rinse and repeat to get home. It could be a bit disorienting the first couple of times you did it, but a regular traveller quickly got used to it.

From outside, you saw the bubble and its passengers vanish as it popped and heard the popping sound that you'd expect, coupled with a slight inward rush of wind as the vacuum the bubble left behind filled with air.

The days eye remained, as if nothing had happened and the hair strands that had been cabled in were reduced to ash. While this provided nitrogen rich food for the plant, it also meant that every trip required a rewiring.

And that was the natural, beautiful, magical marvel that was days eye travel.

Faery Facts.

There's a strange skepticism inherent in humans that precludes the belief in fantastical things, but consider a few subjects they've dabbled in even while living in denial:

botany,

chemistry,

space travel,

the search for extraterrestrial intelligence

and particle physics.

To sum up:

'The study of plants and how they react with other substances to facilitate travel through space to meet other life forms via the transference of matter.'

They're willing to study them individually, but won't accept that using them in more imaginative combinations may bring *wholly* different results.

It's ironic that faeries had managed to attain the last three with only a more profound understanding of the first two.

Just goes to show, it's not about *what* you look at... it's about *how* you look at it.

Its manner was the same as since its discovery, but its purpose had changed. What had been a mechanism to blend cultures and beliefs had been tainted by the fall of man and it had lain dormant for the longest time, contact with humans judged to be unsafe.

When D.O.W.T. was founded and the old routes reopened, the more enlightened meetings of an older time were replaced by missions carried out by teams. Lux's ideology was that humanity had lost its way in the dark and faeries were the spiritual beacon they needed to find their way home. The missions they carried out were tailored to accomplish just that.

The huge part that the days eyes played in making all this possible was reflected in the design of D.O.W.T.'s gardens, its Lea and its headquarters, which created a series of concentric flower heads when viewed from the air.

The gardens defined the boundary of the first flower, leading inward to the wide grassed expanse of the Lea, which shaped the second. The third was created by the immense wooden building which stood at the centre.

The Travel, Health and Legend Offices of D.O.W.T. were striking to say the least.

The structure consisted of a colossal central dome of arched wooden beams, truncated with a flat, grassed roof. Surrounding and attached to the main dome were the petals, eight similar, smaller domes. People were bustling between them, running the last errands of the day.

The wooden framework of the building was encased in a geodesic arrangement of triangular amber resin panes, giving it a yellowish tint that reinforced the illusion of its flower like form.

High up on the flat roofs, there were well-established gardens, with flower beds, shrubs and small trees arranged alongside seating and tables to create beautiful spaces to relax. A lot of the seats were still occupied and the sounds of laughter and chatter drifted through the air as friends and colleagues ended their working day and prepared to go home. The view out over the gardens and into the city beyond was breathtaking from up there and it felt like you could reach out and touch it as though it were a painting.

Buff looked across the grassy Lea at the army of custodians busy at work. They were gently tending the days eyes, examining them for imperfections and making sure they were happy and healthy for each team that popped.

Staying just long enough to see a few teams leave for Earth and some return home, she crossed the Lea, heading for the building and the rather odd appointment she'd been summoned to. The very short notice, 'Be there in an hour,' appointment she'd been told not to breath a word of… to *anyone*.

At Buff's approach, the heavy main doors were slowly opened by two custodians, who welcomed her with bowed heads and hands on their hearts. As with the garden's entrance arch, the doors were lovingly carved with flowers and leaves but in place of the motto was D.O.W.T.'s emblem of a large days eye surrounded by three smaller ones.

The emblem split in two as the doors swung open and smiling her thanks, she walked into the foyer. Beyond the foyer was the hub, the large central dome with its perimeter of arches leading in to the outer domes which housed amongst other things, the three Offices.

There was a line of reception desks and Buff headed for the only one still occupied, recognizing the lady who was sat there. She smiled warmly.

"Hello Violet, how's it Flowing?"

"Good, thanks, Buff, never better in fact, I passed my basic last week. I've just got specialist training to do, then I can pop!"

Buff smiled even more broadly.

"Well done, Vi, that's great news! I bet your family are doing loops, aren't they?"

Vi smiled sheepishly and looked embarrassed. By volunteering, she was following her father, grandfather *and* great grandfather into service. They were extremely proud that Vi was continuing a family tradition.

"Mmm... Dad's chest is so swollen with pride he can't fit through doors any more. His words, not mine. To *anyone* who'll listen."

Each team that popped to Earth for D.O.W.T. was made up of four specialists; a grower, a pusher, a sharer and a polisher, all highly trained individuals in their particular field. Especially growers, who for the most part actually worked *in* a field.

Growers and pushers were the ones responsible for getting their team to Earth and safely back again. A grower took care of the cabling and watering and the jolt of Flow that set off a pop was supplied by a pusher. Sharers and polishers were there to carry out the mission objective, which was ultimately to heal the humans they visited.

The same way humans had traits and talents they excelled at, so too did faeries, but as a different species some of their skills were determined by anatomical gifts that they were blessed with at birth. Faeries were physically a little different to humans and they possessed one or two additions to their nervous systems that they could use to interact with the world around them.

The first, that they all shared in common, were the two brain like wing nodes on either side of their spine under their shoulder blades. Although they *looked* like miniature brains, they weren't as delicate as that, but instead had a tough, transparent membrane over them. Wing nodes absorbed and focused Flow and gave them the gift of flight.

Faery Facts.

So faeries have wings, do they? Not quite.

Wing nodes absorb Flow and use it to 'bloom' two sheets of rainbow~like electromagnetic energy that cancel out or repel the force of gravity, like when you push two magnets together the wrong way round.

Ever seen a picture of the Earth's magnetic field? Just like that. They might LOOK like wings, they might lift you off the ground LIKE wings, they might even be commonly CALLED wings for convenience... but they are in fact, NOT wings.

A bonus of having nodes was that it activated a part of the brain that gave you the ability to actually *feel* the essence of life Flowing through the universe. This left you in no doubt that you were part of something wondrous and larger than yourself. No surprise then that as species went, faeries were one of the most enlightened and reverent of nature.

The second addition, which only presented itself in about nine percent of faery births, was another type of node that could manifest in different parts of the body. This nine percent of the population, known as 'niners,' was made up of the growers, pushers, sharers and polishers and they could not only use their wing nodes to sense Flow and fly, but could also divert energy from them to their secondary nodes to access the abilities they bestowed.

Growers had small nodes at the tip of every finger and had a deep, spiritual affinity with plant life. Through their nodes, they intuitively sensed what a plant needed for its physical health and emotional wellbeing.

Faery Facts.

Still used on Earth today to describe a person's skill with plants, the term 'green fingered' had first been warmly bestowed on growers by their human counterparts, farmers.

Humanity's leap from hunter~gatherer to farmer had already begun by the time faeries and humans met, but the transition was made a glowing success by the wealth of agricultural knowledge faeries had freely shared with them.

Every human farmer had worked closely with a faery grower, learning about the interconnected nature of all living things and gaining a deep respect for the crops they grew.

Together, they learned as much about each other as they did about farming and soon came to realize that humans and faeries loved their connection to the soil and the life within it with an equal passion.

A pusher had a large node at their solar plexus, the bundle of nerves right at the spot where your ribs meet. They could charge this node the same way that an electric eel charges its electrical organs to stun its prey, but with benign Flow instead of electricity.

Once charged, the Flow could be released, or 'pushed' to influence the physical world, either slowly and gently along nerve pathways or in a quick burst from the node.

Quartz crystal was a great example of this, which glowed when pushed, the faery equivalent of a battery powered torch. Seeds could be encouraged to germinate at an almost miraculous rate, metamorphosing from tiny husk to seedling in seconds, something not even the growers could do.

The push they gave a days eye to set off a pop was a different thing altogether. That was more akin to a polite request, after which the plant did the rest.

Faery Facts.

It's thought by some humans that tree hugging is a bit 'hippy.'

Did you know that the origin of tree hugging comes from the fact that a pusher hugs the stem of a days eye to put their solar plexus node in the best possible position to channel a good, hard jolt of Flow into the plant to initiate world to world travel?

Hippy? Hippy?!
Like you wouldn't try it if you had the nodes for it...

Sharers were empaths and had a small but seriously powerful node in the centre of their forehead that they could use to sooth a person's state of mind. Sadness, anger, stress, guilt, grief... all of these could be calmed and depending on their depth, sometimes even totally healed.

Polishers were healers too, but of the body. They used the nodes in the palms of their hands to infuse Flow into their patient's chest, with one hand over the heart and one on the side of the torso over the ribs for good conductivity. The Flow then diffused throughout the body to where it was needed most, directed to sites of injury or disease by the patient's own subconscious mind. It was highly likely that the inventor of the defibrillator had been visited by a team at some point and woken with a *very* clever new idea...

Faery Facts.

It was a true blessing to have a percentage of your people who were genetically gifted healers, but even faeries weren't immune to accidents and injuries, so their culture still had need of medically trained professionals.

The Halls of Healing commanded the same respect and demanded the same dedication to learning you'd expect of any medical school. While the future nurses, doctors and surgeons of lux attended lectures and took exams in the other wings of the Halls, sharer and polisher D.O.W.T. volunteers completed their specialist training in the South Wing, which housed the N.H.S. or Niner Healing School. They took classes in human anatomy and physiology and studied common human ailments and mental health problems ready for active duty on Earth.

These four gifts complemented each other perfectly and some felt that what D.O.W.T. hoped to accomplish was almost guaranteed, as though the universe had deliberately provided the necessary tools to get the job done.

If you were a niner and you volunteered, there was a three-month period of basic training that covered subjects like Earth acclimatization, culture, geography and language studies, as well as fitness training. Then, you graduated into specialist training for a further three months before your service commenced.

Buff wistfully remembered her own training. Advanced escape and evasion had been fun. Twelve days and nights in the Canadian wilderness on Earth, trying not to get caught by the instructors. She'd loved every minute of it.

"When do you start specials?" she asked Vi.

"I've got three weeks before classes start, so I volunteered for a couple of desk duties here to see how things work."

Holding up her palms, she pulsed her polisher's nodes, sending Flow swirling through them.

"Can't *wait* to start using these on a regular basis. Do my bit for the cause an' all that! That's enough about me though, how're *you*? I haven't seen you for moons. Know why you're here?"

"I'm fine thanks, Vi, busy-busy, you know how it is. No work, all play!"

Faery Facts.

'All work, no play.'
Humans had got this one a bit wrong.
It was unfathomable to faeries how humans still thought it was acceptable to work for five days of the week and only get two off, but who were they to judge?
On lux, there's an eight day week and the leisure/work time division is an equal fifty/fifty split, four days of each. This is because faeries are acutely aware that there's more to life than a daily grindstone until they either retire or die.
Not so on Earth. The worst amongst them are quite happy to have a population to overwork and milk for taxes... five days a week.

"Don't know why I'm here though... maybe there's been another loss."

She was talking about the inherent risk in volunteering for service.

Lux sent several thousand missions to Earth daily, each one carrying out, on average, five visits. Tens of thousands of humans were treated every single day. There was an enormous sense of pride in what they did, but it came at a cost.

For the last fifty years during full moon on Earth, a faery went missing. Rarer celestial events like comets, meteor showers and planetary alignments seemed to cause it too, but more often than not the lunar cycle was involved.

At the departure point, from outside the bubble everything *looked* normal. Same on the inside, but in the blink of an eye it took for the bubble to pop, one of the team vanished and just simply didn't appear Earth side.

Apart from linking it to cosmic goings on, it hadn't yet been explained. Prior to fifty years ago, there had been no disappearances and missions had gone ahead without a hitch. As soldiers have to accept there are risks when they sign up, so too did niners.

Faery Facts.

In the fifty years since the disappearances had begun, not one faery volunteer had suggested suspending operations over Earth's full~moon period. Out of a sense of moral responsibility, the Offices had attempted to enforce it on more than one occasion and there had been public uproar each time.

If you took the average daily mission count as approximately seven thousand, with five visits each, this meant that on the full moon thirty five thousand humans that would otherwise have remained untreated had one missing faery to be thankful for... and didn't even know it.

The holistic faery belief was that no one individual was of greater consequence to the universe than another.

In conclusion:

Faeries are selfless, brave and awesome.

"Seven hundred and nineteen faeries missing at the last count," Buff said, shaking her head sadly. "If that's it, maybe I'm being transferred to another team to fill a gap. I hope not. I'm really happy with my lot, we're good together. It feels like family."

"Well, let's hope it's not bad news then," Vi responded, getting to her feet. "Please don't think me rude but Mamma seemed quite keen to see you. I'll take you over. Just to put your mind at rest though, I don't *think* you have to worry about a transfer... the rest of your team are already over there waiting for you."

Buff's head snapped round. "All of 'em?" she asked, surprised and intrigued. It was a rare thing for a whole team to be summoned to see Mamma.

"Yes, I *know!*" Vi whispered in a mock secretive voice, "And on your day off, too. *Very* cloak and dagger!"

They talked as they made their way over to the others, greeting the custodians that tended to the plants that grew there and guessing at the reason for the get-together.

Buff bloomed her wings. Her nodes glowed brightly as two sheets of electromagnetism spread out behind her, lifting her off the ground to about head height. She did a slow, vertical three hundred and sixty degree spin, taking in the always impressive sight of the hub.

She noted how hushed it was here at this time of day. During working hours, D.O.W.T. was a whirlwind of activity as the planning and logistics of missions went on, but after a day of administration most of the staff went home and except for two areas, the building quietened.

The first, that she'd passed through earlier, was the Lea. To keep the risk of detection to a minimum, D.O.W.T. missions were only authorized to arrive on Earth at night while the vast majority of humans were sleeping. To ensure any given part of the Earth could be reached under cover of darkness, there was a constant, twenty-four hour stream of traffic through the Lea.

The second, situated through the first arch on the left as you entered the hub was the

~ Travel Office ~

This was the department that was responsible for planning the elaborate mission timetable, taking into account the sunrises, sunsets and rates of planetary spin on both worlds to keep the whole system running smoothly.

Hanging from the apex of its arch was a large carved and painted plaque. The words 'Travel' and 'Office' curved around the top and bottom edges of a relief of two worlds, one overlapping the other.

The underlying world would have been easily recognizable to most humans... it was an accurate representation of Earth from space. Many years of visits to the human world had given faeries the opportunity to study our textbooks, so their knowledge of our world was quite detailed.

Ironically, although just as stunningly crafted, the overlaying world was at best, an educated guess! Living their more natural, connected life meant that faeries hadn't reached into space with technology as humans had, so their depiction of Lux was based on how high they could fly before the air got too thin. They weren't too disappointed though. It seemed a fair trade when you considered how far days eye travel got you.

In the centre of the Travel Office was the globe, an enormous scale model of the Earth on which the planners tracked the Earth's terminator, the line that separates night and day.

The terminator was represented by an ornate circular ring and as the globe span around its axis on precision carved bearings powered by a counter-weighted clockwork mechanism, the staff closely monitored the all-important T.T.S. or Time To Sunrise.

The surface of the globe was covered in small, individually numbered mission pins denoting active teams. When a team booked on duty, they selected a pin from the board on the way in. The pin number was logged by a planner, then used to mark the location of the mission on the globe. When they arrived home, to book off duty they gave their pin number and the pin was removed. Any pin on the wrong side of the terminator was a team on Earth in daylight, a scenario to be avoided.

The arch next to the Travel Office had a simpler, oval plaque that had no symbol, but was carved with the words

~ Workshop and Stores ~

This was where mission gear was manufactured and stockpiled by Lux's technicians. An enormous, circular, central serving-counter was fed by rows upon rows of rolling racks that stretched outward like the spokes of a giant wheel, ending at a series of rooms that housed the workshops that kept them filled.

Any kit that a team might need could be found here, stored by type; water bottles, ration packs, spindles of hair, tear bottles, trowels, knives and a selection of crystals that a geologist would sell their soul for.

Faery Facts.

Souls and the selling of them.
An interesting topic and a strange concept.
Where did humans get the idea that a soul is something that can be bought or sold for advantage or gain?
Every living thing has Flow, it's gifted to us by the Spark as we enter the universe, but faeries believe that your soul is something else entirely. They believe that your soul develops over the course of your life and the course of your life develops your soul. They also believe that when the last of your Flow passes through the Veil and your soul is ready to join the Ancestors, its quality controls how smooth your journey will be. So the only true advantage or gain to be had from a soul is an easy trip if you have a good one.
This particular soul believes that faeries might have a point.

Stores was the high volume retail outlet of the faery world. The volume of traffic that came through here during working hours was astounding and although faeries were very social creatures, this was one of the few places in their society where a get in, get done, get out attitude was the best tactic to employ. Seven thousand missions a day, remember?

Next to Workshop and Stores was the equally important but frequently less tidy

~ Warehouse and Processing ~

Raw materials collected from Earth were dropped off here by returning teams for inspection, cleaning and processing before they ended up in storage ready for mission issue.

On the other side of the hub, through the first arch on the right next to the foyer, was the

~ Health Office ~

As well as its title, its plaque showed the profiles of two people, a smaller one inside a larger. Its role within D.O.W.T. was to issue mission cards to teams heading Earthwards.

In reality these mission cards, or pop cards as the teams called them, were a kind of medical treatment plan, highlighting which humans were to receive visits and what level of rehabilitation was required. Patient, location, treatment type, dosage and recommended number of visits were all noted on a card, which was then issued to a team. Once a team had their cards and logged a pin number on the globe, they were good to go.

The next two arches led into domes that were simply extensions of the Health Office, but required an enormous amount of space due to what was stored there.

~ Records ~

held filing cabinets; thousands upon thousands of filing cabinets, ranged in back to back banks that swirled from ground level in the centre of the dome outward and upward in an steadily expanding spiral that filled the entire cavernous space.

They held Lux's records on humanity's spiritual and physical progress and individuals, families, even whole communities were categorized and cross referenced here.

These records were the jewel in D.O.W.T.'s crown. They were utterly priceless. The wealth of information they contained was vital in helping to keep track of and heal a whole world, both mentally and physically.

The Health Office used the records to create something like the triage system in a hospital casualty department.

First and foremost, all treatments were based on an individual's level of need, but the ripple effect that treatment was anticipated to have on their closest relationships and in the wider community was considered too.

Whether they believed it, denied it or failed to care at all, humans possessed a deep spiritual connection to each other and it was because of this that the social side effects, as well as the personal, needed to be taken into account when prescribing treatment.

Whilst treating all the humans on record was important, there were also those that needed more help than others. A thankfully small number of the myriad filing cabinets here were set aside for them in a section designated

L.O.S.T.
(Low Odds of Successful Treatment)

D.O.W.T. considered these people a challenge to be risen to. Everyone could be seen as being a product of their own back story, but the events or circumstances that had moulded *these* souls were particularly difficult. However, when these low-odds cases *did* prove successful… wow.

They often ended up becoming D.O.W.T.'s greatest success stories. Seeing the mistakes they'd made in their lives, they often became champions for humanity: the reformed addict that starts a self-help group to free others held in the same trap, or the violent criminal that changes their ways to become the founder of a youth group that gets kids off the streets and away from the influences that could potentially lead them astray. Definitely worth the extra visits.

Sadly though, if you looked deeply enough into the shadows of a particular corner of the dome, you would find a small room of files that children told stories about to scare each other in the dark. It was the only room in Lux with a lock.

It contained the records of several people who were utterly, undeniably, inexcusably

B·A·D·
(Beyond All Deliverance)

B.A.D. files were different. No visits. No treatments. No chance.

After an initial assessment that revealed not only their nature but also a strange immunity to faery treatment, they remained under surveillance at all times, watched but not approached. All you could do was hope *they* passed through the Veil before they caused someone *else* to.

There were some *very* grim people in there. If even D.O.W.T. thought you were B.A.D., you really were.

So that was the humans that Lux was already monitoring taken care of... but what of all the others?

Another responsibility the teams had was to decide which of the ones that were left needed to be put on the books as new patients.

Firstly, the good news was that not all of them even *needed* Lux's intervention. A vast number of human beings were kind, decent creatures who yearned for a better world and the chance for unity and mutual understanding.

To sort the wheat from the chaff and ensure they all got assessed, the average D.O.W.T. mission was split into three parts:

1. Mission.
Following the instructions on your issued mission cards, treat the humans assigned to your team.

2. Reconnaissance.
At your team's discretion, visit unregistered black sites for your sharer to determine the potential treatment needs of the residents therein.

3. Rest and Relaxation.
Ensuring the terminator deadline is not breached, use the R and R portion of your mission to explore, experience and enjoy the human world.
'A happy team is a hardworking team.'

Faery Facts.

Mission Terminology:
A Ready Reckoner For Off~World Volunteers.
Compiled By Giblet Hope.

According to this well~respected D.O.W.T. training manual, a black site can be strictly defined as:
'Any human residence or place of work where all occupants have retired for the evening and have successfully achieved a state of slumber.'

Say the words 'black site' to a human and they'll instantly think of some top secret bunker in the Nevada desert supposedly filled with crashed U.F.O.s and aliens!
There were other worldly travellers at black sites, but they didn't have time to mess about with sci fi.
They had work to do.

Last but most definitely not least, opposite the foyer on the far side of the hub was the

~ Legend Office ~

Bathed in an air of peace and tranquility, it was adorned with a plaque depicting a pair of crossed scrolls.

Before and during the Age of Harmony, it had been the spiritual and historical heart of faery society, a voluminous library that was home to scholars and historians. The truth it contained had provided enlightenment, hope and guidance to all, including humans in the time before the Great Divide. Back then it had simply been called the Library.

Since its relocation when the Offices were built, it was still all of those things, but was also now the driving force behind D.O.W.T.'s efforts on Earth.

As with the other domes, there were side rooms around the perimeter, which included personal studies and meeting areas. Further in, the rows of study desks with their green shaded crystal lamps stretched all the way around the space in three enormous horse shoe shapes, the open ends towards the entrance arch.

This left the centre of the dome free for the repository itself.

Like a mountain of knowledge bursting forth from the ground in eagerness to be learned, the huge hemispherical wooden repository bookcase rose gracefully up to the round help desk of the duty librarians at its peak. Countless thousands of books were cradled within its curving shelves, from ancient manuscripts to recently written works. It was frequented by everyone from school children to scholars.

The wooden top of the help desk was carved all the way around, showing details of the section you were in. Headings and subheadings relating to the segment of bookcase below you helped guide you to whatever you were looking for, but if all else failed you had a shush of librarians to point you in the right direction.

They flitted up and down the banks of shelves, re-homing the last few returned items before they went home, the repository's layout so familiar to them that they barely needed to think about what they were doing.

As they drew nearer, Buff wondered not for the first time if the faery disappearances *were* Legend related. The problem with the Legend was that, as with all good end-of-the-world prophesies, it was just too vague to have complete faith in.

Millennia ago, the fall of mankind was believed to be the time of great loss the Legend spoke of and that human greed would bring about the opening of the Pit. The Legend had gathered a massive following, but in the time since no Nine Keys had been discovered, no Pit had been opened and life in the universe had gone on uninterrupted. Over time, this had convinced many that the Legend was at worst, untrue and at best, exaggerated.

In more recent times, the disappearance of so many faeries had also been considered a time of great loss, but there lay the problem... if it wasn't true then, was it true now? What to believe? One thing was certain. True or not, D.O.W.T.'s mission was still undeniably a noble one.

Buff touched down as they reached the main arch and there it was just ahead of them; mounted in the centre of a sculpted wooden days eye and permanently sealed inside a protective layer of clear, purified resin... the Legend scroll.

Fear of the warnings this single document gave had given faeries a new and deeper purpose. It had provided the impetus for them to build an organization for the benefit of another species on another world and it had reshaped their entire culture. It was the reason Buff did what she did.

They made their way across the dome and over to the far edge to a humble looking doorway, the room behind obscured by a heavy, deep purple curtain draping to the floor.

There was a small waiting area of comfortably plump stuffed seats arranged in a circle in front of it and Buff smiled at the group sitting there. The three faeries she had worked with for two and a half years and had come to regard as family noticed her approach and erupted with loud greetings.

"Way hay, here she is! Alright, Buff?" enquired Squishy, the grower of the group. His mop of dark curly hair surrounded the tanned face of someone who spent most of their time outdoors.

"Ah, look who's decided to turn up at last... we haven't got all day, you know!" quipped Twinkle, a sharer, grinning hugely under her long, wavy red hair and setting her trademark cheekiness to low. It went a *lot* higher.

"Hello, blossom!" called Flo, the team's very accomplished pusher. Wearing her usual purple, she tucked a stray lock of short, dark brown hair behind a delicate ear, stood up and gave her a welcoming hug.

Buff felt the warm glow and slight swell of her heart she always felt around this lot. They were her life.

Faery Facts.

N.I.C.K. names were quite the big deal in faery society. They were derived from a personality trait, a thing you were deeply interested in, a particular skill you demonstrated from an early age... you get the picture.

When you reached school age, which was around 7 years old by human standards, you could opt out and keep your given name, or be commonly known by your 'Name I Choose to Keep' name. It was the first right of passage a faery went through... choosing the title by which the world would know you.

For example;

In a culture where caring and helping were cornerstones, being labeled as the playground care giver was quite the accolade. Buff was always there to tend the scraped knees, the grazed elbows and the bumps, always ready to polish someone up like new.

Hence, Buff.

With a set of grower's nodes and an almost immeasurable delight in bringing seeds to life, Squishy was always destined to work with plants. As a kid, he was as obsessed with the soil they grew in as he was with the plants themselves; farming it, playing with it, coming home smothered in it... to the less than delight of his mother, as you can imagine. His mud pies were some of the most elaborate ever seen.

Hence, Squishy.

The mischief that Twinkle got up to became legendary amongst parents and teachers alike. She had a wonderful gift... the knack of cutting it off just before it became naughtiness, all the while with a bright twinkle in her eye that told you she knew *exactly* what she was up to.

Hence, Twinkle.

Sometimes a person chose to opt out of their N.I.C.K. name at the prescribed age, maybe because they felt that their given name already said enough about them, or that they wanted to honour their parent's choice, or any one of a number of other reasons. Flo had felt that a simple shortening of her full name was enough.

Hence, Flo.

"Hello, guys! Fancy seeing you here!" she joked, flopping into an empty seat and using the cheeky Twinkle's knees as a rest for her crossed ankles as the group said hi to Violet.

When Vi disappeared behind the curtain to announce their arrival, Buff was instantly bombarded with questions.

'No,' she didn't know what was going on.

'Yes,' she'd only been told about the meeting a little while ago, same as the others.

'No,' she didn't think they were getting split up because news of a transfer was always broken in private first and as they were all here, that counted *that* out.

'Yes,' it was all *very* weird.

'No,' she didn't have anything to eat.

"For peat's sake, Squishy, are you ever *not* hungry?"

"No."

Faery Facts.

'For peat's sake?' Shouldn't that be 'for Pete's sake?' A bit of a grey area. It altogether depends on which world you think it originated on. On Earth, it's thought to be a slightly less blasphemous version of 'for God's sake,' a substitute curse to avoid offending people of faith. Faeries would argue that it originated with a society of flow sensitive beings that can communicate with plants.

Discuss.

So, none of them knew anything except that they'd all been summoned here in secret.

Violet's head suddenly reappeared around the edge of the curtain.

"Hey, folks, Mamma's ready for you now," she said quietly and holding the purple fabric to one side, she showed them into Mamma's study.

Time's Up

The curtain fell closed behind them with a soft swish. The room was dimly lit, a peaceful cocoon of a place, overflowing with books and rolled-up parchments, carved wooden ornaments and trinkets.

The walls were draped with warm, soft fabrics and it smelled wonderful thanks to the small incense burner on a shelf by the entrance. It was the lady behind the desk that held your attention though.

"Hello, my dears, welcome! It's lovely to see you again... and all together too!" said Mamma, winking as if to acknowledge the curiosity they all felt.

In her usual fashion Mamma spoke quietly and on hearing her tone, you felt instantly welcome and at ease. Her sharp green eyes studied the world from a caring face that sat atop a slim frame that belied the power within.

She seemed to read you as though she were leafing through the pages of your soul but it was gentle and compassionate, not prying. She was Lux's spiritual leader and everybody loved her unquestioningly.

"It's always lovely to see you Mamma," replied Buff, approaching Mamma's desk, placing her hand on her heart and bowing her head solemnly, the others following suit.

"Come, come, none of that with me," chided Mamma as she rose, her daisy embroidered green dress giving her a floating appearance as she walked around the desk.

She greeted each of them with a big warm hug, first Buff, then Squishy, then Twinkle and lastly Flo.

"Hello, Flo," said Mamma softly, kissing her on the cheek and putting her sharer's node against her daughter's forehead, where it glowed faintly.

"Hi, Mum," she replied, stroking Mamma's face gently and looking deep into her eyes, where something unfamiliar lurked. "You look tired… and scared. What's wrong?"

Mamma's eyes faltered and dropped from Flo's, something neither Flo nor the others had ever seen before. She made her way over to a table beneath a draped window. Hooking back the curtain to let in some orange-tinted, early-evening light, she sat down.

"Oh, that's better. Pull up some chairs, come sit with me, cheer me up. We lost someone else today. Coral didn't arrive on the other side when her team popped early this morning."

She exhaled very slowly, trying to stay composed.

"I spent this morning with her parents, poor things. Poor *Coral*. That makes seven hundred and twenty missing. So that's that…" she said sadly, adding mysteriously, "time's up."

They moved some spare chairs over to the table, heads full of questions but polite enough to let Mamma make her point in her own time.

There was a knock on the arch. Vi had brought them tea and as she put the tray down, Flo reached into her bag, kicked the side of the ever-hungry Squishy's boot with a thonged sandal and secretively passed him a large oat biscuit. He looked at her like she'd just saved his life and mouthed a thank you.

They thanked Vi for the drinks and chatted for a while about day-to-day things, just friends having a cuppa together.

When they'd finished, Mamma got to her feet and went to her desk. She retrieved a scroll and some pebbles and sat back down opposite the group.

"I won't beat around the bush… I have a favour to ask from the four of you."

"A favour? Anything Mamma, just ask it," Buff replied instantly, knowing that she spoke for all of them.

Mamma smiled.

"My dear, loyal Buff… that's an answer I should expect from you. From *any* of you! But don't be so certain, so fast."

Mamma unrolled the parchment, using the polished stones to weigh down the corners. Looking at it laid flat upon the table, they felt a sudden wave of uneasiness.

Seeing a scroll here wasn't strange in itself, but seeing *this* scroll here most definitely was. It was a one of a kind they'd seen before on school trips to the library and in their early training days with D.O.W.T.

This scroll *couldn't* be here, because it was outside in a days eye-shaped, resin-sealed display case.

"It's begun," Mamma said.

The team looked blankly from Mamma's sad face to the scroll and back again, then erupted.

"The Legend?"

"It's real?"

"Are you sure?"

"How do you know?"

Mamma nodded down at the parchment on the tabletop.

"The answers are all here. It's the unabridged Legend and I'm afraid it contains some facts that you need to know."

Buff, briefly missing the crucial word, shook her head, still not following.

"I don't understand… is this a copy? I thought there was only..." She stopped, catching on. "What do you mean, *unabridged?*"

"When the Legend was laid down all those thousands of years ago, every Mamma to follow was entrusted with a task and a secret. The task was to protect and maintain the manuscript to ensure it survived through the ages." She smiled ruefully. "It's only paper after all and resin can only do so much. The *secret* was that there were *two* versions to be protected. The one we learn about as children you already know… everybody does. But there were parts that the Legend itself demanded be deliberately withheld from the general population to allow our culture to exist with a little hope. It was done to protect our kind from living in a cloud of despair under a ticking clock. It was done out of love. Only the current Mamma and the Council know the whole truth. You see… it's all true: The Pit, the Broken Soul, the Nine Keys, the end of life, *everything.* This parchment is the *full* account of the Legend and it gives finer detail. Specifics."

Flo's eyes were like dinner plates.

"What specifics?" she whispered.

"The *public* Legend tells us next to nothing about the Keys except that they open the Pit."

Mamma tapped the scroll with her finger.

"This still doesn't say *what* they are but it does tell us how they work. The Pit is a focal point in the Earth's natural energy system of ley lines, but it's a focal point that formed badly. Any living thing like you or me or even Lux or the Earth has a system of energy lines that allow Flow to, well… flow, but in the Pit instead of flowing it's stored up like a battery. When a critical level's reached, the Keys release all that stored Flow in a powerful surge that short circuits the system. It effectively turns the Veil from a gentle absorber of background level Flow into a conductive network that actively seeks out and feeds on any live Flow in the universe and sends it back to the Source. Then with everything dead, nothing can be born and… well, you get the idea. It's like running a tap into a sink with no plug. As far as bad news goes, it doesn't get much worse."

Mamma paused.

"It also says where the Keys are and how to find them."

"We know where the Keys are?" Buff asked in awe. *That* was a game changer.

"Not precisely, but close. The Isle of Wight, off the south coast of England. I'm sending a carefully chosen team there tonight to find them before the Broken Soul does."

"Why haven't we been searching for them already?" Squishy asked incredulously. "We might've found 'em by now. We could have hidden 'em or destroyed 'em… done *something*."

"Because the scroll gives us a countdown to the one and only sign that will reveal the Keys. It says that as night falls on the day the count ends, a full moon like no other will light the way to the Keys... a moon lit as a spectrum, like white light through a prism. I left instructions with the custodians at the Lea to be passed on to anyone heading Earthwards tonight. The cover story is that the Climate Academy's running a bi-world atmospheric study and teams are to abort their missions and return home to report *anything* out of the ordinary. The countdown's up and the moon's already rising on Earth. All we can do now is wait for that final piece of physical proof."

Twinkle had been leaning forward tensely and now she flopped back against her chair.

"So what's this countdown? What makes it so infallible?" she asked, desperately hoping that somehow this could all still be wrong.

Mamma sighed deeply.

"It's precision. When the Legend was received by our Ancestors, it came in many forms; dreams to be translated, emotions to be worked through, even imagined images. The countdown came in the form of geometric shapes seen while meditating. When this sacred geometry was decoded, it offered an equation. Nine times nine times nine. Seven hundred and twenty nine. It even went so far as to show what that number represented. The seven hundred and twenty sacrifices that need to be made to charge the Pit...and the Nine Keys that overload it."

Twinkle's face drained of colour. "Seven hundred and twenty sacrifices. The missing faeries." She felt sick.

"Like I said… time's up. I've watched that clock ticking the whole time I've been Mamma. My predecessor did too and hers before her. Fifty years in all."

Mamma gathered herself, her tone brightening again.

"But finally, after years of standing helplessly by watching our friends disappear one by one, now's the time for action. Time to gather our little team together, brief them on their mission and get them packed and popped."

Mamma turned the manuscript around.

"There's nothing in here that guarantees sending people will save us, but it definitely says we're supposed to at least try. Look."

She pointed out a section to Squishy who was sat closest and he read it aloud:

'With no warnings, four to send,
Our best, on whom our fates depend,
These selfless souls 'til struggles end,
Our futures and our worlds defend.
Send one with power to heal and mend,
Send one of strength to plant and tend,
A blessed, sharing, loyal friend,
And one to push them home again.'

"So *that's* the favour? You want us to round up the team for you?" asked Buff.

Mamma's small, sad smile didn't go unnoticed by Flo and her face drained in shock as it dawned on her where this was leading.

"No thank you my love, I've already taken care of that. And this *was* the briefing. It's a big favour. I'd give anything not to have to ask it. Find our missing... locate the Keys... save the universe. If you accept, all that remains is for you to kit up and then it's up to the roof to see your families before you leave for Earth."

A stunned silence filled the room and they stared at her in shock.

Them? Save the universe? Surely there was some mistake?

"But it says to send our best," Twinkle pointed out, surprisingly subdued compared to her usual fizz. "Are you *sure* you've got the right people?"

"That's your node talking, that is," Mamma reminded her gently. "Remember you're a sharer, in a room full of people you love and connect with deeply, that have just been given bad news and a huge responsibility. What *you're* feeling is everyone's shock, fear and self-doubt as well as your own. Centre yourself... and then try and tell me these aren't the faeries for the job."

Twinkle took a deep breath and closed her eyes, rebalancing herself amid the flurry of emotions in the room. Her faced relaxed as she sensed the individual auras emanating from her friends.

"Told you, sweetie... our *very* best! I've been watching your careers avidly and I can assure you, you're the best we've got. All *I* had to do was make sure you ended up in a team together. The way you've all bonded just tells me that you're the right choice."

Everything Mamma had told them was subject to them accepting the mission of course, but given the potential consequences, it hardly seemed likely they would refuse. No words were necessary. She got the answer she'd been expecting simply from the look in their eyes.

They spent some time running through the mission objectives together:

1.

Seek out the Nine mysterious and legendary Keys, using directions taken from the secret version of an ancient prophesy that, until *very* recently, had been withheld from almost their entire species.

2.

Prevent a nameless adversary from using them to open a fault in an ancient energy system on another world, unleashing a life-consuming force of incomprehensible power on the universe.

3.

Find seven hundred and twenty missing faeries and bring them home.

4.

Try to make it back alive.

Great… they liked a challenge.

Mamma got to her feet. The green of her dress flowed around her like liquid emerald as she moved to the door, her familiar air of calm and grace fully restored now that all the bad news had been broken.

"As far as the '*no warnings*' bit goes, I'm going to take the Legend's wording at face value. Now the countdown's up, I don't have to keep it a secret any longer. There's no *way* I'm putting you under a days eye tonight without a few hours with your loved ones. They have the right to know who's fighting for us... I'm sure the universe won't begrudge you *that*."

She crooked a finger at the group.

"But before that, follow me, my loves... places to be!"

A Card And Some Presents

First port of call for the chattering group was the Travel Office and Mamma stopped them just inside the arch.

Reaching into a fold of her dress, she pulled out a pop card and held it up, showing it around the group.

There was none of the usual information on it, just a number '9,' the tail of which had been styled into the silhouette of a key.

"More for posterity than necessity," she said cheerily. "This may be a museum piece one day! Back in a tick."

Mamma headed for one of the desks and joined the faery who was sitting there, stamping up his last stack of mission cards for the day.

Bemused, they watched his face change from a healthy pink to ashen as Mamma spoke quietly to him from across the desk.

Squishy pulled a face.

"Poor fella...I know how *that* feels."

The others nodded solemnly.

Mamma handed the card over and he shakily laid it on the desk in front of him. Picking up a stamp he paused for a moment, staring at it, trying to fully grasp what he was being asked to do... and then stamped it quickly,

BOMP!

He opened a drawer, rooting around for a moment before pulling out a second, seldom used stamp and did the same again,

---

KERCHUNK!

He looked over to where the team were stood waiting, then stood up and bowed to them. They waved and nodded back casually as if this sort of thing happened all the time.

Mamma thanked him, cupping his face briefly to offer a little comfort in the face of the news she'd just given him and made her way back to the team. She showed them the card.

Just two words were stamped across the front, one either side of the key; on the left, the oft seen

CLEARED

in green and on the right in red, seeming like a bit of an understatement in the circumstances, was the lesser known

URGENT

Smiling, Mamma handed the card to Buff.

"There you go, it's official now... you've *got* to save the universe!" she joked. "But first, a little foraging trip. I'm treating you kids to some new toys."

"New toys?" repeated Squishy. He liked the sound of that.

"Oh, just a couple of items your average saviour of the universe shouldn't be without," she replied cagily.

Their next stop was next door at Workshop and Stores and after announcing their arrival, Mamma sat them all down in the waiting area.

"When you're done here, you should go straight up to the roof," she said softly. "Your families will have been briefed and be up there waiting for you by then. Don't worry…" she continued, seeing the anxious looks, "they'll be well looked after. Spoilt rotten and treated like royalty in fact!"

Faery Facts.

Faery society doesn't actually have royalty.

Overall, Lux is governed by the Prime Council. It has responsibility for the Societal Code, the set of laws that faeries live by.

Smaller towns, villages and settlements further out from the main city like chicken ranches and farming communities pretty much have autonomy and are trusted to sort themselves out, providing they keep to the Code.

The Council can be brought in to rule on any problems that can't be resolved at community level, but with faery culture the way it was that was almost unheard of.

Four times a year, at summer and winter solstice and the equinoxes in between, summits were held to discuss important matters, but as these were times of celebration anyway, summits tended to end up more of a party than a Council meeting.

No taxes or debt because there was no money; no police or army because there was no crime or war.

Sounds alright, dunnit?

Mamma continued, raising an eyebrow.

"You'd best brace yourselves when you go up though… they're probably going to be a little emotional. There's quite a lot to take in all at once and no easy way to tell it."

"Nicely understated, Mum, just your everyday bit of gossip, really. Don't know what all the fuss is about myself!"

Mamma ruffled Flo's hair, smiling.

"Cheeky! Much as I'd love to stay and hear more of your sauce, I'm afraid I'm going to have to get to the Lea. I want to be there when news comes in that the moon's turned. I'll meet you up on the roof when it does."

"I'd prefer an *if* it does," said Squishy hopefully.

"We all would, my love," Mamma replied, "but things are a little more definite than that. In the meantime, I think you'll find what Trix and Flint have in store for you quite novel, so have fun! And enjoy the time with your families. I'll see you soon."

And with that, she bloomed her wings and was gone, leaving them with plenty to consider.

Have fun? On a day like today? These new toys *must* be good. And then of course, there was the barely masked truth behind the words 'enjoy the time with your families.' Best not to dwell on *that* for too long…

"So… what's the plan, folks?" Twinkle asked.

Buff wrinkled her nose.

"Not sure... but at the very least we have to assume the Broken Soul knows what *we* know and that they'll be on the lookout for the sign to the Keys too. If they are, it might just end up a race to see who gets 'em first."

"That makes me feel better," said Flo, ever the optimist, "we've got a speed advantage!"

Squishy agreed.

"And height too. If the moon's supposed to show the way to the Keys, it's got to be something obvious, surely? If we stay up above the island we should be able to see it first and get a head start."

The team agreed. It was a good strategy, but that's where their planning ended. Assuming they found the Keys, everything after that was reliant on their skills and a healthy dose of improvisation. And luck, if you believed in that sort of thing.

Faery Facts.

'May the wings of the faery kiss the sun
and find your shoulder to light upon,
to bring luck, happiness and riches
today, tomorrow and beyond.'
The Irish could always be relied on for a good ol' lucky blessing and their folklore was overflowing with stories of faeries bestowing good and bad luck upon humans as reward or punishment.
Although widely acknowledged in fairytales, faeries can no more influence luck than a squid can influence the tides, but it does hint at a deep-rooted subconscious memory that faeries were a positive influence.

They were met by a very excited technician, Flint, who strolled up wearing a white lab coat with a pencil behind one ear and goggles pushed up onto his forehead.

"Hello, all, we've been expecting you! Got a message from Mamma to crack out the new gear. How's your grip on reality?"

"Surprisingly tight," said Buff smiling, "I take it you know what's going on?"

Flint nodded.

"I do now. Mamma asked Trix and I to do some hush-hush R&D on a few things a while ago. She came in this afternoon with the finishing touches for them and told us the rest. I always thought the Legend might actually be the real deal... just never thought I'd Flow long enough to see it happen," he said, winking. "I'll take you to Trix."

He bloomed his wings and the others did likewise, following along behind him as he zipped quickly between the storage racks.

They touched down outside a testing bay at the outer edge of the dome and found D.O.W.T.'s senior technician, Trix, waiting inside for them.

Her familiar half-surprised expression from spending too much time around things that went bang changed to one of delight as they entered and her face lit up amid her wild hair as she greeted them.

"Hello, everybody! Well, isn't this exciting! Come along, come through, things to do!" she said enthusiastically, leading them to a long work bench in the middle of the room and motioning for them to line up along it.

On the bench were five black, pouched vests, like the ones used by soldiers for carrying their equipment. Flint picked one up and put it on, doing up the three toggle fastenings at the front. Trix pointed to the other four.

"Find the vest with your name on it, if you would. Put them on, put them on," she prompted. "They should all fit perfectly; they've been individually tailored. You might want to take a closer look at the badges. Just a little finishing touch from Mamma, in keeping with the occasion."

There were two badges on each vest. The first was green and round with a days eye logo in the centre and had the words 'Team' over the top and 'Lux' across the bottom, embroidered in black thread. In the middle of the logo's larger daisy was the stylized '9' key symbol from their pop card, in the same black thread.

The second was a simpler green oval with the wearer's name sewn into it.

"Like 'em!" commented Squishy, openly impressed.

Flo shook her head. "Urgh, boys toys," she said, less so.

"They're very… utilitarian, aren't they? I particularly like the way it looks like we're going to war," said Twinkle, less pleased than anyone.

She was more than happy with D.O.W.T.'s come-as-you-are dress code. She most definitely wasn't impressed with having to wear a uniform, much less a military themed one. It wasn't faery… and it wasn't her.

Trix raised her eyebrows and nodded in total agreement.

"Not a bad analogy. I s'pose you are going into a battle of sorts. It's certainly not your standard mission scenario. You know how you've always only carried the items you need for your niner role? Well, Mamma came to us to ask if we could put something together that comfortably carried everything a team needed for a return pop. Seemed like a good idea… something purely functional that could get *any* faery back home in the event of an emergency."

She pulled a wry face.

"Turned out the emergency had already been happening for fifty years! If, Spark forbid, one or more of you are caught, killed, gets lost or whatever, this'll ensure you still have the kit you need to make it back to Lux. You don't all have Squishy's root skills, so it'd be a rough pop home, but at least you'd get here."

As a safety precaution, every faery that signed up for service was taught the basic knot work for the journey home during training. This meant that if the grower on their team was unable to hook up a bubble for whatever reason, they could still get themselves safely back to Lux, even if it felt like they'd been spun in a tornado on the way there.

"It's not the most stylish item you'll ever wear, I grant you, but this is about getting the job done, not looking good."

She asked Flint to turn around.

"They have the standard flight-friendly tailoring," she continued, pointing to the cut outs in the back of his vest, something that was incorporated into all faery clothing to leave their wing nodes exposed. He pulsed his nodes slightly to demonstrate.

Trix patted the three large pockets at the back. "Medical in the middle... rations and drinking water either side. I know it's more than you're used to carrying, but rather have and not need than need and not have. Over to you, Flint."

Flint faced them again, reached into the inside pocket of his vest and took out a piece of paper. He unfolded it on the bench and they found themselves looking at a map of the Isle of Wight.

"You all have one of these. All major points of interest are marked, except of course where the Keys are, but please feel free to update it with your complimentary free gift… a charcoal pencil!" he joked, taking out a pencil from the same pocket.

"Toggle fixings, one, two and three," he said, pointing to the toggles from top to bottom. "Tear mix and hair in the two front pouches and there's reinforced storage for a knife and a trowel behind them," he continued, pulling out the tools and replacing them.

Squishy pulled the brand new knife out of his vest and laid it on the bench. Lifting up his shirt, he showed Trix and Flint the knife on his belt, left to him when his Dad had passed through the Veil.

"I do appreciate it, but I'll take this if it's all the same to you… it was Dad's and I'm never without it," he said seriously.

"No problem," Flint replied. "Some personal items are fine. A couple of the other items are a little more critical though."

Trix giggled. 'Critical.' Funny. *She* knew what else they had to show them.

Undoing the hair pouch, Flint revealed the drum-shaped wooden device inside and turned to a big storage reel of red hair mounted on the end of the bench.

"S.D.S… Strand Delivery System," he announced with pride, knocking on it with his knuckles.

"Sprung loaded. Just open the cover, lock in a hair strand here, close the cover, release the catch and it winds it onto the reel automatically… like so."

He flipped the catch and there was a high whirring sound as the reel span round, slowing down and finally stopping as it filled up.

"See this lip on the front here? It has a built in blade for trimming."

He tugged some extra hair from the bench reel, looped it under the lip and pulled upward quickly, neatly cutting the hair.

"Once the drum's full, pulling out the hair tightens the ratcheted spring to power the next reload," he said, pulling out another couple of lengths of hair to the smooth clicking sound of the mechanism.

"Nice," said Squishy, impressed, "should save some time if we have to leave somewhere in a hurry."

Flint nodded down at their S.D.S. pouches.

"Give it a go everyone. No real skill involved but it's best to try before you buy!"

Faery Facts.

A side effect of Lux's missions to Earth was cross~cultural contamination. Although faeries didn't use money, even sayings like 'try before you buy' had managed to worm their way into every day life.

Faery culture employed a barter system for personal possessions, but things like food and everyday necessities were dealt with on the basis that if you needed it, you went to a storage dome and asked for it. As faeries had evolved without the genetic flaw of greed, no one took more than their share and if they did end up with an excess of something, they simply gave it to a neighbour who needed it more immediately.

Culturally, this guaranteed three things;

no waste, no shortages and a genuine equality amongst their kind.
Simple stuff really.
Amazing that some people didn't get it.

The room filled with whirring and clicking and sounds of approval as they all tried the new gizmo.

"If you like that, you'll love this," Flint chuckled when they'd finished.

He reached up to the small wooden tube on the shoulder of his vest. He unscrewed the cap, leaving it hanging on its cord and a focused beam of light shone out.

"You've all seen these before... the standard issue crystal torch with one end polished into a lens for a tighter beam. But..." he continued, opening a small pouch on the opposite shoulder, "... we've also been working on ways to maintain the charge a crystal can hold and had a little success, to say the least. It was Trix's breakthrough, so I think she should be the one to show you."

He took a pointed length of quartz from the pouch. It had a dull glow, nowhere near as bright as the torch but it seemed as if the glow was shifting within the crystal. He gave it to Trix and she held it closer to the group.

"Thanks Flint. Look past the glow... see the carvings?" she asked, pointing out the spirals and tracks etched into its surface. "They create energy pathways that either circulate or condense Flow within the crystal depending on their layout."

"*Condense?*" asked Flo. No stranger to pushing a crystal into life, she was excited to see how this had been achieved.

"Yes. Instead of just pushing the crystal to make it glow and it fading slowly over time, the markings act like an electrical circuit that stores the power, looping it until it's needed. Natural dissipation is negligible. It only disperses if you use it and when you do, the new circuitry directs and concentrates the energy to where you want it to manifest."

Flint pulled out a block of wood from under the bench and placed it in front of her. Trix pointed to the middle of the crystal.

"You put your forefinger and thumb on the two spirals in the middle here to complete the circuit and the energy is released highly focused at the tip," she said happily.

Holding the crystal like a pencil, she activated the crackling tip a couple of times for effect, then leant over the block of wood.

As the intensely fierce tip of the crystal touched the surface, wispy smoke instantly began to rise as she worked quickly.

She straightened, and held up the block. The word

LUX

was burnt deeply into the wood. They were amazed. Trix wore a grin that went from ear to ear.

"Cuts through things, starts fires... it's a faery multi-tool! Not bad, eh?"

They agreed. Not bad at all.

"Hang on to your nodes, there's more," Trix went on. "Flint?"

Flint undid one of the two chest pouches on his vest, pulling out an smooth, oval, fist-sized lump of crystal with very similar markings to the one Trix had used on the block of wood. It too glowed softly and as energy coursed along its lines, the fact it had been pushed was unmistakable.

"This," he said seriously, "is your return ticket. It's charged with a push of the right frequency and strength to wake a days eye."

He looked at Flo apologetically. "Sorry, but Mamma did ask us to come up with ways to cover *all* possibilities. This ensures that *everyone* has a way to get back."

He held up the oval. "If you look at the two ends and the two sides, you'll see a spiral on each. When all four are touched *simultaneously*, the crystal goes into overload and you've got to the count of five to hold it against the stem of a days eye before it goes off. Just make sure you've cabled up before you activate it."

Flint looked at Trix expectantly. "Now?"

She nodded. "Oh, I think so, don't you?"

"'Bout time!" he replied excitedly. "One last thing to show you, but we have to go out into the hub. We need the space."

He went to a wall unit filled with woven basket drawers and returned with the one he pulled out.

"Follow me!" he said, then bloomed his wings and shot off once more, leading the group out of Workshop and Stores to the large ornamental fishpond in the centre of the hub.

He put the basket down on the bench that ringed the pond and took out one of several spheres.

"You've all got one of these in your vests, but save 'em... we'll use these," he said, pointing down at the basket. "They're set off the same way, but *whatever* you do, *don't* touch the contacts yet," he instructed. "Help yourselves."

Gingerly, they each took a crystal, peering in fascination at the small pulses of Flow that coursed along the circuit-like markings carved into the surface. They were *very* careful to follow Flint's instructions not to touch the four spirals.

Trix took one and turned to face away from the pond. "Right... on the count of three, set 'em off and throw them as high as you can out towards the edge of the dome."

The four looked nervously at each other at the thought of hurling chunks of crystal about in the hub.

Trix smiled and winked. "Trust me. I don't want to say any more, showing you will be *much* more fun! Here we go then... *one... two... THREE!*" she yelled and touching the contacts with her thumbs and forefingers, she drew her arm back and let fly with as much strength as she could.

The others did likewise.

Six crystals flew through the air in high arcs towards the outside edge of the hub and the team held their breath, waiting to see what would happen and why Trix and Flint were staring at the falling spheres like all their Christmases had come at once.

Faery Facts.

Christmas.
A time closely linked to the notion of goodwill to all, when magical beings allegedly come into your home bearing gifts.

A rather coincidental analogy for the primary faery mission objective, wouldn't you say? Maybe not such a far-fetched concept after all... Many cultures entertained stories about such things, but with their forgotten ancient history being what it was and considering there actually were beings that came into their homes bearing gifts, it was easy to see why humans were predisposed to believe in this stuff.

BOOMF!

The crystals hit the flagstones of the hub and exploded, spraying not fragments of crystal, but five shockwaves of multi coloured Flow that vaporized the quartz to dust and headed outward, crackling through any plants they encountered and sending sparks down their leaves and stems into the soil that cradled them.

They hit the edge of the main dome and spread upwards towards the apex, buzzing along the grain of the wooden beams and sweeping through the warm amber of the resin panels, making them glow briefly as it passed by.

"I forgot to mention... a heavy impact sets them off early!" Trix added ecstatically, just as the waves flashed back through the group one by one, leaving them feeling invigorated and their skin tingling.

The shockwaves faded to nothing with a final few sparks and the group stood looking at each other in wonder at what had just happened.

"Based on the human idea of a grenade, but non-lethal. Rather the opposite in fact, it's actually quite healthy to be on the receiving end of one of these!" gushed Flint proudly. "It sends out a compressed wave of Flow that's designed to disorientate an adversary with, well... *life*. Imagine the shockwave that just travelled through us used at close range against a human unaccustomed to the effects of concentrated Flow. They'd be drunk with it, bless 'em! Dizzy, uncoordinated, easily overcome. *This*," Flint said happily, "is your secret weapon, the thing that hopefully no potential bad guy will be expecting... grenade-toting faeries!"

Faery Facts.

When human/faery relations began to deteriorate at the onset of the Great Divide, faeries had tried to go on extending the hand of friendship long after mankind's steady fall had turned him from friend to foe.

The final nail in the coffin was when faeries began to go missing, taken prisoner or killed as man began to see them as a commodity to be owned and used as he saw fit. It was only then that days eye travel was abandoned, sealing humanity's fate for many thousands of years. Had it been in their natures, faeries would have been well within their rights to arm themselves and exact a terrible revenge for this final betrayal. Can you imagine how devastating a stealthy, vengeful faery army could be, travelling to Earth in the dead of night to seek revenge for past wrongs?

Thankfully, faeries could not.

What they could imagine was taking the basic idea of a human tool of destruction like the grenade and turning it into something that could incapacitate an adversary, but ultimately improve their health.
Clever faeries.

"How'd you figure it out?" asked Flo, impressed.

Flint took out another grenade from the basket and ran his fingers over the patterned surface.

"Once we'd worked the bugs out of Trix's original idea for the engraved circuitry, it was actually quite easy to apply the same rules for different tasks… instead of a focal point like on the cutter, the poppers and the grenades are carved to induce overload when they're set off. Touching the contacts causes positive feedback that makes them go critical. The fact the crystal vaporizes under such a fast release is just an added non-lethal bonus."

"You say easy, I say amazing," said Buff, voicing the surprise they all felt over this new faery tech.

Flint laughed.

"Yeah, fair enough… maybe *easy's* understating it a bit. There was some trial and error. Lots and lots of trial and error in fact."

He pointed to his face.

"And one or two lost eyebrows."

Vindication

With Mrs Cow led up the gulley and tied to the signpost at the head of the footpath, the Raulich family had managed to top off their afternoon of discovery with a good deed.

Mum phoned Cynan Farm in the hope that Jan and John knew who the missing cow belonged to and by the time they'd had a cuppa sat in the back of Daisy, an open-backed truck arrived towing a cattle trailer.

The door of the truck flew open and out leapt a grateful Bertie, very enthusiastic in his thanks for the return of the bovine Kelis. He dragged a large cardboard box full of fresh farm shop produce from the back of the truck.

"Just a little token of my appreciation. She's a good girl, my Kelis... thought the poor love was done for when that cliff went."

The girls watched intrigued as Bertie put down the back of the trailer and led Kelis across the road and up the ramp, her tail swishing back and forth and disappearing from view as he raised the tailgate and locked it.

They waved goodbye as he pulled away, then loaded up and did the same, heading back towards Shanklin, past Cynan Farm and the llama enclosure they'd seen. (Or were they alpacas? They never *could* tell the difference.)

Instead of meeting at the tea room as agreed, they went straight to the Forum and jabbering excitedly, told Freya everything. She sat there in shocked silence until they finished, then stood up.

"Well... come on then! I don't want to have to wait *another* fifty years!"

She dragged on a change of footwear, locked up the Forum and they made their way back to Daisy, climbing aboard and belting up. Freya was giddy with excitement at the thought of traveling in her beloved old VW again.

"Oh my goodness! I'd forgotten how much I loved the sound of that engine. Music to my ears!" she gushed as they left Shanklin behind them.

The little camper and its compliment of happy passengers floated along the roads leading to the cavern, barely noticing the time passing as they chatted about the discovery and what it meant. Having spent so much time and effort on it over the years, Freya was keen to hear everything they could remember in the tiniest detail. Mum and Dad were very happy for her. After so many years, they could barely imagine what a vindication it was for her to find out that her dreams had been true.

When they arrived at the lay by, it was still empty and the road still quiet. They clambered from the camper full of anticipation and crossed the road, the warm, early evening hush broken only by the buzz of crickets in the undergrowth and the sound of birdsong.

The group made their way down the gulley to the beach, the first glow of sunset bouncing off its walls and turning it into a tunnel of orange light, giving the journey an other worldly, magical feel. Not so far from the truth. After all, they *were* about to enter a hidden crystal cavern through a secret tunnel to show it to the lady who'd dreamt of its existence fifty years ago... some would certainly say that qualified as other worldly and magical.

Crossing the flat sand of the beach they approached the tunnel entrance, marveling at the way the steep cliff face took on the same orange hue, creating a wall of colour.

They arrived at the opening and Dad pulled five torches from his pack. Freya's eyes crinkled with mirth as he handed out four head torches, keeping a handheld for himself.

"That's a lot of torches... dark in there, is it?"

"Yeah, I do love torches. It's a sickness, I know. The first step to getting help is admitting you have a problem!" he joked.

Mum snorted with laughter.

"We've still got a long way to go then!"

"Speaking of which," said Dad, showing Freya the on/off button on her torch, "Shall we get started? Floor's a bit rocky... you be alright?"

She pointed down, lifted one of her feet which was wrapped in a very respectable leather hiking boot and smiled broadly.

"Just try to keep up, son."

They set off up the tunnel. A healthy life living in the country had worked its own brand of magic on Freya and they made fast progress, only slowing down as they rounded the last bend and saw a strange light up ahead.

Like the light at the end of a railway tunnel, the opening at the end was filled with the same warm, orange glow they'd seen outside. It seemed to beckon them forward like a campfire in the dark and they didn't realise just how close this similarity was until they emerged into the cave.

The crystal walls had absorbed the colours of the setting sun outside and now pulsated with them. They'd been amazed by the way the sunset had lit up the gulley walls and the cliff face, but this was beyond belief. It was as if they were stood *inside* a fire, but with none of the heat.

Freya stood transfixed.

"Just so you know Freya…" Mum said quietly, with a gentle smile, "*way* better than last time."

Clicking off their lights, they showed their hostess around her newly redesigned, open-topped property, taking her to the waterfall with its deep pool below and walking the whole perimeter of the cavern, before heading towards the centre where the giant crystal stood.

"It must be something new," said Dad to Freya. "I'm into geology and there just isn't *anything* that absorbs light and does what *this* did."

"Freyarite," said Mum.

"Huh?"

"If it's new, it needs a name… freyarite. Freya dreamt about this place, it's her land, her cave… freyarite!"

"You're very kind, lovey, but your family found it," Freya replied generously.

"But only because *you* knew where to look," Mum maintained.

"I think freyarite's *perfect,*" Willow agreed.

"Yup! Freyarite found by family of four! That's alliteration, that is!" added Lea, proving she'd been paying attention in school.

Laughing at that, the five continued their exploration of the cave until the sun had set completely, the opening above them now only a dark patch in the glow of the crystals.

The fiery haze gradually bleached away, leaving a new, colder radiance. They soon realized that the culprit was the light of the full moon as it rose to replace its daytime counterpart. It hadn't quite appeared in the visible patch of sky yet, but everyone agreed that seeing it might be a nice note to end the night on before taking Freya home and going back to the campsite.

While they waited, Mum magicked some snacks from her pack and Dad pulled a small camping stove, some cups and a brew kit from his. In no time at all they were munching away happily on biscuits, with coffees and hot chocolates to drink.

Willow suddenly broke the calm.

"I SEE IT!"

The tiniest sliver was just beginning to peek out from behind the left edge of the hole. As they watched, it grew steadily until it became a full disk, the familiar face of the 'man in the moon' shining steadily down into the cave.

Ordinarily, the moon rises in the east and travels so slowly into the west where it sets that you'd barely notice it was moving. Here though, framed in the opening like it was, they could actually see it moving across the sky, albeit *very* slowly.

It had almost reached the centre of the hole when something caught Freya's eye. Her artist's sense of perspective had been roused and she studied her namesake in the middle of the cave, deeply curious. Tilting her head to one side, she followed the direction it pointed in, out through the roof and up at the moon.

"Is it just me, or is that," she said, pointing at the crystal, "pointing straight up at that?" she finished, pointing at the bright moon above.

They gathered around the crystal and leant on it, intending to sight along its length to see if she was right.

This was exactly the catalyst the universe had been waiting for.

As they all touched it in unison, they felt a tingle of connection between themselves and the giant formation and jumped back, a little unnerved.

Before they had time to react further, an intense beam of light erupted from the crystal, heading out through the cavern roof and piercing the night sky.

There was a pause of a second or two as it traveled at the speed of light toward Earth's nearest celestial neighbour, then the moon flared into life like a school science project.

Over the three hundred and eighty four thousand or so kilometers between the two, the beam had somehow diffused, splitting into a beautiful mottled spectrum of colour. The white disk of the moon had been replaced by a mass of coloured circles that overlapped at their edges to create a beautiful lunar patchwork.

The atmosphere in the cave buzzed with energy and tiny sparks crackled and died in the very air around them, shocking their skin if they happened to cross paths with one.

It was wonderful… but also frightening to know that *they* seemed to be the ones that had caused it.

"At least it was quieter this time," whispered Mum, her voice a little shaky.

Dad, looking terrified, gazed up at the moon the way he had a thousand times before.

"I'm just hoping it doesn't break like the roof did…"

Quality Time

Led by Trix, they made their way up to the roof garden through one of the airborne exits high up in the wall of the hub.

Blessed as they were with flight, faeries weren't always obliged to use doors, so to provide alternative entry and exit points, there were large, porthole like openings around the upper edge of each dome, just below where the gargantuan support beams for their flat roofs began.

Each of these openings was covered by a curved, resin paneled porch that jutted out at the top and tapered down at the sides to cover the opening and keep the wind and rain out. As with most faery construction, this gave the structure an undeniably organic look, in this case, an eyelid.

These 'lids,' as they were commonly called, were very popular amongst the teams. Once they'd picked up their pop cards and kit for a mission, they'd go barreling and spinning upwards at full speed, exploding into the open air outside laughing and pumped up, ready for a spot of off-world travel.

Great start to your working day, unless there also happened to be a faery heading in the opposite direction...

Faery Facts.

Even faeries have to think about traffic control.
They can achieve incredible speeds with their wing nodes, but without the luxury of seatbelts and airbags mid~air collisions can result in damage that not even a polisher can fix.

To make sure that you didn't end up paying a visit to a medical professional, or worse still an emberman, every lid had a coloured rim inside and out, green if you could travel in that direction and red if you couldn't. This one way system worked extremely well, preventing injury and no doubt saving lives.

Another bonus of having the gift of flight was that they didn't have to worry about pollution, parking tickets, the price of petrol, prangs or pricey repairs!

Passing through a green-rimmed lid over the arch of Workshop and Stores, they emerged into the night air outside and hovered silent and unnoticed for a moment, taking in the scene on the roof below.

Mamma had been a *very* busy faery.

The grassed roof garden was spotted with the usual crystal lamps, but extras had been drafted in to lighten the area even further. Now that the sun had crept below the horizon to the last song of the days eyes, several braziers had been lit and were burning fiercely, casting flickering shadows all around.

True to her word, Mamma had organized a 'spoiling' of epic proportions. A large function had been set up in the centre of the roof area and their families were all there, eating, drinking and generally making merry, faces lit up in the firelight. There were long tables piled high with food and refreshments and a well-stocked bar was busily serving drinks to the revelers from jugs and wooden casks.

The lively band that was playing close by already had many of the assembled guests up dancing and the air was filled with the sounds of drums, strings and laughter as, in typical faery style, they celebrated life as though there were no threat to it.

When the team touched down, they were mobbed in a flurry of tears and hugs. When the initial buzz of their arrival had calmed slightly, they grabbed some food and drink and mingled.

Being known as a bit of an entertainer, Twinkle was set upon by an excited pack of youngsters and was quickly bundled beneath a stack of them. She wriggled out from under the pile to answer their questions.

"My uncle is missing... could you bring him back, please?"

"Are there *really* two Legends?"

"Marigold told me the Broken Soul eats faeries... are you gonna get *eaten?*"

"Is it true that the Pit makes your nodes disappear?"

"Nah!" she laughed, wrinkling her nose, "your nodes don't disappear... they go mouldy."

"Eurgh! *Really?*"

"Yeah," she confirmed, nodding enthusiastically. "It's true. That's why we've got to go to Earth tonight... stop you lot turning into *SMELLY LITTLE MUSHROOMS! GRRR!*"

She chased the squealing, giggling kids around the nearest table until they made a break for it, escaping into the crowd to tell anyone who'd listen about the Pit's newly discovered ability to turn children into fungi. She chuckled, wondering how long it would take until the rumour made its way back to *her.*

Grinning cheekily at some older family members who'd been watching the whole thing with disapproval, she wandered off. Her work here was done.

Faery Facts.

Faeries are without doubt the kindest and most generous-spirited of creatures, but their reputation for being mischievous is one of those myths that happens to be 100% correct.
They *do* love a good wind up.

Squishy, engrossed in a piece of cheese and vegetable quiche, laughed and dropped his plate on the table, wiping his mouth as he clocked his mum rushing over from where she'd been singing his praises to his aunts.

She flung her arms around him yet again, then stood back to look at him, stroking his cheek while said group of aunts cooed at the show of motherly affection.

"I see your father in you," she said quietly, "he'd be *so* proud."

Squishy tried, only half successfully, to talk around the lump in his throat.

"I know he would Mum... I just don't know if he'd be right to be. I'm not sure I've got what it takes for this."

"Of course you have. You weren't picked at random, you know. You've all had your names down for this since before you were born... thousands of years before you were born, the way Mamma tells it. Don't worry my darlin', just never do less than your best."

Never do less than your best.

Squishy wrapped his arms round his mum. If anything could get his head in the game, it was those words. He'd heard them all of his life, first from his dad until he'd passed through the Veil, then from his mum as she kept them alive in his honour.

"Look after this one for me while I'm gone, will ya?" he asked, as his younger brother joined them.

Oaklea nodded, looking as if he was about to cry.

"Oi! No, none of that. Come here," Squishy ordered, hugging him and slapping him on the back.

"Don't worry, I'll be back. One more mission, that's all this is. Just a bit different is all, right?"

"Right," Oaklea replied. He desperately hoped his brother *was* right.

Over by the band, Buff's dad gave her a little spin and dipped her as the piece ended, surprisingly graceful considering his broad shoulders. As a new piece began, Buff laid her head on his shoulder and sighed, remembering when he used to have to pick her up so they could dance. Time moved *fast.*

"Little girl moment?" he asked gently.

"No... big girl responsibilities."

He stopped dancing at that, pulling back slightly.

"Not so big that *my* little girl can't deal with 'em," he replied without hesitation. "Healthy?" he asked.

"Never been fitter," she replied, smiling, already knowing the words he'd end on.

"Focused?"

"Like polished quartz, Dad."

"With people you love?"

She looked over his shoulder to where the others were saying their own goodbyes and nodded. "Yeah."

They moved off around the dance floor again, his words comforting her the way they always did when she needed a boost.

"Job done then."

Goodbye

Mamma appeared over the edge of the roof, touched down in front of the band and signalled for them to stop.

The final sign had revealed itself. Impossible though it seemed, a sudden rush of teams flooding back through the Lea were bringing word of a full moon lit by a strange light beam coming from *inside* the Earth. There was no room left for doubt. It was time.

Although no one voiced the thought, they said what could well be their last goodbyes and leaving their proud, teary-eyed families behind, they followed Mamma across the lawn. As they neared the edge of the roof that overlooked the foyer, they swore they could hear *singing*. They weren't mistaken.

The moment the team came in to view, an army of drummers in the gardens below struck up a pounding rhythm and they were greeted by the deafening roar of thousands of cheering faeries that had come to show their appreciation.

"NOW THAT'S SOMETHING YOU DON'T SEE EVERY DAY!" shouted Twinkle over the noise.

Mamma hadn't just gone back to the Lea to wait for news that the moon had turned. She'd done way more than that.

The returning teams had been briefed to bring them up to speed and then given what could well be their last task: to spread word of the Legend's advent to every corner of Lux and tell as many faeries as they could find to make their way to the gardens of D.O.W.T. without delay.

Faery Facts.

171

Bad news travels fast.
Especially on lux.

News as spectacularly bad as *this* had leapt through the population like a brush fire in the height of summer and the streets of the city had soon been buzzing with news of the imminent prophesy. Droves of faeries had converged on D.O.W.T. to fill the gardens and the Lea with their excited chatter and questions.

While the four friends had been with their families on the rooftop, Mamma had orchestrated a little farewell for them with the help of the custodians and was overjoyed to see it had been a complete success. She had *never* seen so many of her kind in the gardens at the same time. It fair took your breath away.

"It seems it's not only your nearest and dearest that want to wish you well on your mission!" she pointed out happily.

Awestruck, they bloomed their wings and slowly floated down to the Lea to be met by a flood of back-slapping and hand-shaking. The sea of hopeful faces made the threat they faced seem suddenly and heart-achingly real. These people were relying on them to save not only their lives, but the lives of their loved ones and in a moment of mutual realization, the team completely understood why Mamma had arranged this send off. Understood and loathed it. It was to burn into their very souls exactly what was at stake.

Four custodians approached with the team's vests and led them to a days eye that had been prepped for their mission, while others moved the crowd back to create a clear space around their departure point.

Buff, Flo, Twinkle and Squishy stepped over the neat furrow that marked the ring of recently knotted and watered hair and roots and took up position inside it, looking back across the clear space at the cheering, shouting crowds. As the custodians helped them into their vests and fastened them, fussing over the team until they were comfortable, thirty paces had *never* seemed so far.

Mamma gently cupped Flo's face with her hands and kissed her.

"You know how much I love you, don't you, Flo?"

"Of *course*," Flo replied with misty eyes. "I love you too."

"I am *so* proud of you," Mamma continued, "and you *know* your father would have been bursting at the nodes with pride too. Our beautiful daughter…"

"Don't worry, Mum, we'll do it. 'Where there's D.O.W.T…'" she said, smiling. "I'll see you when we're done."

Mamma nodded and stepped back out of the ring, her fingertips lingering on Flo's across the boundary for just a second before she bloomed her wings and zipped high above the crowd, raising her hands for quiet.

Seeing her signal, the lead drummer signed off with a slightly different rhythm to the others and they all built to a throbbing crescendo, ending on a powerful, triple beat. Silence fell.

After the music and the noise of the crowd, the quiet was equally deafening. When she spoke, Mamma's words were like balm on the throng's ringing ears.

"My friends, it is with the *greatest* of sorrow that we meet here tonight. The day our kind has feared for millennia has come. The Legend is upon us. We woke this morning to our lives, kissed our loved ones, met our friends, did all the things we've done before, most of us unaware that it was unfolding around us. But unfold it did, as it was always destined to and even as it threatens to darken the light that blazes in us all, we should not surrender hope."

She motioned to the team on the ground below her under their canopy of white petals.

"Remember these faces. When the Broken Soul and the Nine Keys and the menace of the Pit were being foretold, these faces were also being named in that very same scroll. And why else, if not to offer a route to salvation? Why else, if not to give us a fighting chance? So believe what you will, but know that *I* choose to believe *this*... these faces represent the hopes and prayers and futures of each and every one of us," she said, pointing emphatically at the countless faeries before her, "and *I* have faith that's why they were foretold in the first place."

She held her arms wide.

"The living embodiment of our motto, forged in D.O.W.T. and sent forth in hope, I give you... TEAM LUX!"

The Lea erupted with cheering and drumming again as Mamma touched back down onto the lawn, joining the team's families at the front of the crowd.

Flo turned to face the days eye. As her team mates watched, she wrapped her arms around the stem, feeling the roughness of the surface under her fingertips and sensing the Flow within the powerful plant.

She loved this part. Converted to energy and blown through the universe like seeds on the wind... in her opinion, as close to being one with the universe as you could actually get without passing through the Veil and going back to the Source.

She closed her eyes and the others heard her recite the same gentle, hopeful verse she always used before she and her team popped.

'Wise old days eye hear me pray,
take us safely on our way,
through the eye and back today,
returned without a price to pay.'

Speaking so softly that no one else could make it out, she whispered a final private something to the days eye. Hugging the stem tightly, she drew in a huge charge of Flow through her wing nodes and gave one good, strong push out through the node in her chest.

There was a flashing pulse of energy between faery and plant and then the burst of Flow was traveling up to the head of the flower and down into the ground, crackling through the smooth surface of its petals and the intricate lattice of its roots.

As the rush of energy reached the tips of the petals and the ring of hair, there was a sudden PHUT! sound and a sphere of swirling, buzzing Flow materialized instantly around the plant and the group.

Buff looked at each of her friends in turn, consciously trying to imprint this moment on her memory.

'*What a bunch*,' she thought to herself. '*Not one of 'em has even asked what our odds are or questioned whether they should go...*'

Twinkle, seeing the serious expression on her friend's face, didn't think that would do at all. She poked Buff gently in the side with her elbow.

"'Sup, Buff? You look a bit pale... can I get you something? A chair? Some water? Faery Guide to Saving the Universe?"

Squishy snort-laughed and they all giggled as Buff tilted her head to the side, whispering "Very funny."

She looked down at her bare feet, the grass of her beloved Lux still firmly between her toes. Looking up again, she just had time to see the crowd through the shimmering barrier before the bubble flexed slightly as though it were taking a deep breath.

She whispered a quiet, hopeful '*Goodbye*' and...

Introductions

POP!

The bubble of Flow vanished and with the tiniest of wobbles, was instantly replaced with a forest of tall stalks.

They had arrived at the edge of a narrow footpath that cut through a dense meadow of wildflowers and grasses, whose heavy heads swayed and bowed above them in the gentle breeze that brushed their tops.

Their soft swishing should have blended almost musically with the sounds of insects, but something was amiss...the bugs were silent in response to a strange light that filled the sky, in the same manner that birds go quiet during a solar eclipse.

"Been *here* before," said Squish with certainty, seeing the meadow sloping down to some farm buildings and the lights of a small village beyond. He turned around, seeing the familiar stone tower he'd expected.

"Ladies... may I present St Catherine's Oratory, affectionately known by locals as the Pepperpot. We're *definitely* on the Isle of Wight!"

They turned to look at the tall tower with its steep octagonal roof and regarded him with curiosity.

"Before we were teamed up," he explained, "I was here, I mean *right* here, this meadow, working on a wildflower propagation project for the Growers' Mandate." He pointed up at the tower's roof. "Me and my team used to have lunch up there!" he chuckled happily.

Faery Facts.

The term '_G.M. crops' had completely different meanings on the two worlds.

On lux, the _Growers' Mandate, or _G.M. for short, was a document of some importance. It had been put in place to ensure that the care and sustainability of all plant life was given top priority, particularly those that were eaten or used by the indigenous faery population. Very clearly demonstrating the faery belief in taking responsibility for one's own actions, the ethos behind such a document was as follows:

'If you use it, you're accountable for it.'

On Earth, _G.M. sadly stood for something wholly different and faeries regarded human efforts to control nature, increase production and maximize profits with a deep sadness. Seen from a faery perspective, _Genetic Modification was the equivalent of weeing into the town well. Not only did it alter the taste of the water, it also had the potential of causing health problems later on.

"Never looked like that though," he continued, referring to the halo of light that surrounded the top of the tower.

Flo said her usual thank you to the days eye they'd appeared under, with her forehead pressed against its stem, then they bloomed their wings and after carefully poking their heads just above the wildflower 'canopy' to check out their surroundings, they rose higher until the cause of the halo came into view.

The moon was a strange and beautiful sight; scary and magnificent all at once. Its face was a speckled sheet of colour, seemingly caused by the beam of light that struck its surface and drew the eye back to Earth to its point of origin, a hillside in the not-so-distant distance.

Utterly at a loss as to what existed that could cause such a show, but knowing that every second could well mean the difference between success and failure, they powered upward, rolling and spiraling through each other's flight paths towards the source of the beam.

Closer now, they could see that the white, almost solid pillar of light was coming out of some huge space *within* the Earth.

Slowing to a halt about three hundred metres up and getting as close as they dared, the friends stared in wonder at the static like discharges that pulsed and zigzagged inside the beam, heading upwards and outwards.

"Have you ever…?" Buff attempted, trailing off.

"Never," answered Flo, drifting closer, entranced by the energy pulses within the beam.

"Whoa, not too close," said Squish, following her quickly and putting a hand on her arm to stop her, "we don't know what touching it could do."

Twinkle agreed, pointing at the beam.

"Yeah, last thing we need is to get here and get toasted by the signal that…"

Z Z Z !

An arc of static leapt from the column of light to her outstretched finger and she vanished, her voice cut off, vaporized in front of their eyes.

Z Z Z !

"… brought us here," came a voice from below them.

They looked down at Twinkle in shock. She had reappeared a couple of metres further down the beam in another static discharge.

"Argh!" shouted three voices in unison.

Hearing them, Twinkle looked up in horror.

"ARGH!" she shouted back.

A sudden flurry of discharges pulled her frightened, upturned face down the beam in a series of erratic jumps, breaking her cry into a staccato series of sound bites as she went.

As if the first had brought attention to their presence, three more arcs of static zapped from the beam and the others vanished too, their cries of confusion joining with Twinkle's and becoming a disjointed mix of four voices as they arced down the column of light together.

They desperately bloomed their wings larger in an attempt to escape but the arcs held them fast, dragging them downward enveloped in their own light.

Passing through the roof opening, which looked for all the world like a giant, gaping mouth intent on having them for its next meal, they reached the cavern floor in only a few more arcs.

The light beam stuttered as each faery made their final jump, their wings extinguishing as they were deposited with an unceremonious thump on the cave floor. As the last of them hit the ground, the beam died.

The crystal had another surprise in store for them. As it darkened, it liquefied, melting into a glassy puddle before solidifying into a flat, circular plate with a scratchy, crackling sound.

For the first time in thousands of years, since the Great Divide had plunged humanity into its spiritual nosedive, the two species stood facing one another.

The humans stared at the faeries.

The faeries stared at the humans.

No one moved. Or breathed.

The only sound was the almost musical splashing of the waterfall on the other side of the cavern.

Mum put a hand on Dad's arm and leaned towards him, pointing at the forty five centimetre tall figures staring back at them.

"Are those what I think they are?" she asked, hushed.

Dad nodded slowly.

"Think so."

"Well… this is new," quipped Twinkle, seldom short of something to say and always willing to break an awkward silence.

Freya was grinning.

"Faeries. Well I never! Always wondered why my talents lay where they did. Well I *never!*"

"I *told* you… faeries *are* shiny!" Lea said, feeling *very* pleased with herself and hopping with excitement.

"Hello, faeries, my name's Willow and this is my sister, Lea. We're on holiday," said Willow, confidently breaking the ice in her usual fashion. "Are you on holiday too? Could I get wings like yours? Did you really fly here? What are your names?"

Twinkle smiled and replied "Hello! We're working, sweetheart, not on holiday. And only faeries have wings like these…"

She turned around to show them her nodes so they could see as she channeled Flow into them. Blooming her wings in a burst of colour, she whizzed off, relieved to find they were unaffected by what had just happened and circled the cavern quickly before settling back down in front of the girls.

"… but we really did fly here! I'm Twinkle and this is Flo… Buff… and Squishy. We're Team Lux."

She looked over to Mum and Dad.

"Cor, she's full of questions!" she chuckled.

"Oh, I'm sure she's not the only one!" laughed Mum.

After the surreal introductions were over, Buff stepped forward.

"Are you responsible for that?" she asked, pointing up at the moon, which was now pearly white again in the absence of the crystal.

Five humans suddenly looked *very* guilty. Dad decided to take it on the chin for the others.

"Er… we think so. A *lot's* happened today that we think we're the cause of. I don't think it helped that I broke the ceiling," Dad said meekly, pointing upward.

Between them, Mum, Dad, the girls and Freya explained about their meeting the day before, Daisy, Freya's dreams, her sketches and the adventures of today.

Lea ended on the most recent development.

"And then… we met *you!*"

Explanations

Flo decided it was time she joined some dots.

"Well, you can stop worrying about what's happened. You don't have *anything* to feel guilty about. All this," she said, waving around the cave, "was supposed to happen and it appears that you were supposed to be the ones that helped it along."

The humans looked lost.

Flo just looked amused.

Here she was, about to explain to five humans about the part they'd played in a mission that hoped to save all life in the universe, planned by an organization whose purpose was to reunite their two cultures after millennia of separation.

Piece of cake.

"There was a time many thousands of years ago called the Age of Harmony, when our two peoples were friends and shared beliefs and knowledge. The spiritual leaders of our worlds had a series of dreams, a prophesy that we call the Legend. It told of a gateway that would be opened that would end all life. Everywhere. Hardly anyone believed it because the Age of Harmony was so perfect, but that changed. Over time man was corrupted by greed and the cruelty you inflicted on us and each other was too great for us to bear. It made our friendship impossible. We stopped coming here, thinking there was no hope for you. We abandoned you. Eventually, it was decided that it was down to us to guide you back to enlightenment and D.O.W.T. was formed."

Faery Facts.

Lux was the epitome of democracy and majority votes were common at every level of society.

The order of priority for voting was:

1. Local vote,
2. Prime Council vote,
3. Populace vote.

This order had been written into the Societal Code since it was first penned and the last, the populace vote, was put in place as a last resort for when local votes or Prime Council mediation failed to reach a decision. Ironically, the only time in Lux's long history that it had been called into play hadn't even been in response to a failure by the other two.

When the notion of an institution as culturally important as D.O.W.T. had first been thought up, the implications were so far-reaching that it had to be put to the entire population and the local and Prime Council votes were bypassed entirely. Every woman, man and child of school age had their say and after not a single voice of dissension spoke out against the idea, D.O.W.T. was created.

She gestured at herself and her friends.

"That's who we work for... the Department of Off World Travel. It's a major part of our culture. We send teams to Earth to heal your kind of their negative traits so we can eventually reconnect you with the universe and hopefully share knowledge with you again one day. We have a motto... 'Where there is D.O.W.T., there is hope.'"

She stopped for breath and saw she had a *very* attentive audience. '*They'll love this next bit,*' she thought to herself.

"There are three forces in the cycle of life. The Spark, which imbues living things with energy, the Flow, which *is* the energy and the Veil, which exists only to return Flow to the Source after a living thing dies so it can be reused. You can think of the Source as the store for all potential life and the Veil as the gentle, unseen force that absorbs the excess and keeps the store filled. The Legend tells us that the gateway, a place on Earth called the Pit, changes the nature of the Veil and makes it conduct *all* Flow back to the Source. If it's opened, anything alive will die."

She told them about Mamma and her revelation of the secret Legend, the missing faery countdown and the signal their kind had unknowingly been awaiting for fifty years.

Flo regarded the shocked faces with sympathy.

"So you didn't break *anything,* you see? Your being here is all part of the Legend. Everything you did *had* to happen for us to see the signal. It was all meant to be."

"We should just stop being surprised at stuff like this. It's been happening ever since we arrived!" quipped Dad.

"That's called universal engineering, that is," said Squishy. "On our world it's a whole discipline... it's a *very* tangible force. It's the universe making things happen to ensure other events can take place."

Flo nodded in agreement.

"That's right. You were *meant* to reveal this place to us. We had to find it to carry out our mission... to find our missing friends and stop the one the Legend says will activate the Pit by beating them to the Nine Keys that open it."

Know Your Enemy

Mum and Dad looked at each other quickly, their blood chilling. Nine Keys?

"Tell 'em love," Dad said numbly.

"We had dinner last night with the head of the charity we won our holiday from, Luke Borson, only it turns out he lied to get us here. There *is* no charity, just him. He offered us loads of money, diamonds actually, to let him know if we found nine relics. He said they were keys. He told us he wants them to finish his collection of faery folklore and that he'd dreamt that we'd lead him to 'em."

Mum took her purse out of her backpack and held up the diamond Luke had given them.

A very excited Twinkle shot over to Mum.

"He gave you this last night? Did he touch it? Did he hold the stone?"

"Yes, he took it out of a box and passed it to us."

"May I?" asked Twinkle and Mum handed the diamond to her.

Buff joined Twinkle to hover in front of the humans.

"Twinkle's a sharer," she informed them, "an empath. She can sync with a person's consciousness. She can also pick up a little of their aura from the things they've touched. Minerals and such are *particularly* good... the purity of a diamond should retain enough of him to tell her if he's the Broken Soul our Legend speaks of."

Faery Facts.

Akin to human psychiatry, being a sharer was a handy skill to have, but the nature of the work was emotionally taxing.

A sharer working at home on lux could expect their daily work load to maybe include grief over the loss of a family member or a pet, or sadness over a relationship that hadn't worked out. Occasionally, annoyance over an argument... it wasn't like faeries never had differences of opinion.

Working for D.O.W.T. however, they had a whole other world of problems to deal with, some of them quite distressing.

For a sharer, a visit to Earth often ended with a visit to another sharer to help ease the emotions they'd experienced.

That was why sharers generally had the shortest careers in the organization and left earlier than niners with other gifts. A daily dose of negativity could only be managed for so long.

No one understood human nature better than a sharer and no one appreciated the need for human reconnection better than those who regularly felt the lack of it.

Enormous strength of character, sharers.

Twinkle glided over to the flat plate that was all that remained of the giant crystal, settling down in its centre cross legged.

Mentally gritting her teeth, she cupped her hands together around the diamond and making a small opening where her thumbs met, she placed the gap against the node on her forehead and closed her eyes. A faint coloured light began to shine through her fingers and she stayed perfectly still as a stream of images from Luke's life began to fill her mind.

After a few moments, the light faded and she lowered her cupped hands into her lap.

"It's him," she breathed, addressing the other faeries, her voice lowered to a cracked whisper. "The Broken Soul. Such grief. Such *rage*."

She recounted what she'd seen, her voice distant and dreamy as though she were visualising events she'd been present at.

"He hates us. He blames us for his parents' deaths when he was a boy. His father discovered a cavern like this one beneath his estate, but found early on that its crystal floor had the power to kill by touch. He built a wooden platform so he could study it and experiment in safety, but one night, he saw one of our kind appear in its centre. The faery desperately channeled Flow to stay alive, but the cave floor absorbed so much that he couldn't escape. The father realized what was happening and rushed to the faery's aid, but in his haste he tripped. As he fell, his arm went over the edge of the platform and he touched the cave floor. He died instantly. The mother ran to help him thinking he was just hurt, but in her panic, didn't see the deadly connection between her husband and the crystal. As she touched him, her Flow was pulled from her too. The boy sat in that cave all night with the bodies of his mother and father, eyes filled with patient hatred until the faery finally gave up. While he waited, something snapped in his mind."

She sobbed, shaking her head as if trying to free herself of the images she was reliving.

"His father had wanted to keep the cavern's properties a secret until he understood it better, so in a grief-struck attempt to honour his wishes, he tampered with the evidence of their deaths. When the staff finally found him the next morning, he'd cranked the platform up on its winch to separate his parents from the lethal crystal and hidden the body of the dead faery under a blanket. By the time the police arrived, the estate staff had already carried the bodies outside, so apart from a quick look around the cavern for their reports, there was nothing overtly strange to link the deaths to it specifically. All the coroner could do after the post mortems was to record a verdict of unexplained death. The cavern was locked up, written off by the family's solicitor as a tragic curiosity. The boy knew the truth though and would often go there just to sit where his parents had died. When another faery appeared, then another, he saw the pattern. He'd go and watch them every full moon, gloating as they died, then add their remains to his new 'collection.' He's spent his entire life expanding his father's museum and searching for clues that will help him avenge his parents and give him power over us. Some of the artifacts and parchments his father found are old enough to contain at least *some* truth and he's found many more since. Trouble is, the details have been warped over time. Because these discoveries are all from the human world, they're all from a human perspective and he's become convinced that what he's learned is a way to *gain* power, not *unleash* it. He knows enough about the Legend to understand the countdown and that he needs the Keys to open the Pit, but if you tried to convince him it meant the end of all life, he'd never believe it."

She opened her hands and looked at the bright diamond.

"So much hate in something so beautiful..." she said softly, as Dad came over and knelt beside her.

"You finished with that?" he asked.

Twinkle looked up at him, nodding sadly.

"Why do you humans have to be so obsessed with money and power and control?" she asked.

"Not all of us *are*," he responded matter of factly, taking the stone from her.

He held out a chivalrous little finger to help Twinkle to her feet. As she took it and stepped down from the crystal plate, the tiniest pulse of Flow passed between them and she saw behind species and culture and circumstance to the family's soul. He was right. Not all of them *were*.

He held the diamond up to the moonlight, rolling it between his finger and thumb.

"Blood money," he said. "Don't want it."

He stretched his arm back and launched the diamond into the furthest reaches of the cavern. Or at least he *tried* to.

Key Evidence

The diamond curved up and out, glinting in the moonlight as it flew through the air. Gravity should have ensured it followed the curve back down to Earth with a diminishing

DINK
DINK
D-D-DINK

as its journey came to an end on the cavern floor... but gravity wasn't in control any more.

The diamond slowed, came to a halt mid-flight, then shot towards the crystal plate, stopping at a point high above and dead centre of it. It hung there briefly, reflecting beams of moonlight from its facets like a miniscule disco ball, before firing downwards with immense force.

It hit the centre of the plate, puncturing it and causing a shockwave to ripple through the crystal as it liquefied again. A spiral formed around the puncture, slowly pulling downward, deepening and enlarging until it became the cone of a slowly rotating whirlpool. At the same time, wispy tendrils of crystal were drawn up out of the edge of the puddle, binding together to form a ring of individual figures around it.

The vortex began to drag fine, almost web like strands of crystal from the figures towards the hole at its centre. Caught up in the rotation, the strands swept around its edge, spiralling inward and blending together until they were swallowed in an almost solid stream as it fed.

After a few moments of eerie movement, a low crackling signaled the end of this odd spectacle as it froze slowly into place. Being stationary did little to make the image any less unnerving.

Most interesting was that the figures were of varying sizes; three large, two medium and four *very* small. Anyone who'd just had the Legend explained to them could be forgiven for thinking they represented humans and faeries... *nine* humans and faeries to be exact.

"HA!" laughed Mum loudly. "I've been looking *everywhere* for my Keys! Always in the last place you look."

"Nah, I'm not having *that!*" stated Squishy incredulously.

Flo shrugged.

"Weeell... they *did* open the cavern and activate the crystal that showed us where to look. And when we arrived, it *did* pull us down here, forcing us all to meet. All *nine* of us."

Mum was getting into this whole Legend thing quite readily by now and was surprisingly upbeat about the news.

"I always knew we were destined for something big!" she said brightly. "*This* is a bit more than I imagined though!"

Buff smiled.

"It's more than *we* imagined. We've known about this for thousands of years and we thought the Keys were objects the whole time."

"The good news is, Borson thinks the same thing," Dad added helpfully. "He asked us to help him find things, not people."

Twinkle pulled a face.

"Just as well… he knows where you live. If he knew that you were the Keys, you'd be in his collection too. I've *felt* him. I know what he's capable of and you're only here now because he didn't know what you are."

True Colours

"And now I do."

They spun round, startled by the cold voice.

Nine hearts sank as Borson and Neery emerged from the shadows of the tunnel, the latter holding a handgun.

'*Browning 9mm,*' thought Dad. '*Effective at short range.*'

Borson looked smug. They'd arrived in time to witness Dad throwing the diamond away and had seen everything.

"Yes, yes, all very shocking I know. 'What is he doing here? How did he know, etcetera, etcetera?' I had Neery follow you, obviously. The chine, the jeweller's, the old woman's shop, here… I'm not in the habit of striking costly deals without ensuring the terms are adhered to, however amicable the agreement might seem."

He strode closer, his long, spidery legs picking their way across the crystal floor.

"Speaking of our agreement, I'm afraid I can no longer honour it. It required me to pay you for finding the Keys, but as it would appear you *are* the Keys, our contract is now void."

He motioned at the frozen vortex scene.

"Using the nine of you in the way the sculpture here implies can only result in your deaths, so as you can see… I'll have no one *to* pay. I would have taken back my deposit too, if it hadn't already paid such huge dividends."

He pointed up at the open roof.

"So am I to understand that the light show we witnessed on the way here was a signal to summon *them?*" he asked disdainfully, jabbing a finger in the direction of the faeries.

His question was met with a stony, unhelpful silence and he feigned a disappointed look.

"No matter. I have what I need now, regardless of how it came to me. It *was* rewarding to see more evidence of everything my father and I have uncovered though. You'll see for yourself soon enough. For now, Mr Neery will escort you back to Borson House as my guests. It simply wouldn't do to lose the Keys again so soon after their discovery."

With that, he strode off, disappearing into the tunnel. Neery gestured in the same direction with the gun.

"Humans… just one rule. I'll only say it once. *Don't* try anything stupid. I'd prefer not to get my suit dirty dragging you out of here with a bullet in your leg."

"So *kind,*" Twinkle answered back sarcastically, "it's nice to be escorted to our deaths by a thug with our well-being at heart."

He smiled cruelly.

"Faeries… try to fly away and I'll tin up one of your new friends." He held up the pistol for effect. "Maybe one of the kids, to teach you a lesson. Now, *move,*" he said coldly, not noticing the shared looks that passed between the faeries as the group moved off ahead of him.

"This is bad," whispered Mum to Dad, hugging the girls to her. "We need to get away. Now."

"I know," he whispered back, scanning the floor for something to use as a weapon. There was nothing.

Remembering the handheld torch in the back pocket of his jeans, he casually swung his arm behind him, feeling the shape of it with the back of his hand. It wasn't that heavy, but with a bit of power behind it, it might just stun Neery long enough for him to grab the gun.

So, what was the plan? Make a move out here in the cavern, or wait until they rounded the bend in the tunnel? He didn't like the idea of 9mm bullets whizzing around near his family full stop, but having them ricocheting around in a confined space was potentially even worse.

He made a pretense of catching his foot on a rock and slowed, letting Neery catch up ever so slightly. Turning to one side as he 'recovered' from his stumble, he slipped his hand into the pocket where the torch was and pulled it out.

'*Special forces?*' thought Dad. '*Oh dear... I'm gonna get battered... or worse, shot.*'

From that point on, everything became a bit of a blur.

There was a strange flash of light and what felt like a hard shove to the chest and things went muted and sparkly.

The ground seemed to be dropping away from under their feet as a colourful bubble expanded rapidly away from them and they couldn't quite focus their vision enough to figure out why. Someone below was seeing them off. The girls were waving 'bye bye' to whoever it was, as the ground fell further and further and further away...

Escape

… and now, someone was *shouting* at them.

It sounded urgent, but if it was, they *really* shouldn't be doing it through a pillow… it made it *very* hard to understand them.

"NEERY'S BEEN KNOCKED UNCONSCIOUS WITH AN OVERDOSE OF FLOW. HE TOOK THE BRUNT OF IT, BUT YOU'VE ALL BEEN AFFECTED TOO. IT CAN BE…"

The cooler air outside the cavern helped clear their fuzzy heads and muffled hearing. Suddenly, five humans were only *too* aware of what was going on. They were flying.

"… EXTREMELY INCAPACITATING, BUT DON'T WORRY, IT WEARS OFF QUICKLY, LEAVING YOU FEELING PRETTY GOOD! WE'VE EXTENDED OUR WING FIELDS AROUND YOU TO CARRY YOU OUT OF THE CAVE… NO ONE SCARED OF HEIGHTS, ARE THEY? BAD NEWS FOR US THOUGH… EXTENDING OUR WING FIELD ZONKS US OUT. WE USE IT NOW AND THEN TO CARRY LARGER OBJECTS OR HEAVIER WEIGHTS, BUT I'M AFRAID HUMANS QUALIFY AS BOTH. WE'LL MOST LIKELY FALL UNCONSCIOUS WHEN WE STOP CHANNELLING… WE'RE GONNA NEED YOUR HELP!"

Faery Facts.

Wing field physics is a well known subject amongst faeries.

On the ground, their species, Homo faerus, is essentially a smaller version of Homo sapiens, but with some very cool enhancements to their nervous system. They have all the same variations in build and muscle density that humans have and they gauge how much weight they can carry based on individual size and strength, the same way humans do.

In the air however, their node~generated, electromagnetic, gravity~repelling energy field is capable of bearing loads many times their own body weight. Very useful in a society of farmers strong on animal welfare and not reliant upon the internal combustion engine. Although able to process extremely high levels of Flow, even the faery nervous system has a point of overload, as demonstrated by the almost unconscious state faeries are reduced to by channeling too much Flow into too large a wing field. Whilst not necessarily being an unpleasant experience, being what they call 'spangled' leaves them extremely vulnerable.

They'd overdone it a touch on the wing fields, but this had two benefits; not only had they got away quickly, shooting out of the cavern opening at high speed in a tightly packed, tactical escape formation, but they'd gone extremely high, treating the humans to a brief moment of aerial tourism.

Leaving Borson halfway along the tunnel and Neery out for the count on the cavern floor below, they soared over the beach and ended up out over the water. Banking around sharply, they dived steeply towards the waves, pulling up at the last moment and catching spray as they rushed over their crests.

Crossing the flat sand of the beach, they tore up the narrow gulley that led back to the road, shooting over the tarmac and catching a satisfying last look down into the open cavern on the hillside.

Borson's Jaguar was parked at the opposite end of the lay-by to Daisy and they touched down between the two. The Jag's bodywork lit up briefly in the glow of the faeries' wings, before fading back to a ghostly, moonlit white as their fields collapsed and they dropped to the rough gravel, totally spangled.

Mum, the girls and Freya gently scooped up the four faeries as Dad unlocked the camper and pulled open the side door. Smiling at each other in disbelief, they carried them inside and laid them on Mum's and Dad's duvet. Mum pulled a fleece blanket from the tall cupboard next to the bed and covered the four tiny forms, then after making sure that Freya and the children were seated, she pulled the door closed behind her and climbed over the front seat to join Dad.

He started Daisy, completed the fastest three-point turn in VDub history and drove her out of the lay-by around Borson's Jag, her tyres kicking up little spurts of dust as she bumped onto the road and sped away.

Mum kept the two excited girls sidetracked for a while with a string of: 'We beat the bad guys!' 'Wasn't that fun?' and 'We've flown with real faeries!' but they eventually calmed down and the camper was now peaceful.

Mum and Dad had always joked that their children could sleep through the end of the world and now that the end of the world was a distinct possibility, Lea had decided to step up and prove them right. She'd succumbed to all the excitement and was leaning on Freya's arm, dozing. Freya stroked her hair while she slept and listened to Willow singing softly as the dark countryside flitted by outside.

Dad's face was stony with shock and concentration as they flew along the deserted road. Mum put her hand on his leg and he took one of his off the steering wheel to hold hers. He took a deep breath and let it out slowly.

"You OK?" asked Mum.

"Better now," he replied. "That bloke's a loon. You?"

"Yeah, I'm fine. Love, I've been thinking, we can't go back to the farm. He knows we're there. We need to find somewhere else to spend the night."

"You thinking bed and breakfast?" Dad asked.

Mum shook her head.

"Nowhere where there're people. We don't know who he knows or where he might just suddenly turn up. Somewhere quiet. Just us. Until we suss out what to do next."

Dad checked the rearview mirror again, just one more of the many times he'd already done so.

"Let's get off the road now then. We've got food; we've got water; we should just go to ground. At least until daylight. Remember that little chine we were looking at on the map last night? Past the farm, between Blackgang Chine and the lighthouse?"

Mum reached into a pocket in her door and pulled out an Ordnance Survey map. She clicked on the cabin light and after finding the part with the south coast on it, laid it on the seat between them.

"There's the farm," he said, glancing down briefly and pointing out the pencil ring that he'd drawn to mark their campsite. "When you get to the amusement park, Military Road turns into Blackgang Road... it's a track that drops down off that."

Mum ran her fingertip across the map until she found the chine.

"Got it!" she exclaimed.

"Just give me a heads up when we get close, will you?"

They passed the farm with a longing look, then Chale and the amusement park and continued on, up a steep hill that went past a car park with a viewing point.

The map said that the track they needed lay just beyond a tight chicane in the road. Mum had just mentioned this when a zigzag in a red warning triangle and the black and white arrows of a sharp deviation sign flared up in the headlights.

Dad changed down, slowing as he guided Daisy through the sharp bends. There'd been no headlights behind them since the lay by, so he kept Daisy's speed low as they came out of the chicane, thinking that was a better idea than having to stop and reverse back if they missed the track.

The low speed paid off because suddenly there it was, flanked by bushes and almost unrecognizable as another possible route. Good news for anyone wanting to use it as a hiding place.

Braking hard, Dad turned off the road. He drove between the bushes, changing down into first gear to cope with the bumps and bounces of the rough track as it dropped down a winding slope.

This was perfect. Even in daylight, anyone driving past would have to be going at a snail's pace to see it led somewhere. At night, unless they knew it was there and intended to use it, not a prayer... of which, incidentally, Mum was saying a silent one as Dad tried not to hit anything on the way down.

About seventy metres from the road the track opened out into a clearing, overlooking the sea and backed by a rocky crag. Dad turned sharp left and came to a stop, leaving a couple of metres between the side door of the camper and the rock face. The headlights revealed the chine a few metres ahead. It wasn't particularly deep as chines went, but it would still have made a *terrible* parking spot, so he put on the handbrake, clicked off the lights and turned off the ignition.

By this time, Willow had dropped off too and Freya now had a sleeping princess on each shoulder. They looked like a pair of extremely peaceful bookends... and Freya looked more than happy to be the book.

The hot engine hissed and click-click-clicked as it cooled, sounding to Dad like an alarm bell meant to deliberately alert their pursuers.

"I'm going back up to the road to watch for them," Dad said quietly. "Don't want any unwanted visitors, do we?"

He squeezed Mum's hand gently and jumped out. Sliding open the side door, he opened one of the low cupboards and pulled out the big torch, a four cell Maglite. He hefted its weight in his hand, took a practice swipe and looked up to see two unhappy faces looking at him.

"Hey... I'm not chuffed about it either. What's the alternative though?"

"It's not that," said Mum, worried. "Just don't get hurt."

He went to her window and gave her a kiss.

"I love you. Don't worry. If we've lost 'em, we'll stay here for the night, then find a police station first thing in the morning."

"And what are we gonna tell 'em? How much *can* we tell 'em?" asked Mum.

Dad shook his head.

"I have no idea. Start with his staff waving guns about I s'pose. We'll figure it out when I come back."

He leant into the camper, kissed the tops of the sleeping girls' heads and put a hand on Freya's arm.

"You make a cracking pillow, Freya, thanks."

"My pleasure, flower," she responded. "We'll look after these... you look after yourself."

"Will do," he whispered, putting his finger to his lips. "Shhh."

And with that, he turned and ran back up the track as quietly as he could, his footfalls mingling with the clicks of the engine until he disappeared into the night.

Dinner Plans

Finding a good spot to hide while he waited to see if they'd be discovered was the easy part. He was more concerned with the fact that it was so quiet, he could still hear the camper's engine cooling down, even from way up here by the road. Someone would only have to stop and listen for them to be found.

A low noise began to build in the dark and it soon became the sound of an approaching car, its headlights vanishing and reappearing as it moved along the undulating road. Dad closed one eye to protect his night vision, listening for the slightest change in engine pitch that would announce that the vehicle was slowing down. His heart lurched as it *did* slow down, but it was only to negotiate the chicane, after which it accelerated again, sounding like it was almost on top of him. The white car he was expecting went roaring past in a pocket of noise and light... and kept going! YES! They'd missed the track completely.

Dad sighed with relief. With any luck, Borson and Neery thought the camper was heading eastwards at full speed in an attempt to escape. By the time they realized they weren't catching up to them and Daisy had vanished, there'd be too many places she could have hidden and a search would be impossible.

Just to be sure the white car didn't double back, he stayed by the track entrance for another twenty minutes or so before making his way back down to the others.

The girls had recharged by then and were wide awake and waiting when he got back to the clearing. They hugged him as he crouched down to wrap his arms around them.

"Hello, pickles, been looking after our new friends?"

"They're awake now, Dad!" said Willow with barely contained excitement. "They're still a bit floppy, but they're OK."

They led him over to where the faeries were recovering in the back of the camper. Mum had opened the back tailgate in the hope that some fresh air and a bit of a breeze would help to bring them round and it had worked a treat. The four were sitting up, almost back to their old selves.

Mum filled the kettle and while it was boiling the nine of them compared notes on what had happened in the cavern and on the way here.

As Neery herded them towards the tunnel, Buff had signaled a plan to the other faeries by patting her top pocket. She'd taken out her grenade, set it off and thrown it behind her and Neery had glanced down at his feet as it hit the floor in front of him.

After a cautious check of his captives, he'd knelt to see what it was and it had gone off in his face. Bending over it like he was, he'd absorbed almost the whole shockwave and it rocked him backwards, instantly unconscious, his gun still gripped in his outstretched hand.

The Rauliches had only caught the edge of it, but it was still enough to completely disorient them. In their confusion, they missed a lot: a rush of excess Flow being absorbed into the faeries' wing nodes, each faery positioning themselves in front of a human, (except for Twinkle, who took both the littl'uns) the powerful blooming of four sets of enormous, rainbow-like wings and being effortlessly lifted high into the air by a force that seemed to glue them to a sheet of colour.

The faeries had missed their fair share of events too: being carried to the camper after touchdown, the getaway drive, the bumpy downhill ride to their new hiding place and the nervous wait to see if they'd be discovered.

Once everyone was up to speed on the parts they'd missed, Dad went to the open tailgate, slid out a plastic storage box from under the bed and carried it round to the side door. Mum watched him with a half smile, waiting to catch his eye.

After putting out Daisy's awning, he took a sheet from the box and hung it from the side where the breeze was coming from using toggles through the eyelets. He pegged out the bottom edge, et voila… one windbreak.

There was a scraggly, shrubby thing growing out from the rock about halfway up and taking a bungee from the box, he stretched it around its thickest part and hooked it through an eyelet to stop that side of the sheet flapping in the wind. Perfect.

Stepping back to look at his handy work, he nodded approvingly before ambling off to a nearby oak tree to hunt for deadfall. After dumping his fourth armful of firewood in the lee of the windbreak, he caught Mum's smile.

"What?" he said, grinning.

"You know what," she replied, mock serious. "Go on… say, 'I told you so.'"

"Don't know what you mean, sweetheart," Dad chuckled, pulling a fire setting kit out of the plastic box. He took a handful of wood shavings, a ferrocerium rod and a striker from it, then built a little teepee of snapped twigs over the shavings ready for lighting.

Mum saw Buff's quizzical expression and explained.

"Mike was in the army for six years and he's still a bit... well... *boy scout*. Even before we had Daisy, he'd always have blankets, food and water and a stove in the boot of the car 'just in case.' I used to wind him up about it but after this I think I'll be getting a dose of my own!"

Dad used the striker to generate several dense showers of sparks.

CHKKK! CHKKK! CHKKK! CHKKK!

The sparks caught the delicate shavings on the fourth strike and tiny, yellowy-orange flames bloomed and crept outward.

"Would I do that?" Dad asked, looking innocent.

"Yes!" cried Willow and Lea together.

"Traitors!" Dad joked. "My own children, too!"

Laughter filled the air and as the flames took hold, Dad added thicker pieces until the clearing lit up, revealing nine happy faces in the flickering light.

There was no real danger of the fire giving them away; not only were they a good distance from the road, they were also sheltered on three sides by geology and thick vegetation. The only direction they could potentially be spotted from was out on the water and it was highly unlikely that Borson would be out at sea, scanning a small stretch of coastline for them, particularly when he thought they were escaping by road in a highly conspicuous turquoise camper van.

Dad thought that a combination of Daisy's tyre tracks and Neery's training might give away their direction, but that would still put them on a road somewhere, not hiding in a clearing just around the coast from Borson's estate under his very nose. For the time being at least, inside their bubble of friendship and warmth, they felt safe.

With this comforting information in mind, Dad stood and faced the rest of the group.

"Who's hungry?" he asked.

A resounding 'YES!' answered his question and brought up the pressing and crucial matter of faery diet.

Faery Facts.

As you can probably guess, faeries don't eat meat. They are quite fond of milk, cheese and eggs though and have no beef (excuse the pun) with rearing animals for their produce. Faery~reared livestock are some of the happiest and healthiest to be found anywhere.

After a period of sharing their gifts, they are put out to pasture on retirement reservations where they can scratch and chew the cud into old age to finally die free in the wild.

Large communities have sprung up around dairy and egg supply. Cattle care and chicken rangling are two highly~prized professions, attracting faeries from all walks (or flights) of life to the animal husbandry lifestyle.

Some pretty odd traditions have developed from it over the centuries though, the Summer Solstice Cheese Bomb Festival and the Cross Country Chicken Chase Trophy to name but two.

Some people look forward all year to sitting in the sun with their friends and a tankard watching people get covered in soft cheese from a great height, or to watch a crowd of lightning~fast hens go flashing past in a clucking cloud of dust in the hope that their favourite is in the lead!
But I digress… as part of a very healthy balanced diet, faeries do *eat animal produce.*
They just don't *eat animals.*

While Mum got busy with a sharp knife, Dad and the girls got skewering and made some chunky kebabs from an assortment of sweet pepper, mushroom, red onion and halloumi cheese.

A circular grill supported by four sticks around the fire made the perfect platform to roast them on and in no time, the smell of dinner was wafting over them and making their bellies rumble. They gazed into the embers, lost in thought as the sound of quiet sizzling teased their appetites.

When the kebabs were almost done, Mum took one of them apart and diced everything smaller. Dad cut some new wooden skewers from the pack into thirds, then rebuilt Mum's handiwork into mini kebabs on the smaller sticks.

After a moment back on the grill to make sure they were hot, the new and reduced kebabs were handed over to four grateful faeries.

The humans helped themselves to theirs from the grill and after several 'thank you's,' silence descended, broken only by the occasional 'Mmm,' or slurp as someone took a drink between mouthfuls. Apparently, the excitement hadn't dulled anyone's appetite. Quite the opposite in fact.

When they'd finished, Mum fished around in a cupboard and to everyone's delight came out with a pack of blueberry muffins and some fruit for dessert.

Twinkle smiled.

"So this is how humans rough it, is it? Not bad!"

Dad laughed.

"I could've done you a nice nettle and black pepper soup, but the mushrooms needed using up," he replied, taking a big bite out of his apple.

This was the family's favourite sort of camping: under the stars, cooking over a campfire, with the wind blowing through the trees above and the sounds of the night just beyond the orangey-yellow glow and the crackling of the fire... fantastic. Minus a maniac and his henchman hunting them, it would have been idyllic.

"You guys'd do alright working for D.O.W.T." Squishy commented. "You'd be popular with your team at meal times!"

"Some more than others, hollow legs," muttered Twinkle good-naturedly.

After dinner was over they relaxed contentedly around the fire, chatting about possible solutions to their situation and plans for the next day.

Remembering Twinkle's vision, Flo's voice trembled as she verbalised what had been in the other faeries' thoughts for a while. "I was praying the missing were being held prisoner, but from what T saw, it doesn't look like we're here to save them any more... and now we know *we're* the Keys, our last real option is to stop the Pit opening. Destroy it."

Buff suggested that a little reconnaissance might fill in some of the gaps in their knowledge.

"I think we'll have to go to Borson House for a snoop around. We know the Pit's somewhere on the estate, so priority number one is to find out exactly where."

"We should keep numbers low," suggested Squishy quietly. "Two people only, nice and stealthy. Count me in."

Dad stoked the embers of the fire with a branch and put some more wood on. Ignoring the old army adage,

NEVER VOLUNTEER

he raised a hand.

"I'm in too."

Buff was relieved. She hadn't doubted there'd be volunteers, but they did make things easier.

"Thank you. That leaves Twinkle, Flo and myself to get the ladies away if anything happens here."

"No problem," said Dad, looking over at his new partner in crime, "I'm sure we'll find out something useful. Wouldn't we have to get Borson and Neery out of the house somehow though?"

Twinkle smiled.

"I have an idea on that. Borson wants the Keys, right? Offer him *us,* in exchange for your freedom. If he takes the bait, agree to meet him to hand us over. It doesn't *matter* that he needs all nine Keys, or that he'd double-cross you in a heart beat... all that's important is that he believes you're desperate enough to betray us to save yourselves and your kids."

She looked apologetic and a little guilty.

"Sorry, guys, present company excluded, but humans do have a bit of a track record for betrayal. Once they're away from the house, the two of you can sneak in and find out whatever you can."

Mum had a question.

"What about Mrs Raullings? I have a feeling she's not as involved as the others, but she could still be trouble. We *are* gonna be breaking into her employer's house, after all."

"Leave her to me," Squishy said, his eyes positively *gleaming* with mischief. "I'll make sure she's out for the count."

"*Bad* faery!" laughed Buff.

Mum frowned.

"*How?*"

"Medicinal plants. I knock up a *wicked* sleeping draft."

"I'm sorry, am I to understand you're going to *drug* the kindly housekeeper?"

"Let's just say that being a grower imparts a certain skill set on a fellow that Mrs Raullings will benefit from by way of a short, but intensely deep and refreshing afternoon nap."

"So you *are* going to drug her then?"

"Absolutely."

So it was agreed: Mum would ring Borson, playing the not-so-fictional part of a frightened parent desperate to bargain for their children's safety. If he went for it, she'd act as though she believed that meeting in a public place was safer for them and suggest they meet in Shanklin. In truth, they had no intention of being anywhere *near* Shanklin, or Borson. All they needed was to keep him and his henchman busy for long enough to search the house. It made for a convincing blag: Mum and Dad *were* very scared for the girl's safety and the mere *thought* of being surrounded by people in a public place genuinely offered some comfort.

Squishy would make sure the housekeeper was out of action and if anything urgent came up, he would evacuate Dad or fly back to summon the others. Buff, Twinkle, Flo, Mum, Freya and the girls would wait with Daisy, ready to drive, run or fly at a moment's notice.

As Mum pointed out after everyone's part in the plan had been agreed, it was, most definitely, 'On.'

After asking Dad to put a pan of water on to boil for when he returned, Squish left to do a spot of foraging for the plants he needed for Mrs Raulling's little surprise. He wasn't gone long and by the time he floated back into camp, the water was bubbling.

Taking out his father's knife, he began deftly chopping the different things he'd gathered, sometimes using parts of the plants themselves and sometimes only the roots. He placed them into small piles around the edge of a plate as everyone watched.

"Just a little hobby of mine," he began happily, dropping pieces of this and that into the hot water. It looked random, but the human element of his audience suspected it was anything but. It's enlightening to see a true expert at their craft. The casual way they work conceals all the effort that went into attaining the wealth of experience that enables them to appear as though they're not even trying!

"Some of our healers are growers like me, but I've always felt more at home with my hands in the dirt so I didn't end up in the N.H.S. I still dabble a bit though."

Flo rolled her eyes.

"'Dabble a bit?' Talk about an understatement. The N.H.S. offer you a tutoring position at the start of *every* student intake! You've basically got a job there any time you want… you just haven't said, 'Yes' to it yet."

He gave his concoction a stir, reached into a pouch on his belt and held up the wildflower seed he took from it.

"Couldn't do this all the time if I worked in a classroom."

Flo smiled softly as he leant over to a bare patch of earth, dropped the seed into a tiny crack and gave it a sprinkle with the tear bottle from his vest. When she spoke it was jocular, but with a touch of pride.

"Squish has decided it's his personal responsibility to plant up any bare patch of soil he can find here. Every chance he gets, he plants a seed. *He* doesn't make a big deal of it, but *I* will. He's very dedicated."

Squish continued stirring and looked a little embarrassed at the praise.

"It's not like I'm the *only* grower that does it," he said quietly. "I know not all of 'em sprout and not all of the ones that do will last, that's up to the Spark, but seeds want soil and soil wants seeds. I'm just the matchmaker. It's all about creating a root network. The more plants there are, the bigger the network. The bigger the network, the more Flow you lot are surrounded by and the quicker we can get you all reconnected to it."

His look had turned to one of determination.

"Just offsetting all that tarmac you keep laying here," he said with a smirk. "The worst places need the grandest help."

"That's a lovely idea Squish. Like a carpet. A great big Flowing carpet," smiled Mum.

Squishy nodded and pointed at her for emphasis.

"Exactly," he said.

"Or WiFi," added Dad.

"Not so much," laughed Squishy, shaking his head.

Showtime

The sleeping draft was bottled and now sat cooling on the camper worktop, a herbal harbinger of their impending plan.

Dad was sitting in Daisy's doorway watching the girls singing to Flo and Buff. He seemed decidedly unhappy.

Thinking he looked somewhat like a cornered animal, Mum joined him and took his hand. The trapped look melted away.

"I really believe we have to do this," she said quietly. "I *hate* that the girls have been dragged into it, but much as I don't want to, I believe it all."

Dad nodded.

"I know; me too. I have this... *certainty* I can't explain."

"I always knew the girls were destined for great things," joked Mum, "but I was thinking more vet or gymnast."

He smiled half-heartedly.

"Be useful in job interviews, won't it? 'Skills you feel you can bring to the role?' 'Apocalypse Prevention.'"

They kissed, pausing for a moment with their foreheads touching, then got up to join the others around the campfire where they sat on either side of the girls like sentries.

"What if we just went home?" suggested Mum. "Borson can't do anything if there're no Keys, can he?"

Twinkle, who had been gazing out to sea from a niche in the rock face above their heads, drifted down to join them.

"Can't do *that*," she stated matter of factly. "You're still the Keys. He'd just lock you up anyway and make you all a permanent part of his collection in the hope that he'd cross paths with *us* again. Besides, we're all *supposed* to be here. Whatever the Legend might say about someone opening the Pit, don't forget it also gave our kind the clues we needed to get us here so we could meet you. We all saw how hard the universe worked to make *that* happen!"

Dad took a half breath in and raised a forefinger as though to comment, but Twinkle gently interrupted him.

"I know what you're thinking, because it's what every mortal, sentient being does out of hope for the future… you're thinking that means the universe is putting things in place to ensure a positive outcome, aren't you?"

"No one likes a smarty pants," replied Dad and Twinkle chuckled.

"I'm sorry, but none of that points to success or failure. We want to survive… Borson equally wants things to go *his* way. Doesn't matter to the universe, it's already got ideas of its own. The universe isn't good or evil, just neutral, so it'll only do what's holistically best for the greater good. If that means we live, cool, but it could also just be wiping the slate clean to start again."

Freya wrinkled her nose.

"Typical. Fate gives you its plans in writing and *still* no one knows what's going on. And you seem so calm about it! I'm normally a pretty positive person but I tell you, I'm having trouble seeing a light at the end of *this* tunnel. I wish I could see things from your perspective."

Flo threw the pebble she'd been tossing and catching at Twinkle's boot. She raised a questioning eyebrow at her. Twinkle nodded.

"Don't see why not… hasn't been done for thousands of years, but if it's ever going to be done again, now's certainly the time!"

"Time for what?" Mum asked.

Buff explained, wearing an enormous smile.

"An awakening. Faeries giving humans the ability to sense Flow. It was done all the time during the Age of Harmony, but *never* since. This is a big deal! If you accept, you'll be the first humans to be awoken since the Great Divide."

"Is it dangerous?" Mum wanted to know, thinking of the girls.

"Absolutely not. Our brain structures are actually very similar. An awakening just bypasses the fact you weren't blessed with nodes and stimulates a couple of inactive areas that process Flow consciously."

Buff wiggled her fingers.

"You'd be able to see it and feel it through your nerve endings. Lets you receive but not send, I s'pose you could say."

Faery Facts.

When the friendship between faeries and humans was in its infancy, a healer from Lux and a highly~respected herbalist from Earth had speculated on the anatomical similarities between their two brains. They had come to the conclusion that apart from the obvious difference in relative size, the two were almost identical in function and the concept of 'waking up' the human mind was born.

Unsure of the outcome, the herbalist had selflessly volunteered himself as a guinea pig and their theory was tested. It was a resounding success and he became the first human to experience Flow as faeries did.

The process took the two cultures by storm and the expression 'everything's looking rosy' appeared overnight to honour a new and wondrous way of experiencing the world. Strange, until you consider that the faery healer's name all those years ago was... yes, of course it was... Rose.

At first glance, it appeared that only one of these geniuses had been immortalized with a popular saying, but as the herbalist graciously acceded at the time, 'everything's looking merliny' just didn't have the same ring to it.

Flo took over from Buff.

"It's pretty special. It's a bit like the tingle you get from static electricity, but *so* much more. You have to feel it to understand. You'll see auras and patterns in living things too. I have to warn you though... If you do this, you'll be changed until the day you pass through the Veil. You can turn it on and off as easily as opening and closing your eyes, but I can almost guarantee you won't want to. Your view of the world will *never* be the same again."

Dad was curious.

"But we can already see it... your wings."

"You can only see *that* because it's channeled through our nodes. When it affects the environment in a concentrated form, it's visible to anyone, like... uh... like how you can only see electricity when it makes a spark."

"Or rainbows," added Buff, enjoying the surprised looks for a second or two. "It's not *all* about refracted light you know."

Flo paused and smiled, a small secret smile that spoke of the wonders to come.

"There's what you know... and everything else! *This* is the full extras package... a more beautiful way of experiencing the universe. Who's in?"

They all were, of course.

"Could I have the assistance of a member of the audience then, please?" asked Twinkle, almost as excited to be doing it as the humans were by the offer.

Freya couldn't volunteer fast enough. She couldn't *wait* to see what the world looked like through faery eyes.

"This'll definitely give your artistic flare a little tweak," Twinkle said lightly, before explaining what was involved.

Forehead to forehead, she would direct a steady stream of Flow into the pineal gland deep inside Freya's brain at the top of her spinal cord, to gently stimulate her nervous system and unlock the sleeping portion of her mind.

At the same time, Flo would give a powerful push to the part of the brain responsible for vision and imagination, the occipital lobe at the back of her head. It needed a hefty nudge to wake it up and the effect would be akin to throwing open a pair of heavy curtains to let in the sunshine.

Flo suggested she might like to lie down on her side, so Mum laid a blanket and a pillow next to the fire and Freya made herself comfortable.

Kneeling close to her face, Twinkle placed a hand on her cheek.

"You'll see colours, then there'll be a flash of light, but it's only inside your head. Your vision will white out for a moment, but as it comes back… well… things'll be different. OK?"

"Bit nervous," said Freya.

"You'll be fine," Twinkle replied with a wink and lay on the pillow in front of her with their foreheads touching.

Flo got into position behind her head, lining up her node with the base of Freya's skull and the two faeries closed their eyes.

Twinkle then delighted everyone by singing a verse that hadn't been heard outside a history lesson since the Great Divide:

> ' Grant vision to this human face,
> to see the wonder of this place,
> in friendship, hope and love and grace,
> we share our blessings with your race.
> From faith to knowledge in one leap,
> a soul brought hence from blissful sleep,
> the gift of truth profound and deep,
> a treasure long for you to keep.'

"That's *beautiful*," whispered Freya.

"You ain't seen nothing yet, kid," Twinkle whispered back, then filled her mind with Flow.

Her head bloomed with warmth and filled with a confused, dappled aura of colour that she somehow felt rather than saw in a brief moment of synaesthesia. It swelled, filling her mind until she thought there couldn't *possibly* be room for more.

There was a sudden sensation like a balloon full of bright light popping at the base of her skull as Flo pushed, then she felt nothing at all as the lights went out and she lost consciousness.

New Perspective

She came round to the sight of eight blurry, concerned faces leaning over her.

While she'd been out, Twinkle had assured them she was OK. Flow was essentially the raw energy of life and by definition a healing energy, so she couldn't be harmed by it, just a little overcome by the amount received or where it was directed. Freya was about to wake up with the ability to actually see and feel it, so thirty seconds of unconsciousness seemed a fair price. Even so, Twinkle was relieved when her eyes flickered open again.

As her vision sharpened, Freya realized that her friends' faces had gained something extra. They were all surrounded by a haze of muted rainbow light that radiated tiny, waving filaments steadily outward, like the tentacles of sea anemones that hunted for morsels of food in the water around them. The filaments pulsed silently to some regular rhythm which she felt certain were their heart beats. As she peered closer, she realized that the tip of each filament was dissolving, evaporating away before her eyes.

She raised herself up on one elbow and made a circular gesture towards them with her forefinger, narrowing her eyes.

"You've got a…" she began.

"We know," responded Buff, delightedly.

"But it's all around…"

"That's right!" added Flo, grinning.

"But that's not…"

"Yes it is," finished Squishy, "and if you like *that*, check out everything *else!*"

With a helping hand from Mum, she sat up slowly, realizing that the haze of colour around her friends wasn't limited to their heads. A cocoon of energy emanated from them from tip to toe, extending a few centimeters from their skin, shining through even their clothing.

She dragged her eyes away from this fascinating sight to find that the night wasn't nearly as dark as it had been before she'd lain down.

Until recently, aside from the bright moon and its reflection on the English Channel, the fire had been the only other Earthbound light source. There had been a definite edge to its sphere of influence though, everything outside its welcoming glow disappearing into the darkness beyond. But now, to a lesser or greater degree, *everything* was visible thanks to nature's own brand of night vision.

The aura of a big, healthy dog fox shone out from the undergrowth several metres off, as he eyed with suspicion the group of strangers that had infiltrated his territory. The glowing rabbits hopping around the entrance to their warren some way down the slope were granted a temporary reprieve from becoming his evening meal as curiosity briefly got the better of hunger.

Bolts of colour flitted overhead as bats in search of an evening meal took advantage of the warm, insect-filled sky. Their impressive speed created dense, colourful trails that stretched out behind them and lit up their flight paths before fading away to nothing in their wake. Even the insects themselves, tiny pinpricks of luminescence high above, swept and span in swirling clouds like flocks of swallows at dusk.

She held her hand up and spread her fingers, comparing herself to the trees and bushes that surrounded their campsite, awash with light. The same filaments of Flow that shone from her shone from the vegetation, but instead of the tremble of heart beats, they simply glowed slowly and steadily around the leaves and twigs as the energy dissolved away from their tips.

Even the lichen on the rocks shone brightly, but although it glowed, it barely seemed to be radiating Flow away at all.

Freya was overcome with the wonder of it all and dabbed away a few mildly self-conscious tears of joy. It was the most magical thing she thought she'd ever seen, but even in the midst of this splendour, she was still together enough to notice the differences in Flow behaviour.

Faery Facts.

Everything alive has Flow.
The average life~span of a given species is determined by the rate its Flow returns to the environment for recycling by the Veil. In the case of something with a short life~span it dissipates in a torrent, but with extremely long~lived species you'd be lucky to see it happen at all.

For example: a human gets about eighty years, a dog about fifteen and if you're a tree or a lichen, you might get somewhere between the high hundreds or the low thousands. So the lesson for today is that if you like to chill out and take things easy, be a lichen. If you like chasing your own tail and scratching your butt, be a dog. You'll have much more fun, chasing sticks and cats and such... you just won't see as many beautiful sunrises. 'The candle that burns twice as bright, burns half as long,' an' all that. Could be worse... if you were a mayfly, you only got twenty~four hours!

As you can imagine, this is a big topic in faery society. A couple of systems had been developed to document the phenomenon, but the systems themselves caused endless debate over whether one was too simple and the other, too complicated.

One system, the Species Longevity Register, or S.L.R. had been used for what seemed like forever and was essentially a list of living things in order of average life span, a nice simple way of presenting the information.

The other, the Flow Dispersal Index, or F.D.I. had only been introduced recently (if you could call two hundred and sixty~two years ago recently) and was a far more detailed system, cross referencing Flow dispersal rates with the many factors that affected them. It had gained popularity due to its more measurable, statistical approach. The debate had been known to get quite heated on occasion, with the old school and the new blood having very different opinions on which should be officially recognized and used.

As the F.D.I. clearly demonstrates, stress is known to affect Flow dispersal like a match affects gunpowder, so to avoid these disagreements faeries decided to put their house in order and compile both schools of thought into one definitive work. In the time since, the concise and more simply named

LONGEVITY INDEX:
The Combined S.L.R. and F.D.I. Compendium.
The One Stop Shop For All Your Life Span Queries.

had no doubt kept stress levels down and increased a few life spans.
Live stress free... live longer!

The faeries explained Flow dispersal and how it governed life spans while they quickly worked their way through the others, until all of the humans had received their own awakening and stood surveying a new world through new eyes.

With their fae friends looking on gleefully they lost themselves on a voyage of discovery, gazing closely at flora and fauna, nervously touching plants and trees as though they expected a jolt of electricity and using their auras to interact with the life around them. They had never felt so alive, so connected, so *one*.

Mum even managed to overcome her life-long phobia of spiders.

Faery Facts.

Some people would swear under oath that they suffer from a phobia when really, they just have a mild fear or an extreme dislike of something.

Drama, drama, drama!

Genuine phobias often manifest physical symptoms; from the sweat you break into when the dog in the park runs your way, to the frozen in terror, heart pounding, sick to the pit of your stomach feeling you get glimpsing a spider crawling across the carpet from the corner of your eye.

Stripping it right back to basics, getting over a phobia depends on just two things:

1. Severity.

If you're lucky, it's mild and you either grow out of it, or cure it by confronting the thing you fear.

2. Treatment.

Although M.O.P.s (Mission Operating Procedures) dictate that more serious psychological conditions such as aggression, paranoia, depression, grief and guilt take priority, phobias are one of many things that can be treated by a sharer.

Don't worry, they're on call every night... they'll get to you eventually.

She was following a low-lying branch on a beech tree, using her own aura like a magnet to make little spirals from the filaments coming off the leaves, when there it was... a stonking great common British spider, glowing away in the centre of a beautiful web.

In one of the segments of the web, a daddy long-legs had become trapped on the sticky silken threads. It struggled vainly to escape, but each movement only made its plight worse.

Pulses of Flow were coming off the spider and running faintly down the strands of the web, fading away at the points where they were anchored, but also bouncing back to the spider much more brightly from the daddy long-legs, announcing its presence.

The spider eyed Mum suspiciously with its many eyes. She wondered if it saw her as competition for its next meal. Mum had no such hankering for the juicy daddy long-legs, but in lieu of telling the spider that, she settled for shuddering involuntarily while leaning in for a closer look.

She looked at the spider.

The spider looked back.

Twinkle smiled gently. "What if I told you I could help you with that?"

"Oh, I don't think even *you* guys could do *that*... I've only got to *look* at one of these things and my skin crawls. They're just so... *silent*."

She shuddered again.

"Is it how they can sneak up on you without you noticing?"

"Yup."

"The eight hairy legs?"

"Uh huh."

"How about the beady eyes? Always watching?"

"Pretty much. And don't forget some of them *jump*, too. Is this s'posed to be helping?" asked Mum, unimpressed by faery phobia therapy.

"You *know* none of that is actually a reason to be scared of 'em, right?" asked Twinkle, more rhetorically than quizzically.

Mum nodded begrudgingly.

"Yeah, but *you* know that doesn't help, right?"

Twinkle laughed.

"Two minutes of your time and you'll never feel like that again," she guaranteed, pointing at her node. "Twinkle, sharer, at your service."

Although Mum was always one to rise to a challenge, when it came to her arachnid-y nemesis she was less than confident that even a faery intervention would be successful.

She'd heard the whole range of well-meaning 'beat your phobia' clichés, from your entry level 'It's probably more scared of you than you are of it,' to the *particularly* unhelpful, 'Oh, go on… it won't bite.'

She knew people meant well, but she'd never quite understood why they would think reminding her that spiders have fangs would be beneficial?

Years ago at an animal encounter day, she managed to fight her fear enough to let a handler put a tarantula on her shoulder. The idea was to demonstrate to the girls that there was nothing to be scared of and ensure that she didn't pass her fear on to them. It had worked, because the pair of them had been proper little nature buffs ever since, who liked nothing more than catching bugs to study.

The story didn't end well though. Mum had been so proud of herself that later that day she'd had another go. Everything went swimmingly until the handler got distracted for a moment and the spider decided to go for a wander.

Sometimes, late at night, Dad could still hear the screaming...

Realistically though, Mum knew she fell somewhere near the middle of the phobia scale, so exhibiting her usual tact and diplomacy, she politely accepted Twinkle's offer.

"Great!" Twinkle exclaimed delightedly. "It's as simple as this... I'm gonna absorb some of what the spider's feeling, then use my node to transfer it to you."

"That's *it?*" Mum asked.

Twinkle nodded.

"No holding it, or letting it crawl up my arm, or any of that nonsense?"

"That's it," stated Twinkle. "You just need to get as close as you can to the web, so the spider knows you're there. For this to work, the spider has to sense your presence."

Keeping a *very* close eye on the web's occupant, Mum moved closer, until she could feel the hairs on the back of her neck standing up.

Closing her eyes, Twinkle reached out and touched the end of a strand where Flow was dissipating into the bark of the tree. As Mum watched, she saw the node in the centre of her forehead grow increasingly bright, then she opened her eyes, floated over to Mum and placed her forehead against hers without a word.

The effect was instant.

"*Oh...*" Mum said sadly, realizing that in the grand scheme of things her fear of beady eyes and silent movement had no comparison to a deep and perpetual fear of being eaten alive.

"'xac'ly," answered Twinkle quietly, grateful her demonstration had been so successful. She gestured at their surroundings.

"It's a war zone out there when you're small and juicy… a constant battle to avoid predators and hang on to the Flow you were blessed with. We've got it *easy* in comparison."

Mum's reality had altered twice that night: firstly when she'd been gifted with the ability to see something that'd always been hidden from her view and again with the knowledge that a phobia can sometimes merely be a lack of perspective; your *phobia's* perspective.

Turns out they really *are* more scared of you than you are of them!

She touched her forehead lightly.

"Weird feeling. It felt like two people saying the same thing at the same time."

"There's more than one creature in the web and they're both worried about what's for dinner."

Mum's attention was suddenly focused back on the daddy long-legs. At least the spider was only *worrying* about being eaten… for D. L. L. it was a distinct likelihood.

"Poor little fella," she said, looking sadly at the trapped daddy, "should we save it?"

"Not our job, lovey. This would've prob'ly happened whether we were here or not and if not *this* insect, then another. It's how things work. It's too hard to choose between an insect eaten or a spider starved, so we don't. We leave those decisions up to nature."

She waved at… *everything*.

"Don't let it upset you. All this was set up *waaay* before you and I had an opinion on it."

"It's still very sad," Mum declared. "I always assumed this stuff was going on but feeling it is a *whole* other thing."

Twinkle patted Mum's knee.

"Yeah... that would be a side effect of *knowing* stuff. Sucks, dunnit?"

Click

Flo beckoned them over to a rotten log she'd discovered on the outskirts of their camp that was home to something she thought might interest them.

"Who wants to see a trick?" she enquired.

Everyone did.

"Parents teach their children this back home... woodlouse racing!"

Flo charged her pusher's node and sent energy down her nerves to her fingertip, causing Flow to seep into the log and enticing woodlice from their hiding places beneath the old bark.

They scurried frantically to where Flo was touching the wood and when several were herded around her finger, she moved it steadily along the log as they jostled each other for first place.

Twinkle did her best to commentate.

"Aaand... THEY'RE OFF! A close pack as they leave the bark behind... but Green Spot pulling away and quickly gaining a handsome leeeead... the pack falling behind steadily as they pass the first fungal fence... oh, One Antennae has stopped completely... and Green Spot miles ahead as the pack join her on the home straight... but here's Wriggly Butt coming up on the inside vying for the lead! It's Wriggly Butt and Green Spot neck and neck as they approach the faery fingertip finish line and... OHHH, MY DAAAYS... Wriggly Butt takes the flaaag! See you in the winner's enclosure, Wriggly Butt!"

Wriggly Butt, the winning woodlouse, walked onto Flo's hand to the sounds of cheering and she laughed as its tiny legs tickled her.

Mum suddenly burst out laughing.

"Little Louse on the Faerie!" she announced delightedly, thinking of a favourite childhood TV show of hers that she'd introduced the girls to a few months before the holiday.

Flo let the woodlouse crawl on to her other hand and placed it back on the log. As it headed back towards her for another try, she moved to a different spot and used her forefinger to draw a large circle of Flow on the bark. As the herd gathered to follow it, Flow glowed from the joints in their shells as they absorbed it from the pathway she'd made.

"Ooooo!" said Willow and Lea in unison, making Mum and Dad smile and say "Aahhh..." in unison, which made Squishy laugh and slip off the end of the log and then of course, everyone was roaring!

They may have already bonded during their time together, but in that instant of joyful mirth the jigsaw pieces of the Legend clicked together irreversibly. Events beyond their control might have led them here, but right now none of them could imagine *anywhere* they'd rather be.

Shared Advice

It was getting *very* late, so Mum and Dad shepherded the girls into the camper to get them bedded down for the night.

Their adrenaline had finally run out, leaving them in that tired, floppy state that children get into at the end of an extremely busy day.

Mum and Dad could tell they were exhausted; considering the company they were in, they collapsed into their rooftop bed with barely an argument.

Mum popped up through the hatch to kiss them goodnight and found Lea breathing on her window, drawing a love heart and some kisses in the condensation.

"Watcha doing, baby?"

"Goodnight kisses for the faeries," Lea replied sleepily, finishing the last one.

Mum gave her a hug and a kiss of her own. "They'll love that... I'll see you in the morning, honey. Love you."

She kissed Willow goodnight too and after Dad had been in, Freya, taking her new role of Proxy Grandma very seriously, offered to see them off to sleep with a story. She read less than two pages before both girls were out for the count.

The fire was getting low by then and as Dad headed for the woodpile to build it up again, he noticed Flo kneeling by the seed that Squishy had planted.

As he approached, she cupped her hands over it and pushed. She raised her hands slowly as something swelled from the earth beneath them, then took them away to reveal a perfect, healthy seedling and a fading patch of Flow in the earth surrounding it.

Dad's eyes widened in astonishment. He looked around hopefully, with a 'Did anyone just see that?' look on his face.

As he turned back to Flo, he nearly jumped out of his skin... she was hovering right in front of him, smiling warmly and holding her finger to her lips. The glow of her wings lit up his face.

"Shhh," she said softly. "You mustn't tell Squishy. He doesn't know I do that. I love the way he's trying to carpet the Earth. The quicker they grow, the quicker they seed and the quicker they spread, so anything I can do to help is *really* no trouble."

"I promise," said Dad seriously, "but that was *awesome*. Can I at least tell Katy?"

"Of course. Wondrous things *should* be shared with someone you love," replied Flo, smiling happily.

Sudden realization hit Dad. Before he could say anything else, she flitted away and busied herself with anything that did the job of avoiding his next question.

Smiling at this rather unexpected insight, he built the fire back up again, amused by the fact that even spiritually enlightened beings like faeries had trouble letting on that they liked someone. He shook his head.

'*Not so different*,' he thought.

He watched the flames grow for a while, until his fire-gazing was cut short by the sound of Squishy using a sharpening stone across the clearing. He'd collected everyone's vests for a final contents check and had begun making sure everything was in order by honing their knives for them.

Being a bush craft enthusiast, Dad was over there like a shot, keen to see what his new friend was up to. He was into all the same kit... maybe not the *grenades* so much, but certainly the knives and torches.

"Looks interesting," he said, doing a poor job of concealing his intense interest.

Squish held up the blade, edge uppermost, looking along its length towards the fire.

"Final kit check. Looking good so far," he affirmed.

With a satisfied nod, he sheathed the knife again.

Dad watched as he went through the remaining vests, nodding sagely along with him as he counted grenades, checked crystals and tested spool ratchets. They looked for all the world like two blokes staring down at a car engine with folded arms and lauding the benefits of a timing chain over a cam belt.

"Boys and their toys!" called Mum from where she was sat watching.

Dad blew a raspberry at her and she giggled.

"Just making sure everyone's safe, Ma'am," Squishy joked, gazing softly across the camp.

Dad followed his look to where Flo was sat, gently pushing a moth's antennae with her fingertips.

They watched for a moment before the moth took to the air, its wings glowing and shimmering with Flow as it flapped away, leaving a little trail behind it.

"Amazing," said Dad.

"Yeeeah," Squish agreed, but there was a dreamy quality to his voice that made Dad look back at him.

He wasn't talking about the moth.

Dad leant over and lowered his voice.

"Man to man, Squish. How long have you loved her?"

Squishy looked at him, startled, about to protest, then relaxed with a resigned sigh.

"Oh, I don't know... a long time. Since we got teamed together."

"What d'ya love about her?"

Squishy looked at him like he was mad.

"*Look* at her... she's a *goddess.* She's kind and gentle, she's clever, she's beautiful... *and* she pushes everything I plant. She might not know it, but my last breath and heartbeat are hers and without her soul to grace it, my life'd be incomplete."

"*Wow.* Squish... you *have* to tell her how you feel." Dad paused. "You already knew she does the thing with the seeds?"

"Pushing? Uh huh. She's too sweet to be much good at sneaky. Best to let her keep her secret though, don't you think?"

"I'm not sure about *that,* mate. All I know is, life's short and you shouldn't waste time hiding stuff. 'Specially love. You might wake up one day and realise it's too late."

"D'ya think she feels the same way?" asked Squishy hopefully.

Put on the spot, Dad was suddenly very mindful of Flo's finger on lips 'Shhh,' from earlier. Fighting an overwhelming desire to tell Squishy the truth, in lieu of going against her wishes he said the only other thing that felt right.

"I think you should find out. Katy and I were friends for a long time before we were a couple. We were at a barbeque and a friend told me everyone was wondering when we were gonna get together. I told her what they'd said and she just kissed me. Years later we're happily married with two beautiful little girls who just happen to be two of the Nine Keys. Sounds like your universal engineering thingy to me. What if they hadn't said anything? Or I hadn't told Katy? Or she hadn't kissed me? Doesn't bear thinking about. Sometimes you've just got to do what feels right. Maybe us talking like this is the universe giving *you* a little nudge. Or me, to *help* you. Or to help you and Flo, *via* me."

Squishy looked genuinely taken aback.

"Not bad for a human… if we get through this, I'll have to see about getting you enrolled in a universal engineering class!"

He suddenly looked determined.

"You're right… I should stop messing about and let her know. Not 'til we're done with all this though. If she turns me down, I don't want to be moping about, no good to the mission."

"Very responsible," said Dad gently. "Or… you could be flying high with more to fight for if she tells you she feels the same. The ball's in your court, my friend. Seize the day an' all that. Faery fist bump." Dad held out his fist and Squishy bumped it, both of them smiling from ear to ear.

Carpe Diem

Vests and contents checked, Squishy returned all but one then drifted back to Dad.

"Have you seen Flo?" he asked, looking a bit embarrassed. "I'm, uh… she… er… she needs her vest."

Dad regarded him thoughtfully for a second or two, then pointed upwards.

"Good choice, Squish, you won't regret it," he said, smiling gently at his friend.

"Dunno what you mean," said Squishy, trying to hide his grin as he fully bloomed his wings and headed upwards, leaving Dad below, smirking and shaking his head.

He found Flo on a ledge set back into the cliff, facing out to sea. She was whittling something with her knife, her head bowed and her face etched with concentration.

When she saw who it was, her features softened and giving the last letter of her carving a final flick of the knife, she gave him a bright smile.

He put her vest down next to her.

"Wondered where that was," Squishy said, pointing at the knife. "You're all set, unless it needs sharpening? Crystals polished, tools checked, nothing missing."

"No, it's fine, thanks."

She reached over to slip the blade into its sheath in her vest, then patted the ground next to her and he settled down.

"Can I ask you something, Squish?" Flo said, looking out to sea.

"Anything."

"Tell me again why you plant? Not in Lux, I mean here, everywhere you can find." She looked back at him. "In the most unlikely of spots?"

Squishy laughed softly. "'Cause I can. Because if you can, you should. 'Cause if only one seed in a hundred grows that's one little corner healed. Even if *that* dies, the earth gains nutrients where it was and maybe the next one will live and make *more* seeds." Squishy's eyes gleamed. "Got to start somewhere."

"So you *really* believe what you said about the worst places?"

"Completely."

Flo laid her hand over his and sighed deeply. "Me too, Squish… me too."

Looking down at their interlaced fingers, Squishy took a deep breath. "Can I ask *you* something?"

"Of course."

"Why do you push everything I plant?"

Flo looked surprised for just a second, then took his face in both hands and kissed him square on the lips. His face was a picture.

He knew in that instant that this was *their* story. For the rest of their lives, every time they were asked how they got together, this would be the story they told until it became as familiar to them as their own names.

"Because you're my friend," she finally answered. "Because every seed that's placed with such hope *deserves* a little push. Because I admire your dedication to healing this world. But mostly because I love you."

Squishy stood and pulled Flo to her feet. They kissed again, the two of them floating high up off the ledge, spinning lazily. Against the full moon, their combined glow made it hard to tell if there were two sets of wings… or just one.

Sentries

The camp was almost silent, save for the low crackle of the fire and the hoot of an owl some way off to the west. Not even the 'ke-wick hoo-hoo-oooo' of a pair, just the lonely 'hoo-hoo-oooo' of a solitary male. It was a surreal quiet, but it had a serenity of sorts. The lull before the storm.

For all its tranquility, in the circumstances, posting guards had seemed the sensible thing to do and Mum and Flo were the only ones still up, having taken the first watch. They chatted quietly about their two worlds.

Mum told Flo about their lives together back home and Flo listened spellbound as she learnt, face to face, all about human hopes and dreams and fears. Faeries knew an astonishing amount about their Earth-bound sisters and brothers, but until now, everything she'd heard had seemed second-hand. Hearing it from the horse's mouth was *very* different.

Seeing the passion and emotion that shone from her eyes as she talked about her girls and her husband, their love of nature and their beliefs, Flo realized how similar their peoples were in some ways.

She was left feeling that deep down her kind and humans valued all the same things… love, family, friendship, trust, loyalty, kindness… and that there really *might* be hope for a united future.

In turn, Flo did a first rate job of describing her world and the organization they worked for. They compared Lux and Earth's history, economics, architecture, flora and fauna, arts, relationships, farming, spirituality and politics.

By the time they were done, Mum was a curious combination of frazzled and unsurprised. She'd heard a *lot* of amazing stuff in a short space of time and although it was a bit much to take in, most of it actually made a lot of sense.

She was left feeling that deep down her kind and faeries valued all the same things… love, family, friendship, trust, loyalty, kindness… and that there really *might* be hope for a united future.

She shivered suddenly. The fresh night air and a sudden sea-swept breeze joined forces to remind her that the fire had died while they'd been talking. She built up a new teepee of firewood from the woodpile and thick smoke instantly spiralled upward as the intense heat from the deep embers worked its magic. In no time at all, the fire was blazing again.

The extra warmth was extremely welcome and when they'd toasted themselves enough, they headed for the camper together to check on their sleeping loved ones.

Freya had been given the main bed and was wrapped up in a sleeping bag. She looked very peaceful.

Upstairs, the girls had barely moved position since they'd fallen asleep to Freya's bedtime story and were catching flies like a pair of horizontal and very beautiful statues. The only thing that spoiled the statue illusion was the gentle snoring that escaped them. Buff and Twinkle were up in the roof with them, curled into the ends of their duvets like cats.

Dad was laid along the big front seat of the camper, with one blanket over him and a second rolled up under his head as a pillow. Despite the limited space, he was doing a quite respectable imitation of a starfish. A snoring starfish. Mum could almost hear his denial.

'But I don't snore.'

Yeah, *right*. She tutted quietly.

"Good job I'm turfing him out for the next watch," she whispered to Flo, who stifled a giggle.

Squishy was laid on his back on a folded blanket on the kitchen worktop, his arms over his head and his face buried in the crook of one elbow.

Although Daisy was technically only a four berth, she was doing an admirable job of sleeping seven people. The fact that some of them were a tad smaller than she was used to helped of course. And to think, Mum and Dad had actually been worried about whether there'd be enough space for just the *four* of them.

They watched in silence for a while as their beloved sardines slept peacefully. Now they'd entered R.E.M. sleep and their brainwaves had changed, so had their auras. The dominant colour of the tendrils had shifted to an almost electric blue and instead of slowly diffusing away at their tips, they had become thinner and wound themselves into tight coils. Every so often one would extend outward lightning fast, snapping out at some invisible target like a snake striking.

One uncoiled as they watched and there was a tiny but intense white flash as it found its mark, leaving the ghost of its brief presence on their vision.

Flo nudged Mum and smiled.

"The closest you'll ever get to actually seeing someone's dreams," she whispered.

Faery Facts.

We are All connected.

Human, faery, animal, tree or flower... we're all drinking from an infinitely deep well of energy that connects us in mostly subtle, but sometimes obvious ways.

You're never more connected to this than when your unconscious mind is free of your body while you sleep. In this state you can tap into the universe and even touch other souls. Dream up a new clean energy source to save the planet, empathize with your pet, dart through the waves like a fish... all possible in your dreams, because in your dreams, all things are possible.

That little white flash at the end of a tendril is your sleeping soul joining the party.

After a time, Flo suggested that Mum get some sleep.

"Don't worry about waking the others, petal," she said, as Mum made a move towards the front seat where Dad was, "I'll stay on watch."

"Well, *that's* not fair, is it." Mum stated.

Flo laughed. "Another perk of having nodes... I can absorb Flow to keep me awake. You humans need your rest though. If I need some company, I'll wake someone up, but I'll be fine, honestly. I was just happy we could have our chat!"

Mum looked doubtful, but she was tired by now, so she reluctantly agreed and slid gratefully under her duvet next to Freya. She let out a long, deep sigh as the wonder of the day washed over her like a gentle wave and without even realizing she was falling, she was asleep.

The moment her aura changed, Flo bloomed her wings and glided up into the roof to gently wake Twinkle. This was where her friend got to shine and do what she did best.

Twinkle worked her way around their human companions, using her node to give them all a much-needed mental boost of fear-dispelling, positivity-generating Flow.

Leaving a trail of contented sighs and peaceful smiles behind her, she packed Flo off to sleep at the foot of the roof bed and took a shift by the fire. She sat cross-legged close to the low flames, bathed in their warm glow and lost in her own thoughts about the coming ordeal.

Eventually, she roused herself and did a final round of the camp, making sure that it wasn't only the humans that had received an extra jolt of the good stuff. Content that she'd done all she could for her friends, she threw some more wood on the fire and settled down to see in the fast-approaching dawn.

This was Twinkle's favourite time of day. She watched in wonder as the sky slowly lightened, the stars vanishing one by one until only the brightest remained. As the first rays of the sun crept above the horizon, a rush of goose bumps washed over her at the familiar sound of the days eye's morning song and she felt a twinge of regret that the humans weren't awake to experience it with their newly-awoken senses.

She said a little prayer to the Spark that after today, they'd get another chance.

Recon

Considering what the day had in store for them, everyone was *incredibly* upbeat when they emerged from Daisy, rubbing their eyes in the bright sunlight.

Feeling rested, ready for anything and completely ignorant of the fact that Twinkle had zapped 'em, the general consensus amongst the humans was that a good night's sleep was responsible. The faeries however, not having expected the same treatment, all shot Twinkle 'I know what you've been up to,' looks of gratitude.

Before they woke, Twinkle had loaded up the fire again so they could warm themselves against the last of the morning chill. As they gathered eagerly around it, she greeted them with a broad smile, glad to be in their company again.

They got on with the important business of breakfast egg muffins without delay, then had a quick splash and brushed their teeth.

The mood changed as Mum fetched a phone and Borson's business card. She dialled and they heard a faint voice on the end of the line.

"I'd like to speak to your boss, please," she stated, with as little emotion in her voice as she could manage. There was a pause and she took the opportunity to put the call on speakerphone.

"Mrs Raulich, what a delight. I've been expecting your call."

"Have you?"

"Of course, my dear. A wife and mother can always be relied on to protect those she loves. We are only speaking because you wish to bargain for their safety."

His smug, confident air was unsettling, but Mum kept it together.

"So you *are* willing to bargain then?"

Borson chuckled mirthlessly.

"Touché, Mrs Raulich. Yes, I am. What do you have in mind?"

Mum paused for a long moment for effect.

"What if... what if we gave you the faeries?" she answered in a low voice. "They told us you've been collecting them for years anyway; can't you just get a few more of them instead of us? We did our bit; we helped you find what you were looking for. Just *please* don't hurt my family."

Impressed at her suggestion of using more faeries, Buff gave her a thumbs up, silently mouthing the word 'Yes!'

Mildly curious as to how they knew of his collection, but unsurprised that someone, somewhere had noticed the disappearances, Borson sighed theatrically.

"Oh, very well. In the scheme of things, replacing you with them may raise fewer questions than your disappearance, I suppose. Give me your new friends and you are free to go back to your lives."

"Just hand 'em over and that's that?"

"Bring them to me at Borson House and our business is concluded."

"No. Not Borson House. Somewhere more public. How about the main car park in Shanklin?"

"More *public?* To deliver a quartet of *faeries?*" challenged Borson, sounding almost incredulous.

"Quite frankly, I couldn't care less. The more people are around, the safer we are."

Safer? Knowing what he had planned, Borson strained not to laugh condescendingly at this. Their gullibility would be their downfall. When no one had emerged from the tunnel, he had gone back to the cavern to discover an unconscious Neery and no Keys. He had *no* intention of letting them escape a second time. At the point at which Neery had them in his sights again, they would either come quietly and remain uninjured, or... well, Neery had his orders.

In lieu of laughter, Borson replied, "Shanklin it is, then."

"I'll call again when I have them," finished Mum and promptly hung up.

Twinkle looked impressed.

"Nice! If I didn't know better, I'd have believed every word," she said, winking.

"That's my deep-rooted love of am-dram showing," Mum laughed. "It was easier than I thought it'd be. I know the whole point was for him to think we're stupid enough to meet him, but I can't help feeling a little insulted he'd think we're that daft. I guess that was the idea though... bluffees bluffing the bluffer. Wish we could see his face when he realizes he's been 'ad." She grinned mischievously. "Now we just leave him stewing for a couple of hours while we 'catch' the four of you, then I'll ring him back."

They had drinks while they strung out an hour and fifty minutes of fake faery capture, then Mum called Borson back with the news that they'd grabbed the four of them and bundled them into a storage box. He sounded very pleased. They were to meet at three pm on the grass verge in front of Shanklin car park, safely surrounded by the dense throng of tourists on the High Street.

Dad and Squishy had a good long coastal walk ahead of them, so they set off way before then. They made their way down the incline and headed east along the coast in the direction of Borson House, hugging the cliffs until they reached the point where the gardens sloped down to the beach.

Using as much cover as they could find, they crept up through the gardens to within forty metres of the house and found a good spot to secrete themselves under the lower branches of an ornamental shrub.

Peering out on to a side view of Borson House, they could see Borson's white Jaguar parked near the front door with the engine running.

After a bit of a wait, the front door swung open briskly and out stepped Neery in a chauffeur's cap and driving gloves. As they held their breath in their leafy hiding place, he made his way to the highly polished Jag and opened the back door for Borson, who strode out of the house behind him like a flamingo and folded his skinny frame into the back seat. Neery closed the door and climbed into the driving seat, revving the engine with a low, throaty growl before gliding up the driveway and disappearing into the trees.

Dad and Squishy watched intently until the car was out of sight, then left their hiding place and ran to the back of the house.

After sneaking under a couple of windows, they came to an open one through which Mrs Raullings could clearly be heard destroying Tom Jones' 'It's Not Unusual,' above the clattering of pots and pans. They sat on their haunches for a while with their backs against the wall, hands over mouths, desperately trying not to alert her with their laughter.

Her singing faded as she went into a pantry, its door banging shut behind her. Two heads appeared slowly over the window sill, taking this opportunity to scan the big kitchen.

"Look," said Squishy in a hushed voice, pointing at a jug of lemonade and a half-full glass on the work top by the sink. He took out the sleeping draught and held it up.

"No time like the present!" he whispered happily and was gone, up through the window and tipping the contents into Mrs Raulling's glass before Dad could even respond.

No sooner had he poured it into her glass than the pantry door banged open again and she reversed out with her arms full of bread-making ingredients. Dad ducked down again as fast as he could, gulping. Squishy!

Thankfully, the housekeeper had seen nothing. By the time she'd turned around to walk to the island in the middle of the kitchen, Squishy had shot upwards and spread-eagled himself on the ceiling. Suspended over her head, he watched as she unburdened herself and went to the sink.

She gave a contented sigh as she looked out on the sun drenched garden, considering how lucky she was that her 'office' had such a pretty view... then picked up her drink and gulped it down in one. Thirsty work it was, baking in a hot kitchen on a sunny day.

Up on the ceiling, Squishy smiled. *'Yup... that should do it.'*

She went back to the island and managed to messily weigh out some flour, spill the salt and drop a large knob of butter on the floor before coming to the conclusion that she really, really, REALLY needed to lie down for a bit. She wandered out of the kitchen in a wobbly zigzag, a hand on her forehead, seeking somewhere horizontal and sofa like to 'rest her eyes' for a bit.

Squishy flew out through the kitchen window to rejoin Dad and the two of them carried on along the wall, weaving behind shrubs and bushes where they could. They soon came to a small flight of stone stairs leading down to a window and a cellar door, offering a possible way in. Although the door was locked, the window was held open a crack on its stay, so Dad flicked the arm up and pulled it open.

Taking his torch out of his pocket, he shone it into the room, over shelves full of old boxes and paint cans. There was a workbench under the window and after Squishy had floated in, Dad put the torch in his mouth and clambered through.

After partly closing the window again, they crossed the room to the only other door and listened for activity on the other side. Nothing. The handle turned easily and silently and the door swung open on to a *very* different room. Clean and well maintained, they found themselves in Borson's wine cellar.

There was a wooden tasting table in the centre of the room equipped with a shaded light and a rack of glasses and off to the sides, under vaulted stone arches, were rack upon rack of bottles, corks down. No £4.99 supermarket special offers here though. The contents must have equated to tens of thousands of pounds.

Despite everything that had already happened and everything Borson still had planned for them, Dad felt suddenly and surprisingly sorry for him. For all the material wealth he had, Borson had been robbed of the one thing that might have saved him: Love. Instead of a happy childhood with his loving parents, he'd been consumed by anger and hatred.

But here was the annoying clincher… according to their new friends, the universe had *engineered* that. It could have ensured the Borson family didn't buy the land the Pit was on, kept the Pit hidden, or not created a place like the Pit in the first place for goodness' sake, but oh, no… instead, it had sacrificed a loving family and caused this whole complicated mess. Dad had never been annoyed at the universe before. It was novel.

Reminding himself that however sad Borson's past was, the lanky old insect probably wouldn't think twice about killing them, he and Squishy made their way through another smaller room, past cheeses and rings of sausage. Squishy's stomach growled loud enough for Dad to hear.

"Mate… seriously? I thought *I* was the one that thought with my stomach!"

"Dunno what to tell you… I *love* cheese."

They reached the far side of the cellar and climbed the set of wooden stairs there, opening the door at the top slowly and slipping out into a wood-panelled corridor. The sound of a radio drifted from one end, the sound of impossibly loud snoring from the other. They knew the radio was in the kitchen, so they turned left and headed toward the snoring.

Sudden recognition washed over Dad. They had entered the main entrance hall, so at least he now had a rough idea of his bearings.

The snoring was reverberating from the drawing room where they'd waited for Borson. As they popped their heads round the door frame, they were treated to the sight of Mrs Raullings draped across a chaise lounge, head back, mouth open, putting a chain saw to shame with the volume she was producing.

The spacious hall was making them feel very exposed so they crossed it into the corridor on the other side. This led to the morning room and the garden eventually, but between them they tried every door until they got halfway along and found a study.

Slipping inside, they went straight to the desk and began looking in drawers. Nothing except stationery. The wooden filing cabinet in the corner was equally unenlightening, as was the writing bureau. The bookshelves held some interesting titles relating to faeries, but nothing that helped. One entitled

The Pit And Its Precise Location
On The Borson Family Estate

would have been handy... it was disappointingly absent.

Frustrated, they headed towards the door to leave and Dad tripped on the edge of the large Indian rug that covered the study floor between the desk and the door. Cursing his clumsiness, he bent down to straighten it and stopped, staring in disbelief at the intricately reproduced arch of the main gate, staring back up at him.

Excitedly, he rolled up the rug all the way to the door and stepped back to get a better view of the beautiful map of the estate that had been inlaid into the parquee floor of the study!

From the gate, it depicted the long driveway that led through the grounds to the house and the ornamental portion of the gardens and even detailed several of the estate's outbuildings.

Between the house and the coast, there was a reproduction of the solid oak dining suite where they'd enjoyed dinner together. In itself, not strange to see in a lovingly crafted map of the Borson family estate, but what *was* odd was how it was titled.

~ Cavern ~

There was a small brass ring inset into the wood. Dad ran his fingertips over it, exchanged a raised eyebrows look with Squishy, then tilted it up on its hinge and pulled.

A circular section of the map with a thinner piece resembling a tail came away to reveal a subterranean space hidden beneath the garden. The larger section exposed a cave with a wooden structure centered over a strange spiral motif, while the tail uncovered a tunnel that ran south away from the cave, toward the beach and a beautifully crafted chine. A single, understated word marked a greenhouse-like structure at the chine's head.

~ Entrance ~

They could barely believe their luck. It couldn't reasonably be anything else *but* the Pit, but if they felt any last twinges of doubt, they were soon dispelled by the inscription inlaid around the outer edge of the cave.

Two Souls, Stolen Too Soon

Elizabeth Isabella Borson
&
Oscar Robert Borson

Much Loved, Never Forgotten

Dad shook his head, dumbfounded. They'd been sat directly above it as Borson had made his strange offer about the Keys over dinner!

Excitedly, he took his mobile out of his jean's pocket and took several photos of the floor map to show the others. When he felt like he had enough, he replaced the cavern panel and rolled the rug back into position. After a quick glance round to make sure they hadn't left anything out of place, Dad looked at his watch.

"Hour and twenty two minutes left," he said, voice hushed.

"Let's go then... I still wanna see this cavern and we don't want the bad guys rolling up while we're mid-trespass!" Squishy replied, chuckling quietly.

They'd given themselves two hours; the time it would take for Borson to get to Shanklin and back, with a little extra added to allow for his impatient wait for a delivery that would never arrive. How Borson would react when they didn't show up at all and what their next move would have to be was anyone's guess.

Maybe they'd go into hiding. Borson must be in his early sixties, so they'd probably only have to drop out of society and live a life on the run living in fear of kidnap, imprisonment and sacrifice for twenty or thirty years or so until he died. Two or three decades. Doable, when you considered the alternative was the end of all life in the universe. It wasn't a good plan, but it was the only one of two that sprang to mind.

The other, that Dad was keeping to himself for the time being, was to enlist the help of an old friend of his. An army engineer friend, with a penchant for demolition. Dave was a last resort.

A life on the run... or blowing stuff up... Dad *really* hoped someone came up with a better idea.

They ran and flew out of the morning room at the back of the house, down the stone steps and most of the way across the garden, relieved to be outside again. They stopped when they got to the canopied wooden dining suite. It felt very odd to be crouched there, knowing what was beneath their feet waiting to be brought to life. After a quick look at the photo of the map on Dad's phone, they veered off slightly through a copse of trees and came out close to the chine.

There was a round, metal framed glasshouse near the cliff edge with a protrusion that seemed to overhang the sheer drop. As they got nearer they realized why. The section that overhung the cliff edge was open-bottomed, with a metal spiral staircase that disappeared downward into what was, for them, the unknown.

The glasshouse was unlocked and they wove their way through tall, tropical plants that had flourished into giants in their south-facing home. When they got to the base of the stairs where they ended at a small, flat plateau deep in the chine, they were greeted by a thick steel grate with a door incorporated into it, secured with a heavy padlock. Behind the grate was a tunnel and they both shivered at the prospect of what lay at the end of it.

An open-sided gazebo had been set up in front of the entrance with a folding chair and table under it. It looked unsettlingly like a comfortable place from which a guard might stand watch.

Dad shone the torch into the dark, but could see no more than rock walls and a rough floor receding into pitch blackness. Whatever was at the end remained tantalizingly out of sight. And reach, due to the lock.

"Cover your eyes," commanded Squishy and there was an intense flash as his cutting crystal went to work, melting through the tempered steel of the padlock amid a shower of sparks like the proverbial hot knife through butter.

"That… is… *awesome!*" exclaimed Dad, "I could do with one of those."

Squishy smiled as he melted through the last of the padlock's shackle and the pieces fell to the rocky floor.

"I'll have a word with Workshop and Stores, see if I can get you one. They don't normally like stuff like this being left here, but given the circumstances, they'd prob'ly not mind *you* having one!"

Dad swung open the weighty metal door and stepped over the threshold into the tunnel. There was a power breaker on the wall and he pulled the handle, lighting a string of bulkhead lights which ran along the ceiling.

The tunnel proved to be much shorter than the one that led to Freya's cavern and they reached the other end in no time at all. While Squishy floated along, unfazed by their surroundings, (to remain unseen, fairies often found themselves in odd, hidden places where hardly anyone goes) Dad spent the walk experiencing an almost overwhelming feeling of déjà vu. Unsurprising really, when you considered that this was the second secret tunnel in less than forty-eight hours he had found himself in.

Familiarity or unfamiliarity aside, no amount of planning could have prepared either of them for the sight that met them when they emerged from the tunnel… into the Pit.

Tricked

The electric lights from the tunnel continued into the cavern, circling it and providing a full three hundred and sixty degrees of illumination. The cold electric light brought a stark clarity to the horror they'd discovered.

All the way around the rock walls was a welded frame incorporating hundreds of metal rings and in each of these nestled a glass globe of the type that Borson had stored in his summer house in the garden.

The strangeness of their new surroundings was outweighed only by one horrible fact. In each globe, in various sad, unceremonious positions, was a tiny body.

There were hundreds.

The cavern itself was much smaller than Freya's, but with the same squashed bubble shape. There were no giant formations, no cascading waterfall and in place of the beautiful crystalline walls there was only smooth, bare rock.

The floor did become crystal further in however, with a very defined point at which it changed from bare rock to what at first glance looked like dark, smoky glass. On closer inspection, it had a rough surface made up of tiny, equally-sized crystals and was crisscrossed with lines that resembled fork lightning, or the veins of a leaf. These intricate lines were visible only because they were lit, although it was impossible to tell if their glow was picked up from the lights arranged around the walls, or a natural phenomenon from within.

A ramp spanned the first section of exposed crystal like a drawbridge over a moat and led onto Oscar Borson's wooden study platform.

The platform was suspended above the floor on thick chains that attached to a colossal structure made up of eight thick iron girders. These arched out over the whole platform and straddled it like the spindly legs of a giant, mechanical spider.

It was just as Twinkle had described it from her vision, complete with a large open space at the centre where the missing appeared every month. The platform and the supporting frame were very obviously old and original and it was easy to picture Mr and Mrs Borson working here all those years ago, assisted by their young son, as they tried to fathom the mystery of how and why the crystal did what it did.

A modern electric winch was bolted to a section of wall frame by the entrance and a steel cable ran from it and through a pulley high up in the centre of the spider. It was attached to a shackle that suspended a circular wire mesh cage above the open section of the platform. The floor of the cage, weirdly, was lined with turf.

Before the true weight of their find had a chance to properly sink in, there was a gasp from the cage and a row of familiar faces appeared, peering down at them from behind the mesh. Mum, Willow, Lea, Freya, Buff, Twinkle and Flo were all locked inside.

"Mike!"

"Daddy!"

"Squish!"

The two of them hurried up the ramp to a soft jingling sound as the platform bounced almost imperceptibly on its chains. As they crossed the platform itself, they saw work benches dotted about at various points. On one, in amongst the books and tools and notepads and test tubes, Dad caught sight of a pile of vests that until a couple of days ago, he would have thought belonged to an Action Man.

The boys stared up at their out-of-reach loved ones, checking that everyone was OK and just plain confused as to how they were even here.

"We thought we'd never see you again!" said Mum, as happily as their predicament would allow. "Neery turned up about 5 minutes after you left us," she explained. "He'd been spying on us most of the night and he and Borson knew the whole plan. He made me drive everyone back to the house in Daisy and brought us all here."

"Did he hurt anyone?"

"No, we're all fine. Surprisingly calm, considering."

Dad quickly scanned the walls, found what he was looking for and raced back across the platform, down the ramp and over to the winch control. There was an UP and a DOWN button and a big red mushroom shaped EMERGENCY STOP.

After a short push on the DOWN and STOP buttons to test them, he pushed the DOWN button again and the winch whirred into life, humming efficiently as the heavy cage lowered. He stopped the winch just before the turf floor drew level with the wooden planks of the platform and ran back to the others.

They grasped each others' fingers through the mesh of the cage, ecstatic to be together again, until Squishy, sad to break up the reunion, got his cutting crystal out and told everyone to move back.

"Have you out in a sec," he said confidently.

"He really will," assured Dad. "These guys have some *very* cool toys."

There was a brilliant flash as Squish activated his cutter, but before he could start work they were interrupted by a low, cold chuckling and nine heads spun in the direction the sound came from.

Neery stepped out of the tunnel into the cavern, wearing a victorious, spiteful grin, not really much more than a baring of his teeth. He made his way up the ramp to where they were.

"Mr Borson will be here presently, but in the meantime, I should thank you," he mocked. "You've saved me a job, making your own way here. You," he barked at Squishy, "Lose the crystal and the vest and throw 'em over."

Scowling at him, Squishy slipped the crystal back into its pouch, untoggled his vest and threw it at Neery's feet.

Neery leveled his pistol at Dad.

"Mr Raulich... empty out your pockets, lift your shirt and give me a spin would you?"

Dad put his phone, torch, keys and wallet on the platform floor, lifted the hem of his tee shirt and turned around slowly.

Neery nodded. "That'll do... wouldn't want any surprises *this* time, would we?"

"How did you find us?" Dad asked sullenly.

"I know the island doesn't give the impression of needing much in the way of high security, but I'm paid to provide it nonetheless. I tagged your camper with a tracer the moment we parked next to you. We knew *exactly* where you were holed up last night. Much better to have you believe you'd outsmarted us and keep you all in one place than to have you all bumbling around in the dark trying to escape." He pointed at some welding gear and clamps scattered over the platform. "Mr Borson spent the night audio-surveilling you and while you were busy telling him all about your plan, I was down here, knocking up your new room."

Laughing maliciously, he gloated, "When you left to come here to the house, I bundled this lot into your camper at gunpoint and had 'em banged up here before you'd even made it off the beach. We left like you expected, but only to watch your little tour of the house and gardens on CCTV in the guest cottage. I was s'posed to intercept you at the house, but who'd have thought your little fact-finding mission would bring you straight here? Very bad form by the way, drugging Mrs Raullings. Tut tut."

Dad refused to be provoked.

"What's your deal, Neery? Really? You don't come across as the sort of bloke that just follows orders and doesn't think for himself. Do you really believe that killing us will give Borson some sort of power? *Please.* He's cuckoo and you *know* it."

Neery snorted. "OK, Mr Raulich, I'll humour you. No... I *don't* just follow orders, because yes... I *can* think for myself. And no... I don't think Mr Borson will become magically all-powerful. I do think he's found something formidable though... and that's something I *can* get on board with.'

Dad was taken aback. He was surprised he'd actually got him to engage in conversation at all, let alone admit he thought his boss was wrong. He pressed his advantage.

"These guys have told us what the Legend really means... he doesn't gain power by opening the Pit; it drains the life out of the universe. We all die. Whatever he's found that says anything different has been distorted by humans over time. If we don't stop him he's gonna kill us all."

Neery smirked coldly.

"You'd say anything to save yourselves now, though, wouldn't you? After all his years of research, I'm more inclined to believe him than anything any of *you* say. I couldn't care less if he takes over the world and uses faeries as garnish for his next meal. Before you waste any more time trying to convince me I'm on the wrong team or my life choices are leading me down a bad path in some attempt at shifting my allegiance, save yourself the effort. My being on Mr Borson's payroll buys him a surprising level of loyalty and open-mindedness."

"So you're no better than a mercenary then... just follow orders and get paid, yeah?"

Shaking his head with amusement, Neery laughed derisively.

"Oh, Mr Raulich... you were in the army yourself. How did *you* get paid? By following orders. The only thing different about my situation is that my employer has changed. Mr Borson pays much better than Her Majesty ever did. Of course I'm a mercenary. An extremely well-paid one."

So Neery genuinely didn't give a damn what the outcome was. As long as he thought he could maintain his personal status quo, which seemed to be thug for hire, then that was enough for him.

Just *perfect*. A man who enjoyed cruelty and couldn't be reasoned with due to his personal greed.

"And your pay packet justifies killing children and a whole new species?" Mum asked furiously. "We should be befriending them and instead you want to be loyal to some nutter on a power trip!"

Neery looked at her with dead eyes and his reply was cold and calculating, that of a conflict-hardened soldier who had developed too zealous a taste for his work.

"If this place can be weaponised, there's no army, no *country* that could stand up to it. A few innocent deaths to ensure military dominance is well worth it. Just collateral damage."

Borson applauded this as he appeared in the tunnel entrance. He strode in, his long, thin legs covering the distance to the base of the ramp in no time.

"Quite so, Mr Neery. Though to my mind, foreign powers are merely the tip of the iceberg. Once I have the resources of *this* world at my disposal, the *real* work begins. I'm well aware that Mr Neery has some reservations about the outcome of this evening's proceedings, but while he favours the idea of a weapon for dominance here, I hope for the subjugation of another world entirely."

Neery looked awkwardly at the floor.

"Fret not, Mr Neery, I suspect we'll both be granted our wish."

Borson walked up the ramp. He opened his arms wide and span around theatrically, gesturing at the globes.

"How do you like the mausoleum wing of my collection? The globes were my idea, but I have Mr Neery to thank for the engineering side of things. Sets the tone rather well for this evening's official opening, wouldn't you say?

"Well, I won't be recommending it on Trip Advisor, if that's what you're after," retorted Mum with a level of sarcasm she rarely used.

Borson shook his head.

"You're not here to review it, my dear... the nine of you are to become its main exhibit. I have arrangements in place for the likes of you," he said, waving a hand flippantly at the faeries, "but I will have to arrange something more bespoke for the five of *you.*"

He paused to let their imaginations run riot with thoughts of what *that* meant.

"You'll have to forgive the crudity of the final addition," he continued, pointing at the cage, "its necessity was only discovered *very* recently. I think Mr Neery has done a splendid job. A little industrial in appearance, I know, but still rather good."

He turned to Neery.

"Mr Neery... let's show our guests to their accommodation, shall we?"

"Yes, sir."

Neery ordered Dad and Squishy to stand aside while he unlocked the cage door. With a flick of his head, he ordered them inside with a monotone, "In."

Squishy glided in front of Dad, his wing field spitting furious red sparks, about as angry as a faery had been in a good few thousand years. Probably since the time of the Great Divide.

"And if we don't?"

Neery swung the pistol directly at him. It was a very big gun in comparison to a very small faery.

"I still don't think you understand the rules of the game," said Neery calmly. "If you refuse to play, I shoot someone... don't care who... and we play anyway. Last warning. What's it to be?"

"Just do as he says, Squish. Don't do anything we'll regret," Flo implored. "We'll think of something else."

Dad gently touched his friend's arm.

"Yeah, come on, fella, she's right. It's not like he can kill one of the Keys."

"Very true," said Neery, "but I *can* make one of them *very* uncomfortable before the end."

Without a second's hesitation, he moved the pistol up and to the left and shot Dad once, high up in the right shoulder.

Trapped

The gunshot was deafening in the enclosed space of the cavern, leaving their ears ringing with the power of it. With a scream of pain, Dad dropped to the wooden platform holding his arm in agony as eight voices shouted, "NOOO!" in unison.

The ladies moved as one towards the open cage door to get to Dad, but Neery stopped them in their tracks with a waggle of the gun and a 'Na ah ahhh.'

His calmness evaporated like steam escaping a kettle. "IN… NOW!"

Squishy went first and Dad was bundled roughly in after him. The door swung shut with a clang and Neery snapped the lock shut. Click.

That was that. The Keys were trapped.

Twinkle immediately went to Dad's forehead and used her node to minimize as much of the pain as she could, while Mum put pressure on the wound with a folded sleeve from one of the girls' hoodies. Buff laid her hands either side of Mum's makeshift dressing and started infusing his shoulder with a massive dose of Flow to kick start the natural healing process.

Squishy was beside himself with guilt.

"I'm sorry! I'm sorry! I'm SO sorry, if I'd have just done what he said, this…"

"Don't you *dare*," Dad said through gritted teeth. The pain was fading after Twinkle's treatment, but hadn't vanished entirely just yet. "Don't you *dare* blame yourself for this."

"Yeah, don't give it another thought, *Squishy*," Neery butted in, putting extra sarcasm into Squishy's name. "It's a flesh wound. Like he said, it's not like I can kill any of you. That comes later."

Neery stepped to one side as Borson joined them by the cage. He gave a heavy sigh.

"I would have much preferred to have avoided such unpleasantness, but a lesson had to be learnt to hurry things along," he said, looking almost like he meant it.

"Now that everyone is tucked up safe and sound, I feel it would only be fair to explain what your part in all this is going to be. You are to be sacrificed in the name of a prophesy that promises the one who fulfils it access to a force of unimaginable power. I would like to be that person. I've continued my late father's work and dedicated my entire life to acquiring enough knowledge on the subject to ensure just that."

He knelt down in front of the locked door.

"Through extensive testing, my father discovered quickly that while life essence is as different from electricity as water is from air, they both share similarities. Conductivity, for example. The defining quality that makes something able to conduct life essence is both simple and obvious... it has to be *alive*. I'm sure you've noticed that the floor of your accommodation has been lined with fresh turfs?"

He touched a finger to the floor of the cage.

It was essentially two layers of mesh, with a thick layer of turf sandwiched between them. The roots dangled down from the underside of the cage while the long grass stems poked up through the holes in the mesh on the inside.

"It would appear that all living things radiate some kind of life field beyond the confines of their physical bodies. While the processed material of the cage may have prevented the desired effect, this turf will create a living conductor that will bring your life fields within reach of the influence of the crystal. When that happens, this place will reveal its secrets. I'm hoping for access to their home, but I'll settle for Neery's weapon if I must."

Borson had thought of everything. His father's research and his own years of study, watching hundreds of faeries having their life force consumed by the Pit, had given him a horrible understanding of how the system worked. He shook his head in mild disbelief.

"And to think... my father's peers *mocked* him for his notions. Such a tragedy that he and mother lost their lives just as they found the place that could have provided irrefutable evidence of his theories... a creature, believed to be merely mythical, but instead real and living amongst us! You should be proud that you will be helping him receive the kudos he is due. Posthumously, sadly, but still... better late than never."

Freya spoke, tight lipped and angry.

"And d'ya think he'd be proud of what you've done with his discovery, or ashamed?"

Borson's eyes flashed.

"I don't pretend to *be* my father... *he* had a different set of priorities for this place, hoping to reverse its nature and use its power to heal. But *he* didn't have to watch his parents stolen from him... *he* didn't grow up dreaming of revenge, dedicating every waking hour to its realisation. I will take his discovery and use it to subjugate the species responsible for his and mother's deaths. The world will finally know he was right. I'll see to it."

"You can't control this, Luke," said Twinkle softly. "It's not a door, it's not a weapon... our Legend tells of the end of all things if the Pit's opened, not mastery by one being... your quest for power has been based on a massive misinterpretation. I understand your grief and rage at the loss of your parents, but we didn't take them from you... the accident that took them was a side effect of the universe bringing our kind here as part of the Legend. It breaks my heart that you lost them the way you did, but we've lost friends and family too." She pointed at the globes around the walls. "So many have already died, Luke... *please* try to see past your loss and help us stop the Legend coming true. Give it up before you take any more lives."

"I have *fifty* years, my entire adult life, invested in this moment. What makes you think that anything you might say, today of all days, would dissuade me from my goal?" Borson asked, smiling contemptuously. The smile dropped away. "You give it up."

He turned to Neery.

"In deference to my mother and father and the night they died, we'll begin when the moon is at its highest point. In the meantime, see to it that the Rauliches' transportation is properly concealed. I'll instruct Mrs Raullings to leave some supplies for you in the glasshouse above."

And with that, he turned on his heel and strode away over the platform, down the ramp and out of the cavern.

Neery followed him out, stopping only to add Dad's possessions to the pile on the workbench and raise the cage back up with the winch. After the sound of his footsteps had receded down the tunnel, the lights suddenly went out, leaving them in the pitch dark. The kind of darkness you experience when you visit a cave and the guide turns their lamp out to demonstrate exactly what pitch darkness *really* looks like. A darkness that seems to seep into your skin and your very bones.

There was a booming, metallic

CLANG

as the gate at the end of the tunnel was slammed shut and they realized that this could well be the end of the road for them.

Buff bloomed her wings, banishing the dark to the farthest reaches of the cavern and they watched in dejected silence as gentle reflections played on the hundreds of glass globes that surrounded their prison.

Like candles lit to remember the dead.

Suspicions

Mrs Raullings woke to find herself on the chaise lounge in Borson's study. She remembered being overcome by drowsiness and needing to find somewhere to lie down to rest her eyes for a bit, but for the life of her couldn't recall *this* being the place she'd decided to do it!

She may not have been able to bring to mind making it to the study, but she could certainly remember the dream she'd been having whilst there. It had been both vivid and unpleasant, traits best not experienced together in the same dream, one of those dreams that stays with you for a good long while after your eyes have opened.

It had been dark and awful. She could still feel the cold metal of the cage she was locked in and hear the echoes bouncing from the walls around her. The only comfort to be had came from a multitude of tiny rainbow coloured lights that seemed to surround her, mysterious and out of reach. In the darkness there was no scale and no frame of reference and each one could just as easily have been a Christmas-tree light as it could have been the end of a railway tunnel seen from far away. Even so, they were still the only thing about the dream that felt *good*.

Flustered, she pulled herself upright with a hand on the plush upholstery and gave her head a shake that wobbled her rosy cheeks.

"My!" she said aloud, relieved to be awake, but also that she'd woken before she was found by Mr Borson. It was *highly* inappropriate behaviour for a housekeeper to be snoozing around their employer's home.

She stretched the most enormous stretch, accompanied to the sound of joints cracking, then yawned and swayed unsteadily out of the study, aiming for the kitchen and the water she desperately needed to ease the dryness in her mouth.

She leant on the edge of the sink, before turning on the tap and swilling out the glass that had held her last drink. She filled it and downed the whole thing. It didn't touch the sides and she drank two more, one after another, almost without a breath.

Her thirst quenched, she put down her glass with a satisfied gasp and was about to go about the business of tidying the mess she'd made before her nap when something in the garden off to the left caught her eye.

It was Mr Borson, heading towards the house from the bottom of the gardens.

'The gardens?'

She hoped that didn't mean he'd returned while she was asleep and witnessed her inadvertent forty winks!

Apparently, he hadn't. He seemed unperturbed as he caught her eye and raised a hand in greeting, then took the steps up to the patio two at a time. A moment later he came into the kitchen.

"I shan't be requiring supper this evening, thank you, Mrs Raullings. I shall be otherwise engaged, but if you'd be so kind and please prepare something for Mr Neery? He is working on something for me in the garden, so if you could leave it in the glasshouse by the chine, he will pick it up later."

"Yes sir. I'll put something nice together."

"Of that I have *no* doubt… I'm forever in awe of your culinary skills. When you've done that, perhaps you could take the evening off and take in a show or some such? Consider it my little treat for your consistently first-class service."

"That's very kind, sir, thank you," she replied sincerely. She'd been expecting a telling-off rather than a compliment and a bonus, so her inward sigh of relief was a deep one.

He nodded and left and she heard footfalls on the main staircase as he went upstairs. A distant door closed somewhere on the first floor.

She went to a cupboard and took out a wicker picnic basket with two flapped lids. No sooner had she put it on a worktop and opened one side, than more activity drew her eyes back into the garden.

Mr Neery had swung open the doors on the barn that was used to store the estate's sit-on lawnmower and the quad bike that he used to patrol the estate boundary.

He went inside, pulling the doors almost closed behind him, but not before Mrs Raullings had seen a turquoise camper inside.

'What was the Raulich's camper doing here?'

Through the gap in the doors, she caught a glimpse or two of Neery dragging a dusty tarpaulin over the VW, then he came back outside, closed the barn doors and dropped the locking bar back into place in its metal brackets.

He looked down at himself, pulling a face at the pigeon poo and dust he was covered in from the old tarp, made a half-hearted attempt to brush himself off, then headed for the house, presumably to wash his hands and get changed.

Now, Mrs Raullings wasn't suspicious by nature. She was a jovial, kind, generous and trusting soul. She wasn't paranoid, a conspiracy theorist or generally taken to bouts of skepticism, but something about this whole situation was making her feel *extremely* uncomfortable.

Why was her work colleague hiding a vehicle that didn't belong to him? She considered her employers use of the expression 'otherwise engaged' and his offer of a night off. Why did he want her off the estate and out of the way?

Suddenly feeling very determined and not a little disobedient, she threw together a rushed packed meal that included a large flask of coffee and bustled out of the kitchen.

Leaving the house, she made her way straight to the barn and lifting the locking bar, she slipped inside, feeling, it has to be said, a bit like a secret agent.

She went straight to the sheet and lifted it high enough to get a good look at the vehicle beneath. Her heart sank. It was the Raulich's VW camper van alright, with its keys still in the ignition.

She dropped the cover back into place and left quickly, hurrying through the gardens to the glasshouse.

On the way, her head buzzed with a confused jumble of thoughts and questions, but there was one thought in particular, a memory actually, that kept niggling at her like a thorn in her thumb.

It was a glimpse she'd had of a drawing on Mr Borson's desk as she'd taken him tea in his study this morning. More a rough scribbling than anything artistic, it was of a tin-can shaped object. Its rounded outer wall had a checkered pattern and a smattering of arrows were dotted around the sketch, accompanied by comments and measurements.

She'd only picked up one detail clearly as she'd caught that quick glimpse. Three words, with an arrow pointing to the checkered pattern.

One inch mesh

She shuddered as her dream oozed its way back to the front of her mind. As she remembered the sensation of the cage beneath her finger tips. The way her fingertips could fit through the gaps. Gaps of about one inch.

Reaching the glasshouse, she pushed open the door and made her way through the lush plants, depositing the picnic basket on a small wrought iron table next to the spiral staircase.

She looked down to the plateau below for a good long while, half of her wanting desperately to believe that she was imagining the whole impossible, coincidental thing and the other half knowing she should trust her instincts that all was not well on the Borson estate today.

Her indecision lingered only until the feeling of hopelessness from her dream resurfaced. She put a foot on the first tread, then the second and the third, her resolve increasing with each step. By the fourth, there was no turning back.

Surprising Ally

Dad clawed the fingers of the hand on his uninjured side through the mesh, rattling it to test its strength. It seemed solid. He and Mum moved back as far as they could in the confines of the cage and began kicking the sides, but while they managed to bend the grid out of shape, none of the thick welds at the joints gave any signs of giving. Neery didn't seem the type to do a shoddy job, but it had been worth a try.

"Where's an angle grinder when you need one?" he asked despondently.

"Or a crystal?" added Squishy, looking over at the bench where their things were piled.

Dad sat back down, the exertion of trying to escape reminding his shoulder that it recently had a bullet pass through it. He winced as Mum checked the makeshift dressing and Twinkle gave him another small dose of Flow to keep the pain at bay.

Mum went back to work, kicking the cage at various spots hoping to discover a weak point, but her destructive efforts were cut short when the cavern lights winked back on. They froze, afraid, listening as the echoing of footsteps grew louder; afraid that their escape attempts had drawn Neery back, afraid that Borson had decided it was time to go ahead with opening the Pit.

It was a complete shock when Mrs Raullings popped her head tentatively into the cavern, her eyes widening as they settled on the cage and its occupants.

With the unshakeable 'seen it all' composure that can only be mustered by the truly old school, she bustled up the ramp and over to the group, shaking her head.

"Well!" she exclaimed. "This *is* a first."

She folded her arms, like a mother about to listen to an excuse from her children.

"So," she asked, "how *did* we get ourselves into *this* pickle then?"

They explained everything as quickly as they could: The Pit. The missing in the globes. Borson's plan to add the nine of them to his collection. His belief that doing so would grant him power. What would *really* happen when he opened the Pit. When they were done, Mrs Raullings took a deep breath and puffed it out from between pursed lips.

"I always thought it was a strange hobby for a man of his age. What can I do to help?" she asked, making it more a statement of intent than a question.

Still impressed by the fact that she hadn't batted an eyelid at the fact that four of their number were half-metre tall faeries, Squishy pointed at the bench where their possessions were.

"We could really do with those vests on the bench over there," he said gratefully. "There's a control by the tunnel that drops the cage, but don't let it go lower than the floor boards or you'll be doing your boss's job for him!"

She shot him a look. Apparently, gallows' humour wasn't something Mrs Raullings found the slightest bit amusing. She hurried over to the winch control and lowered their prison, but when she fetched the mission vests they wouldn't fit through the mesh, so she held them up to the cage one at a time as Squishy reached through, undid the tiny toggles and took out what he needed.

She was returning the vests to the bench when a voice echoed down the tunnel.

"Oh, Mrs Raaaullings? Hellooo?!"

Borson appeared in the mouth of the tunnel. He looked reprovingly at his housekeeper as Neery joined him.

"Ah, my dear Mrs Raullings, I'm afraid your absence was noted by the ever-watchful Mr Neery. I have to admit, I'm a little saddened to see you *here.* What to do? What… to… do?"

She drew herself up proudly, all of her years of loyalty to him dissolving instantly.

"You should be *utterly* ashamed of yourself! I know what you're up to. I know what you plan to do to these poor people… your mother and father would be *furious,* rest their souls."

Borson was unprepared for this and quite taken aback by her outburst.

"I'm not sure you are in any position to be lec…"

"I'm in the *best* position to be lecturing you, actually," she interrupted, not caring a jot about the employer/employee boundary any more. She'd left that *way* behind.

"I've been in service to your family most of my life, since my mother kept house here for your parents. I saw you after they died… saw you change from the lovely boy I used to share jam sandwiches and play hide and seek with, into a cold, unloving man. Well *enough* is enough!"

"How *dare*…"

He needn't have bothered… she was in full lioness mode now.

"How *dare* I? I'll tell you how I *dare*, shall I? I understood how deeply you were hurt so I stayed *despite* how you changed. I stayed out of loyalty to you *all* and now you're about to make a mockery of their memory and my loyalty by murdering a loving family and… and… well, *look* at them! *FAERIES,* for goodness sake!"

She finished, angry and breathless. There was a long pause before Borson spoke and when he did, it was almost with affection.

"You *have* always been there for me, Mrs Raullings… the same was true of your mother for my parents and me, for which I *am* truly grateful. You'll find things have moved along apace since then though and the unfortunate fact remains that you cast a shadow over your loyalty by intruding where you had no right to. I will forgive your indiscretion if you decide to stay, but if you decide to leave, so be it. Come the morning, the decision as to whether you wish to remain at Borson House is entirely yours, but I suspect that when you witness the power of what lies here, you may feel more secure in the service of the one who commands it. Be under *no* illusion… tonight *will* go ahead as planned. The Rauliches, Ms Redfin and the faeries? Merely a means to an end."

"You know that quote about the end justifying the means?" Freya called from the cage. "It's not always true, you know."

The Main Event

With the air of a circus ringmaster, Borson raised his arms and addressed his captives.

"ISN'T IT MAGNIFICENT?" he bellowed. "Nature's power, in a perfect balance of geology and physics, harnessed by the simplest of human engineering. A window into a new realm, to one purpose and one alone." He glared at the faeries, lowering his voice almost to a snarl. "To make me your master."

"It's not a 'perfect balance,'" piped up Twinkle in disgust. "It's an accident of creation that should never have happened. And *'one purpose?'* That's about the only thing you've got right so far and you're too blind to see what it even *is!*"

He was beyond insults now. The culmination of a lifetime's work was upon him and twisted though it was, this was the closest to happiness he had been since his parents had died. Many aspects of his psyche had broken the night his parents were taken from him and Borson had spent decades perfecting the behaviour of an emotionally functional human being. He could play the game and put on a show of normality when the occasion or company called for it, but truth be told, he didn't feel love or compassion or joy on any level. He felt no loss at this handicap. The lack of such distractions suited him. Empathy and kindness would only have got in the way of his dogged determination to complete his father's work. Instead, he made do with a single-minded, driven hatred for those he held accountable.

"Blind? I think not. I can see clearly what needs to be done and since we've had to traipse down here earlier than planned to find Mrs Raullings, I see no sense in delaying it any further. Let's begin, shall we?"

With a distinct lack of ceremony, Borson reached over to the winch control with a boney hand and pressed the down button.

The winch activated and as he and Neery made their way on to the platform for a better view, the cage began its final, short descent to desperate begging and shouting from all of the Keys but one; gritting her teeth, Flo grabbed the mesh behind her with both hands and as the roots of the turf connected with the crystal of the cavern floor, she drew in as much Flow as she could without damaging her nodes and fully bloomed her wings.

It was incredible.

Instead of the usual electromagnetic field pattern of a pair of wings, her field went *way* beyond that, the edges meeting and stitching together in a blaze of white light. When the light faded, what was left was a bubble large enough to wrap around the entire cage and its occupants, fed from the heavy, twin streams of Flow that poured from her nodes. Buzzing with power, it sent sparks of energy up the cable and into the shackle, the chains and the spider like legs of the frame.

The cage came to a halt on the cavern floor, but the crystal it now rested on seemed to have taken on a motion all of its own. The crystal *itself* was as still as ever, but it was as though something *within* the crystal were pulling downward. Like thick, cold treacle this inner energy began to spin, slowly at first, then faster, twisting itself inexorably into a spiral beneath them, a vortex that opened directly into the Veil.

The colours of the fluxing, swirling bubble around them began to drain downward, contorting into a spiral of their own before vanishing through the boards. When the Flow hit the crystal beneath the planks, the colours were spun deep into the vortex, merging together until they rushed away in a stream of pure white light, consumed by the Veil's deep hunger.

Flo kept the barrier replenished and held the relentless feeding at bay for a while by drawing on the seemingly limitless supply of energy coming through her nodes, but the supply only *seemed* limitless; if this were a battle, it was one that could only be lost... the Pit was open now and the Veil's hunger was insatiable.

The changes it had undergone had granted the Veil a surprising trait. A physical form. Sensing a rich food source, tiny, oily black tentacles crept up from the vortex, juddering in shock as they experienced this plane of existence for the first time.

They began to feed from the bubble slowly and tentatively, pulsing and throbbing as they absorbed Flow from it and as they fed, they grew, swaying back and forth like weed in the current of a stream. The larger they grew the more voraciously they fed, grasping their way further up the bubble's surface, breaching the barrier wherever they touched. White flashes filled the cavern as Flow poured into the voids they left behind, self-healing the damage.

With such a powerful source to nourish them, the tentacles were growing too quickly. In only a few seconds they had become writhing, two metre tall monsters that surrounded the Keys, filling them with dread as they watched the wall that protected them being steadily overrun.

Flo knew she had to act now, or the barrier would fail. Filled with fear and full of doubt that she could channel more Flow than she already was, she also knew what would happen if she didn't try. The thought of that alone gave her the strength she needed and there was a colourful flare as she doubled her efforts, dragging in more Flow than she would have ever thought she was capable of, her face a grimace as her overloaded nodes began to feel like they were on fire.

Borson looked annoyed.

"Mr Neery, bring this unbearable stalling to an end," he instructed coldly.

With cruel delight, Neery approached the bubble, planning on taking a shot at one of Flo's legs, which would have been an utterly devastating injury to someone the size of a faery. Thankfully, he never got the chance. It was then that Flo released the extra energy she'd absorbed in one massive surge of awesome power.

The effect on the bubble was immediate. It inflated like an enormous balloon, the creeping tentacles of life-sucking Veil pushed aside and forced beneath it as it swelled across the wooden platform. As it expanded, it engulfed some of the workbenches, an extremely calm housekeeper (considering the circumstances) and one gun-toting henchman.

Neery rocked backwards as the barrier blew through him, then looked back in panic to see the buzzing, colourful wall *behind* him, realising that he was now *inside* the bubble.

The vortex responded to the extra energy by not only increasing in speed, but expanding in size too. The rotating hub of the Pit stretched to match the bubble and was now almost half the diameter of the platform.

Larger, hungrier tentacles of Veil slid up from the base of the bubble once again, blocking any escape back through the barrier that Neery might have been considering. If he tried to pass through the barrier now, he'd be passing through a swaying screen of Veil too... he would hardly break the surface before hitting the floor, drained and dead.

He shook off his fear, burying it beneath the only instincts he thought he could trust... those of a trained soldier. He'd got through some pretty hairy moments in combat thanks to his training and right now seemed as good a time as any to apply it.

He was in enemy territory, under attack from hostile forces and thankfully, armed. If he did nothing, it was highly likely he'd be overrun and killed, so he'd orchestrate a tactical diversion... by shooting the faery that was generating the bubble. This time to kill, not injure.

With luck, when he shot her the bubble would collapse and an opportunity to escape would present itself. Better yet, the weird tentacle things would go for the ones in the cage first. Not *much* of a plan, but at least he *had* a plan. He raised the pistol.

Squishy had plans of his own. Grabbing Buff's shoulder to get her attention, he handed her one of the crystals he'd taken from the vests Mrs Raullings had brought him.

"I've got Neery," he said flatly.

In unison, they hit the contact points on their grenades and reached through the mesh, launching one across the platform at Borson and dropping the other at Neery's feet.

The first went soaring over the top of the swaying wall of tentacles, punching through the bubble wall and leaving a set of ripples in its surface, like a pebble thrown into a pond. Sensing the concentrated Flow within it, the closest tentacle shot out a hungry tendril of Veil in an attempt to consume it, but the crystal was a hair's breadth out of reach and continued on its way until it hit the platform and skittered to a halt a metre or two in front of Borson.

The second had no such distance to travel.

DONK
DONK
DONK

Neery looked down.
"OH SH..!"

BOOMF! BOOMF!

The two grenades detonated almost simultaneously. The double shockwaves, one inside the bubble and one outside, fizzed like bonfire night sparklers as they passed through the barrier and each other. The bubble and the tentacles absorbed much of their power, but they still packed enough of a punch to reduce Borson and Neery to stunned heaps.

Flo saw all of this unfolding before her and a sudden realization dawned. This was why the opening of the Pit meant the end of everything. The freed Veil would simply... *grow*. Now it had the ability to leave behind its other dimensional realm, it would just reach out, growing exponentially across the universe until there was nothing left to consume. The doorway was open now and like a cork in a bottle, the only thing stopping the Veil feeding unchecked was the bubble she was channeling.

In the midst of all this chaos, through the pain in her nodes and the sadness in her heart, a memory surfaced in Flo's mind. What Mamma had once told her as a child about love. How it was the most powerful force in the universe. She could hear Mamma's voice, feel the warmth of her hand wrapped around hers, smell the blossom of the orchard, even feel the grass under her toes as they walked. The memory was so vivid it felt as though she were *living* it, rather than remembering it.

"It's *all* about love, Flo… it's the reason we're all here. There's *nothing* bigger or stronger, not even death. If you share your love completely, you can change the world, yours and everyone else's. It's infinite. It doesn't matter how much of it you give away, you can still give more and the people you share it with can do *exactly* the same. It just goes on and on growing. All *you* have to do is give it and the rest takes care of itself. Embrace it, little one. We're built for it."

She sobbed once, violently, shocked by the depth of the memory and in that instant, she knew what she had to do. She'd considered it as an option some time ago and now the time had come, she saw it for what it was… their only hope.

She looked around her companions: Mum, Dad and Freya hugging the girls in a last protective act… Twinkle, Buff and Squishy, her kin, whom she knew would rather die than fail, huddled around them. Closing her eyes, she visualized all of her love, her compassion and her joy radiating outward into the other Keys and beyond her closed eyelids, the thing she was visualizing was becoming reality; her node glowed blindingly, bathing the others in its light.

And then she pushed. Everything.

Sacrifice

POP!

The bubble and all of its passengers vanished in a rush of air and Borson was suddenly alone in the Pit.

Stunned, he tried and failed to stand, opting instead to drag himself down the ramp towards the tunnel, but his impaired motor functions and spangled mental state were not making his exit an easy one.

The few bulkhead lights that hadn't blown flickered their protest at the darkness. One of the remaining bulbs blew amid a shower of sparks, then another, as residual Flow arced into the electrical cables that ringed the cavern and buzzed down the legs of the spider, before dissipating over the floor.

With no reason to remain vertical, the wall of tentacles flopped on to the platform, slithering across it as they homed in on the next most abundant food source in the room... Borson. Anywhere there was a gap or a crack in the platform, they poured through it like tar, oozing to the ground and reforming into tentacles again before resuming their hunt for prey at ground level.

The concussive shockwave from Flo's push had smashed a circular depression into the Pit where the edge of the bubble had been sat, reducing the crystal there to a ring of dust. The force of this had set off a chain reaction that was spreading rapidly across the surface of the Pit, tiny fragments of sparkling crystal exploding upwards, accompanied to a sound like a mouthful of popping candy.

As powerful as the Pit was, it was still reliant on its crystalline structure to generate the conduit the Veil needed to reach Earth and this ability was deteriorating as the splintering spread and the Pit shrank. One by one, the tentacles evaporated away into harmless, smoke-like wisps as the crystal they emanated from was reduced to grit.

By the time the Pit had shrunk to barely a metre across, only three tentacles remained, still oozing their way across the cavern floor towards Borson in a last-ditch effort to feed. As the shrinking went on, the first melted away, then the second, the intact crystal almost gone. With a final, desperate stretch, the third shot out a thin tendril from its tip and latched on to Borson's foot. Unfortunately for him, the catastrophic damage the Pit had suffered had slowed the speed at which it could absorb Flow to a crawl.

In the beginning, it had been instantaneous; Flow had been whisked away so quickly that, with the exception of faeries that could channel Flow to delay the effect, a living thing didn't have time to comprehend what was happening, indeed that anything *was* happening, before it was over. Now though, the process had slowed so significantly that his life force was dragged from his physical body intact and still resembling him.

Leaving his lifeless body slumped on the rocky floor a short distance from the ramp, his Flow was compressed into the outline of the feeding tentacle in a misshapen, shadowy form. Screaming soundlessly, he was dragged along the tentacle's length, drawn into the shadows beneath the platform towards the lip of the Pit in greedy, slurping pulses.

He slipped over the event horizon of the shrinking vortex, spiraling downward on his way back to the Source just as the last crystals succumbed to the chain reaction and the Pit sealed with a final

CRACK!

and a shower of crystal shards.

Three metres down, frozen like a hologram in the shattered crystal, Borson's contorted, upturned face stared back at the world he'd left behind. His Flow would never be returned to the Source. His soul would never begin its long journey of atonement on the way to join the Ancestors, stopping at the memory of each wrong he had done to correct it, before moving on to the next. He would never attain the purity he needed to take his place in the consciousness of the universe. Trapped between dimensions as he was, his soul would remain broken. Forever.

Topside, the Keys and the housekeeper were near the dining suite, sprawled on the cool, mown grass where they'd materialized under the bright moonlight of a balmy evening. The oppressive cave felt a million miles away from where they were now, even if it was still only a relatively few metres beneath them.

Their heads were reeling, though whether this was down to the euphoria of being free of the claustrophobic cavern or from the excess of Flow they'd been exposed to was uncertain. It was probably a good-sized dose of both.

Buff struggled to clear her mind as she dizzily dragged herself up and tried to stand.

"Nnno… that ain't gonna happen," she slurred and flopped back to her knees.

She remembered surrounding the humans along with the others. Seeing her friend smiling, eyes closed, radiating Flow out of her node into everyone within the bubble. Feeling her ears pop as, impossibly, they traveled... and then feeling the warm night air up *here*.

All of them were having a similar time of it, doing their best to understand what had just happened, while at the same time being grateful it had. Memories started to seep back, but they were strangely not all their own. They were an odd mix of their own recollections and an almost out-of-body version of events blended with intense feelings of love and loss.

The point of view of these other memories began to make sense. What they were recalling was what Flo must have been experiencing as she pushed. Some kind of emotional absorption, a sharing of her inner thoughts caught up by the fluxing life force and then imprinted on their minds as it soaked into their bodies. Flow had some pretty special side effects at the best of times, let alone when you channeled enough of it to generate a protective bubble strong enough to save the lives of your friends!

No faery had *ever* generated a travel bubble without the aid of a days eye before though. There was no doubt that this new discovery would be debated by scholars and end up in textbooks throughout Lux. Flo had better be ready for the fame that would come with discovering something so groundbreaking.

As the group dealt with their mixed memories in their own ways, Squishy lay in the grass, dealing with his the best he could. Flo had saved something extra for him. Her hopes and dreams.

In the fragment of time it took to pop from the cavern to the gardens, he experienced every second of their life together. The day of their hand fasting, their joy at the news they were having a baby, holding hands at the birth, watching their little girl play and grow, birthdays, clinging to each other as they watched her marry, the grandchildren, holding hands, flowers, laughter, music and...

... and he would *have* to have a word with her about spoilers.

He was wrenched from these thoughts by an anguished scream from the dining table. They stood unsteadily to find that Flo had pushed Neery out too, saving him the horror of being consumed by the Veil in the Pit, but whether by accident or design, the universe had meted out a worse fate. Even the unshakeable Mrs Raullings put a hand to her mouth in horrified shock.

Neery had rematerialized at garden level blended with the table and one of the carved seats of the dining suite.

His left knee and most of that leg jutted up from the flat surface of the table, peppered with shards of splintered wood that jutted from his skin and clothing like the pins in a pincushion. His left arm was half in and half out of the wood and his right hand reached upward out of the oak, making a tense claw that shook and twitched. His torso was angled out of the table at forty five degrees and his right shoulder, neck and head were merged with one of the chair backs, the ear of the chair bursting out through the side of his head and the socket of his left eye. He wailed desperately.

Twinkle rushed to his upturned forehead and dosed him with a wave of Flow so intense that it took *almost* all of the pain away, *almost* instantly. He gasped for breath as the pain became tolerable and a single, slow tear of understanding rolled down his right cheek between the splinters that punctured his face.

"It's OK," Twinkle whispered gently, feeling his gratitude and better-late-than-never regret, "it's gonna be easier where you're going, I promise. Just keep your eyes on mine, Sweetie… I won't leave you."

She kept her word, stroking his face and holding his gaze until mercifully quickly, she saw the light fade from his good eye. There was a weak flare in his aura as his Flow burst outward from the visible parts of his body and she watched it fade as the Veil, restored to normal service, did its job of universal recycling. He was gone, or at least the *physical* 'he' was. His soul still had a *very* long journey ahead of it.

She sighed deeply and turned back to the others. The humans were filled with pride, assuming it must have been difficult to treat him with even the tiniest shred of kindness after all he'd put them through. The faeries had expected nothing less of her.

They had no time to reflect on their emotional differences just yet though. Down in the cavern, the chain reaction in the Pit may have ended, but the energy released into the surrounding rock structure had taken its toll also and had one final geological surprise in store for them.

In a different reality, Borson's frozen image may have remained the subject of curiosity and study for years to come. Instead, a series of wide cracks opened up around the plate of dust that had been the Pit, spreading through the floor and up the walls to the domed ceiling. The cracking continued around the ceiling's perimeter until it was ringed by a deep fault line, a perforated tear-off slip in solid rock.

When the cavern finally caved in, it was something of an anticlimax, as though nature were denying the Pit more limelight than it had already stolen.

With no structural integrity left, the roof simply *sank*, filling the space the cave had occupied with a grinding, rumbling sound. It took a large section of the lawn, some flower beds, the dining suite and everyone there with it, leaving everything in position, only several metres further down in a newly formed depression ringed by steep, high walls of rock strata and raw earth.

Accelerating sharply as some critical point of failure was reached, it buckled the spider and the cage, squashing them flat as it dropped the last few metres to its final resting place with a thudding crunch, burying the faeries in their glass jars and Borson beneath thousands upon thousands of tonnes of soil and stone. A powerful pressure wave blasted down the tunnel, carrying with it a crystal laden dust cloud that erupted into the chine, blossoming into a haze that danced and sparkled in the bright moonlight as it drifted out to sea.

The sudden extra kick of adrenaline from being dropped several metres back down into the remains of their subterranean prison had quite the restorative effect on them all. After making sure the girls were unhurt, Mum stood and looked around the rest of the group.

"Is everyone alright?" she asked, warmed to receive a string of affirmatives.

"All good here," replied Squishy, looking around to check on Flo. "How 'bout you, Flower?" he asked, using her full name.

There was no reply.

"Flo?"

He leant round the edge of the dining suite, catching sight of her foot and the beaded ankle bracelet that Twinkle made for her last birthday.

She was completely still. With a knot in his stomach, he rushed to her side. She was lying on her back, her head to one side, one knee drawn up, with one arm straight out to the side and a hand clutched around her necklace. He turned her face towards his and although her beautiful eyes were wide open, the sparkle had left them.

"Flo!" he called, shaking her shoulder. "*FLO!*" He paused. "Flo… please. *Please.* I saw. I want it too, Flo, *please* don't go."

He lifted her up into his arms, shaking her gently, putting his cheek against hers, kissing her, but even as he begged her not to leave him, some inner part of himself understood that she was already beyond his reach.

Twinkle joined him, filled with dread as she gently brushed her node against Flo's forehead. She pulled back quickly. No trace of Flow remained, not even the nominal background levels of someone who had just died. It was as though she'd been emptied, but surely not by the Pit? If *they* were alive, so should *she* be.

In a sudden epiphany, Twinkle was seized by the implications of Flo's shared memories. Certainly the love, but in particular the feelings of loss. *She'd done it to herself...*

With no days eye to awaken, no plant network to temper the immense amount of channeled Flow and no complicated root address guiding them, the only tools at Flo's disposal had been her boundless love and the desire to save her friends. They'd been enough to allow her to do miraculous things, but she'd have had no way to gauge how hard to push. She *must* have known what could happen if she went too far and she'd done it anyway. She'd gambled and lost her life to save theirs.

She caught Squishy's eye, shaking her head ever so slightly. With grief etched into her face, Twinkle turned to face the others, who stood hugging and crying as the full weight of Flo's sacrifice overpowered them.

"Do you understand? She gave her Flow to save us. *All* of it."

The stars and moon had disappeared behind a blanket of cloud, bringing real darkness to the deeper darkness they felt inside. As though the sky knew what was expected of it, there was a sudden, bone-jarring thunderclap and it started to rain. Heavy rain that washed the tears from their faces and cooled the heat of their anger and sorrow.

It rained for hours. Even the Earth had found a way to grieve.

Understanding

After clambering their way out of the hole and liberating Daisy from the barn, the surviving Keys left Mrs Raullings at the house and made their way forlornly back to the Faery Forum, knowing nothing more than that they needed somewhere private where they could be together.

To say the faeries were shocked to see what it was that Freya did for a living was beyond an understatement.

It wasn't the theme or the quality of her work that affected them so deeply. The reason why the carvings shocked them and bathed them in new waves of grief was that many of her sculptures were of their missing.

As they drifted around the shop naming the people they recognized, slowly but surely, light dawned on Freya. Each carving that the faeries named was also one of her keepers.

It didn't take her long to put two and two together and she told the others about her dreams, who in turn explained who the ones they recognized were.

"So let me get this straight," she said incredulously, "I've been dreaming of *real people?* My keepers are the poor souls we saw in the Pit?"

Overcome with sorrow at this, she slumped onto the stool behind the counter.

"'Fraid so," answered Buff.

"I'm not sure I know what to do with that," Freya croaked bleakly.

Twinkle sat down cross-legged next to her on the counter and gently held one of her fingertips in both of her hands.

"That's the universe for you. It may not be able to speak to us, but if it needs to make itself heard it'll do it in other ways, like through serendipity or inspiration."

"Pretty lousy message," Freya stated, frowning. "What good was it? Didn't save any of them, did it?

Twinkle raised an eyebrow.

"No… but it might just have saved everyone else."

Hmmm. Freya couldn't argue with that. Instead, she drew herself upright again, an idea unfolding in her mind. She finally understood why she'd been blessed with her artistic talent and why she'd spent fifty years using her gift to carve her dreams.

She hoped her own gift would be considered appropriate.

Words From Beyond

Squishy walked through the arch of the gate, up the flower-lined path and knocked on Mamma's front door.

He was *very* nervous. It was the day of Flo's freeing and it wasn't traditional for him to be here at the family home so close to the ceremony. He felt slightly less awkward because Mamma had asked him to come, but he also planned to return something of Flo's. It would probably only make Mamma sadder and that was the last thing he wanted to do.

Faery Facts.

Death, in faery culture as in others, was a strange mix of joy and grief. Joy, because they had known their loved one's face, voice, smell, personality and soul... and grief, at the loss of those very same things. Faeries, of course, had the advantage of the absolute knowledge that their loved one's Flow would surround them again in the soil, the flowers and the very air they breathed. It made their grief *no* easier. Faery funerals, or 'freeings,' were all by cremation, quite literally the freeing of the deceased from this plane of existence. There was no team of paid funeral directors like on Earth. An emberman organized the building of the funeral pyre and acted as a largely superfluous master of ceremonies, but the bearing of the dead, the eulogies and the lighting of the pyre were taken care of by the family and if necessary, friends too. Traditionally, the closest family member lit the pyre, giving them a deep sense of closure and responsibility for their lost one's final journey. The day before the freeing, the family were left to themselves to contemplate their loss and prepare for their duties the following day.

The 'Show Of Undying Love' celebration after the freeing was loud, joyous and most importantly, an opportunity to laugh, cry, shout and revel in the miracle that we're all blessed to be a part of... life. Like the wake that often follows a human funeral, a S.O.U.L. party was a time to honour your lost one by sharing tales of the ways their life had touched yours. There was singing, dancing, food, cider and beer. Lots and lots of beer. They went on 'til quite late. Or early. Depending on how long the beer lasted. Did I mention there was beer?

The door opened and Mamma's face brightened very slightly when she saw it was him. He bowed his head, his hand covering his heart.

"Hello, sweetheart, come in," she said, taking a step back so he could enter. She closed the door behind him.

"I'm sorry I'm a little early, Mamma, but I have something for you before we leave. I didn't know whether you'd want to take it to the freeing or not and as this is the last chance before..." He broke off and Mamma squeezed his arm.

"You'd better come through, then. I was just about to grab a quick drink before we left... would you like one?"

"Erm... OK then, thank you."

They walked through the house, stopping in the kitchen for some juice and water before going out on to the patio and sitting on a bench between two shrubs heavy with fiery red flower heads. Squishy took a sip from his drink and put the cup between his feet. He took off the days eye pendant that hung around his neck and held it out to Mamma.

"I made this for Flo just after we teamed up," he explained softly. "Twinkle took it off and gave it back to me, but it was a gift and I don't feel like I can keep it. I'd let Flo take it with her, but I know personal possessions aren't left with people when they're freed, so I'd like you to have it. I'm so *very* sorry, Mamma... I'd take her place if I could," said Squishy, looking down, his voice breaking.

Mamma lifted his chin tenderly.

"I absolutely believe you would, my love. You honour her, but we both know what Flo would have to say about it, don't we?"

She turned the pendant over in her hands, admiring the fine craftsmanship. It had obviously been carved with love and care and it broke her heart a little more to think that she wouldn't get to see it age around her daughter's neck with this young man by her side. She remembered when Flo had first shown it to her and the shine in her eyes when she'd said who it was from. Mamma felt an almost physical sting of regret that she hadn't pointed out the obvious to her daughter at the time.

"This really is beautiful, Squishy. I love the words... never noticed them before," she said, tracing the letters around its edge with her fingertips.

"Words? I didn't do any," he replied and Mamma turned the pendant, holding it so he could see what was inscribed on it.

He breathed in deeply and sighed as he read the three words carved there. The three words that Flo must have been carving just before they kissed.

His words.

"Oh, Flo," Squishy whispered.

The worst places really *had* needed the grandest help… and Flo had given it.

Parting Gift

Freya and the Rauliches left the Avebury Lodge B&B and headed up the High Street towards the Red Lion Pub. They had dinner reservations there later, but they had somewhere *much* more important to be first.

After greeting a lady walking a rather boisterous pair of black and blond, yin and yang labradors, they crossed the main road through the village at the chicane that ran in front of the pub car park.

Joining the old Herepath on the other side, they passed the Avebury Chapel and the male and female Cove stones of the northern inner circle as they continued up the road, heading for the place where the road cut through the high bank of the henge.

An outsider watching them would have seen nothing out of the ordinary. Just a family taking a stroll around Avebury stone circle at sun set, enjoying an ancient site on a beautiful evening.

What an outsider couldn't have even *begun* to imagine was what awaited them, or the enormity of the occasion.

"There's another one!" squealed Willow excitedly.

"Ooo, yes!" replied Freya, bending to look closely at the days eye she'd found. Once you knew what to look for, you realized the eyes were *everywhere*.

The girls hunted for days eyes until they reached the cut through, then the group left the lane and joined a path that took them through a wooden gate.

The path climbed steeply up the side of the henge, but instead of following it to the top where it continued all the way around the circle, they broke off and ducked under the lower branches of the Tolkien trees, the four enormous, grandparent copper beech trees that had looked out over the neolithic stone circle for hundreds of years. It was here that they had been asked to come.

A small, but infinitely more hopeful percentage of humans had used these trees over the years as a place to leave their hopes, dreams and prayers to be heard. Their lower branches were festooned in tied ribbons, trinkets and even offerings of food and drink in hopes that the universe, the divine, or whatever else you chose to call it would hear those prayers and answer them.

Faery Facts.

Prayer.

Sometimes it worked, sometimes it didn't, but the universe was *always* listening.

If you tried to quantify the effectiveness of prayer for the average Earth dweller, you'd often come up against a very human wall of cynicism, or end up in an argument about who or what you were praying to. A large percentage of people simply didn't believe in that sort of thing anymore and an equally large percentage of people were dogmatic about their version of it.

Same thing, folks… we're *all* praying to the same thing. It's only each other we argue and fight with about it.

Faeries called it the Spark.

It doesn't care what you call it.

It would much rather we all just loved each other.

~

Squishy opened the front door for Mamma and she came outside into the bright colours of the garden to find Buff and Twinkle waiting for her.

They greeted her with hugs and kisses as she joined them on the flagstone path, then escorted her through the gate with its thick covering of roses into the street beyond.

Mamma gasped in surprise at the sight before her. She'd known today would be special, given what Flo had done, but *this?*

From her garden gate, as far as the eye could see and then beyond, marking the route all the way from her house to the Faer Well, faeries lined the streets. Every child, every woman, every man.

And not just from the city of Lux.

Every faery community had come to honour the sacrifice Flo had made. Villages, animal ranches, farming communities, the tiniest of hamlets out in the sticks and lone crystal prospectors living in cabins by the remotest rivers in the deepest of forests… all had come.

And not just faeries.

Chicken ranglers sat astride their clucking hens at intervals, holding banners that fluttered in the breeze as they waited expectantly for the mother of their saviour to pass by. As they waited, the hens strained against their reins and scratched their claws impatiently.

Rats, the guard dogs of the faery world, given leave from their duties guarding hatcheries throughout Lux, sat by their faery's side, as well trained as the best of their Earthly canine counterparts. Rats are quite empathic. It's why they make good hatchery guards. Whenever there's a fox about, they can sense the danger, or more precisely, the fear, or even more precisely, emotion in general. Right now, their whiskers were twitching feverishly as they sensed the mix of love and grief in the air.

Although the crowds were such an eclectic mix of ages, professions and communities, every single one of them, from old timer to new born baby, was dressed in purple. All that were old enough had a hand over their heart and their wings bloomed in salute, creating a rainbow hued pathway for Mamma and the others as they began the long walk to the freeing circle, meandering through the crowded streets and parks until they reached the boundary of the gardens there.

The circle was arranged in rings; the gardens were outermost, to symbolize the journey through life as you approached death, then there was a vast canopied ring of seating for the mourners to meet and bear witness to the transition between the two and lastly, in the centre, was the imposing rocky outcrop of the Faer Well where death became final.

Following some great tectonic upheaval in a time before faeries had evolved, the jagged shard of rock had been thrust out from Lux's crust like an arrow head through a target. The outcrop included a geological oddity. It was home to a vent shaft that disappeared almost vertically into the depths of Lux.

It had been discovered at a time when faery spirituality and culture were blossoming into something more permanent and it was quickly decided that this vent was a gift, a universal sign that this was the way they should send their dead back to Lux. Since that day, it had become the resting place for the cremated remains of all faeries. Because of that, no one knew where it led, because no one considered it an appropriate place to explore.

There were stories and myths of course, not least of which was that the vent was home to the Cloud, an oracle born of the combined ancestral memories of all the faeries that had ever passed through the Well. Tales of travelers meeting the Cloud to seek wisdom abounded, usually with a 'moral of the story' ending, often along the lines that you shouldn't have sought out the Cloud in the first place. But they were just stories. After all, no one had actually ever been there.

The Well sat in a field of lush, carefully tended grass that stretched from its rocky face back to the canopy area, which creaked and billowed like the rigging and sails of a tall ship as they walked beneath it. It's irregular bulk drew their eyes as they approached. A stone stairway, using natural features in the rock to augment its many hand carved steps, led up to a plateau at the very top where the opening of the vent was to be found. For safety and practicality, the vent was capped with an iron grating and it was on this grating that funeral pyres were built.

The Faer Well was a place of truly final goodbyes. Of course, faeries *knew* their loved one's Flow had already passed through the Veil and returned to the Source, but there was still the need to say goodbye to their body.

That was the purpose of the Faer Well. To let go and to give back to nature at death what was given at birth. It was also important that you went back to the Source as you had arrived in the world... no clothing, no possessions, free of worldly goods and ready to be received into nature again. The *only* exception was the light cotton shroud that the deceased was wrapped in to preserve their dignity.

When a pyre had burnt down, taking the remains of its solitary passenger with it through the grate, the cycle of Spark, Flow and Veil was considered complete, but there was one group of faeries that had been denied this last rite. With no bodies to free, the families of the missing had been robbed of the opportunity to complete the cycle.

This blow had been softened by a gift that had given Lux a way to honour and memorialise them. It was with mixed feelings of sadness and gratitude that they passed through the ring of life-size wooden sculptures that had recently been installed around the Well.

When Freya had the idea of giving her keepers to Lux, she'd simply hoped they would offer some comfort, however small. She couldn't have imagined then that they would end up here, standing watch over the final chapter in the lives of faeries. Their likenesses would ensure the part they had played in the Legend wasn't forgotten.

Mamma stopped to face the keeper that had been unanimously agreed amongst scholars to be different to the others. It was different because it portrayed *two* faeries, a mother and a baby. Although clearly a depiction of Flo, her face was hidden so it was believed that the sculpture wasn't intended to represent her... it was sent to Freya to symbolize the baby.

Freya had carved a total of seven hundred and twenty *one* keepers throughout the fifty years she'd received her dreams. She had carved this one about two and a half years ago... around the time Flo and Squishy had met for the first time. In a mark of respect, the universe had sent her a dream that represented the innocent new life that would never be, because of the sacrifice its mother would make.

Mamma knelt for a second in sorrow for her beloved daughter and the grandchild she would never meet, then rose and moved onward to the Well.

~

The time was approaching.

Dad glanced at his watch for the hundredth time, apprehension making him a little edgy.

Mum reached out and took his hand.

"Take a leaf out of their book," she said, pointing at the girls and Freya, who'd laid out a picnic blanket and were busy herding ants around the mat of exposed roots that surrounded the trees.

He smiled and took a nice big, calming breath. The smile quickly faded as the mixture of dry summer soil and chalk from the earthworks of the henge began to levitate from the root mat, as if the area in the shade of the huge beeches had been isolated from gravity.

The air was vibrating.

Almost tripping on some of the bare roots, the five of them backed off nervously as they realized there was a very definite shape to the area that was affected, a large circle that filled the space under the trees with a domed haze that reached up into the branches above their heads.

There was a sudden flash as though someone had reflected the sun at them in a mirror and they recoiled, shielding their eyes. When they opened them again, they were looking directly into another world.

~

After the revelation that Flow could be channeled in vastly greater quantities, it had been suggested that there might be a way in which the other Keys, the *human* Keys, could be included in Flo's freeing ceremony.

To this end, a rather impressive number of days eyes had been transplanted from the Lea into the freeing circle and now sprouted from the grass around the Well. An army of growers had spent nearly three days weaving rope like thicknesses of hair and cabling them together into a new configuration designed to conduct higher levels of energy. Almost all of Lux's supply of red hair had been used in the task.

Like fingerprints, each days eye's Flow pattern was infinitesimally different. Workshop and Stores had come up with the rather brilliant idea of linking a vast quantity of days eyes and balancing the frequency of each pattern so they all matched.

The newly discovered crystal circuitry had played a major part in the idea. By introducing a carefully pre-charged quartz crystal into the buried cabling around every plant, each frequency could be adjusted and all the plants pattern-matched to each other, generating one large bubble instead of many smaller, individual ones.

Under normal circumstances, a travel bubble had one purpose… to pop. To prevent this happening, pairs of crystals were mounted on logs at the junctions where the rings around the plants met; one at Earth's background frequency and one at Lux's.

A bag-like net of woven hair encapsulated the two crystals, enveloping them in an elongated sausage shape that spanned the space between the logs. At the midway point between the two, the bottom of the net tapered downward into a funnel shape and reduced finally into a thick, braided cable that was coupled to the junction. As Flow circulated through this expanded network, this had the effect of confusing the origin and destination points, creating a stable bubble that was open at both ends and granting the humans a window onto the ceremony.

Of course, it was all *highly* theoretical.

The other possibility was that it might all end in a lot of wasted red hair.

Mamma stroked the tall stem of a days eye, then stepped over the freshly dug trench of the toughened and expanded network, hoping that this *wouldn't* all end in a lot of wasted red hair.

She paused for a second to admire the knot work of the shroud that encased the huge junction crystals. The drain on them was expected to be incredibly heavy, so as well as being especially large, they had also been pushed almost to the point of fracture to ensure they carried enough charge to hold the bubble open for as long as possible. Even so, they were only expected to last a precious few minutes before they drained or failed destructively.

She leant and pressed her ear against one, hearing the crackling sound inside the quartz as it fought to contain the energy and hold itself together. Standing and joining her companions, the four of them passed through the plant boundary and turned back to watch what, if anything, would happen next.

At a signal, the pushers stationed at each plant filled their nodes and pushed. There was a communal holding of breath and a flash, then the Well was awash with the light of the largest bubble ever brought into being. It towered above them, cloaking the entire Well and Flo's pyre in its shifting colours as they craned their necks to take it all in.

Most astonishing was the vista outside the wall of the bubble. Still the inhabitants of Lux as before, but now merged with five humans under a canopy of trees. Two worlds, presented in one view. It had worked! They waved at each other across the boundary, across who knew what incomprehensible distance, but only briefly, as the emberman's polite cough reminded them that now the bubble was active, time was not on their side.

Greeting them at the base of the steps, he led them up without delay to the scrape of fabric on stone as each footfall took them closer to the top. They'd always remember today's tiniest details; the gritty feel of the stone walls beneath their fingertips as they climbed, how the echoes sounded as they passed through tunnel sections of the stairway, the smell of damp from the moss and ferns that adorned the walls... things that would come back to them later, at the oddest of times, in the way only memories draped in grief did.

They broke out onto the plateau, noting with a rush of sadness the torchbearer waiting patiently to one side of the pyre. He held a staff fashioned from oak, carved with a pictorial version of how the Spark had brought life into the universe and how it had Flowed there ever since, showing the Veil as a final barrier at the top. Above that, the lit flame burned gently and steadily as it waited to fulfill its purpose. The bearer's role was brief but essential; guardian of the first flame, responsible for ensuring the torch was lit and ready for handing to the nearest relative.

They'd expected the bearer, but nothing had prepared them for the beauty of Flo's pyre.

The emberman had prepared it using the usual lattice of logs running in alternate directions, but in addition to being interwoven with flowers, every single log that made up the structure had been covered in carved personal tributes. Even smaller stock, intended to catch more easily and act as kindling was decorated or carved into expressions of love.

All of Lux had been desperate to show their gratitude for the one who had voluntarily given her life in exchange for their safety, so in the days leading up to the freeing, woodcarving tools and wood for the pyre had been left in public places throughout Lux so that people could add their condolences in a societal demonstration of thanks and admiration. What had ultimately been created was unlike any funeral pyre that had come before it.

The torchbearer approached Mamma, but she shook her head and gestured to Squishy. His eyes widened in surprise. There was an order to be followed. If there was a spouse it went to them, then the children, the parents, the siblings and so on to friends, but only if there were no family.

"Don't look so shocked," she said softly, putting a consoling hand on his arm, "You earned her love. You've certainly earned the right to free her. In a few precious seconds, you shared all of the things that would have earned you the honour in time anyway."

Squishy was overcome. With shaking hands, he took the torch and the two of them approached the pyre, their eyes fixed on Flo's form wrapped tightly in its delicate purple cotton shroud. She was in her favourite colour, one last time.

Mamma reached up and placed a hand over her daughter's heart. When she took it away, the necklace Squishy had made was laid across her chest. He looked at her questioningly.

"I know... 'out as in...' but if you still feel you want Flo to keep it, I think it's the right thing to do. Let's just call it another natural expression of love," she finished, touching the ornate carved logs of the pyre.

He gently stroked Flo's forehead, then knelt by the triangular opening built into the base to receive the lit torch, smelling the rich oils the wood had been treated with to accelerate lighting.

This was the point of no return, the point where a loved one's loss became truth. This was why the lighting of the pyre was reserved for the closest loved ones. It was acceptance.

He pushed the torch into the opening and there was a flare as the tinder and oil caught. Handing the staff back to the torchbearer, he joined the others, where they clung to each other watching the flames take hold. His voice breaking, he began to recite 'The circle,' the freeing prayer.

'This is not the first time I've held your gentle hand,
nor will it be the last time we'll rest upon this land.
A journey so familiar down a path we're blindly led,
the thousand times we've been around, the echoes in our head.
With our story far from over, we earn another name,
dust or raindrops, wind or fire, I'll hold your hand the same.
More than you've imagined, but less than what will be,
my soul resides within you... and yours is safe, in me.'

Behind and all around them, the crowd was utterly silent, wearing its grief like a heavy blanket, the quiet only broken by the crackling of wood as the fire rose. Even the animals amongst them were subdued, as though someone had explained the gravitas of this part of the ceremony to them.

Very quickly indeed, the piled logs all but disappeared into the blaze, mercifully concealing Flo's outline behind a curtain of heat and light and bathing those on top of the Well in the radiance of her freeing.

Buff, who was stood behind Mamma with a hand on her shoulder, looked down at her fingertips. They were giving off *colour*. She hadn't been trying to see her own aura, but as it streamed away from her towards the fire, she couldn't help but notice. She showed the others and they realized it was not only happening to her, Twinkle and Squishy, but flooding through the barrier from the five humans too, growing from smoky wisps into thick streams that poured from the eight remaining Keys into the pyre, imbuing the flames with strange colours.

They condensed into a single, powerful point at the crown of the woodpile where Flo lay, as a lifetime's worth of Flow and love, stored temporarily in her friends, coalesced in her necklace as a power source intended for one last act.

A sound began to rise. Unnoticeable at first, it crept up in volume until it reached the ears of the gathered mourners across the freeing circle and those at the top of the Well, building and filling the air until it became a wall of noise that affected the ears and the vision with the pulsing, vibrating energy it held.

The days eyes were singing.

The glow increased until it outshone the funeral pyre and then suddenly, beautifully, the pendant exploded in a shower of embers. Freed from the confines of the carving, a surge of Flow pulsed through everyone stood on the Well and into the walls of the bubble where it was absorbed, changing it from a swirling rainbow to a pure white globe of light. It sang as the flowers did, as though it were vibrating like the diaphragm of a speaker.

Mamma and those with her looked out wide-eyed from the peak of the outcrop at the solid, singing wall of light that surrounded them, while the mourners outside the bubble stared in awe at the gigantic, harmonic blazing white globe in the centre of the freeing circle, praying that those inside were safe.

~

Watching all of this from Earth, the humans saw the pulse, witnessed the bubble turn white and were suddenly bathed in the song of the days eyes. Not understanding quite what it was that they were seeing and hearing, they took some very nervous steps away, unsure whether the bubble's behaviour was normal, or a reason to fear for their lives.

The blazing white bubble flexed just once, as though it was taking a deep breath... then popped.

On Lux, it just vanished.

On Earth, something rather more profound occurred.

When it popped, the energy held in the barrier crossed the distance between the two worlds instantaneously, exploding in a buzzing, multi-coloured shockwave of Flow that blasted through the family and the grandparent trees on its journey outward. They watched in awe as the tidal wave of light passed through the village and travelled across the surrounding countryside into the world beyond.

A little way off from the Tolkien trees, in a small, tidy cottage with an immaculate lawn and flowerbeds in Avebury village, an elderly gentleman who went by the name of Albert stood frowning by his open door. He'd been regarding the glow coming from the direction of the trees with a distinct look of displeasure on his tanned gardener's face.

"DORIS!" he called to his wife, who was making a pot of tea in the kitchen.

"Yes, dear?" she called back patiently, putting the tea cosy on the pot.

"Those damned hippies are lighting fires again!" he yelled, annoyed.

Chairman of the Residents' Association and the local Neighbourhood Watch Scheme, Albert was feeling invaded. He had grown up in Avebury; lived there his whole life in fact and had spent many years fighting to stop the flood of campervans that parked up in the village overnight.

A barrier on the main tourist car park just outside the village had stopped *some* of that. Locking off the fresh water tap outside the village's public toilets had helped further, but the area had *still* attracted ardent explorers that seemed to want to be around the mysterious stones after dark. The village's roads and small car park had been made 'Resident Only Parking' and signs threatening the horrors of wheel clamping were fixed everywhere as a warning to anyone *still* determined enough to want to stay for a spell.

The thought of all these steps not being enough to prevent 'those damned hippies' from lighting their fires in his beloved village made his blood boil. If he had to miss Eastenders because he had to turf them off the henge and put another fire out, he'd be *most* annoyed.

They'd turn up here with their long hair and tie dye, claiming they were drawn here by the power of ley lines, touching the stones and going on about healing energy, leaving their silly crystals all over the place trying to 'charge' them... *ridiculous*.

What *idiot* would believe that you could charge a *crystal?* Or heal people with *energy?* He shook his head, exasperated.

There was a bright flash from the area he was watching, which alarmed him briefly as he considered the possibility that they'd actually set fire to the trees, but the thought vanished as quickly as the glow did. Maybe he'd been wrong after all. He leant forward, squinting, looking confused for a moment at the sight of something racing toward him, then the shockwave blasted through him and the cottage amid a flare of rainbow colour. He rocked back in his Crocs as it passed and vanished on its way outward, his confused look fading and turning to one of relaxed interest.

Doris came around from where the kitchen was at the back of the cottage with the tea tray.

"Sorry, dear, did you say something about hippies?"

Albert took the tray from her and placed it on a small table on the front lawn. He pulled a chair out for her.

"Not to worry. Just thought they were lighting fires again, but apparently not. I do hope they'll clean up after themselves this time," he said. "I can't bear to see tourist rubbish around the stones, 'specially near the grandparents."

Smiling, she sat down and took the tea cosy off the pot, as ever, enjoying the sight of the daisies it was decorated with. She poured them both a nice cup of tea. Their favourite... chamomile.

"I'm sure they will dear. People are generally quite good. Did you see that beautiful rainbow-thingy just now?"

~

Willow and Lea waved as the energy pulse faded into the distance, making everyone feel, quite rightly, as though they had just said goodbye to a dear friend.

With its purpose realized, Flo's soul raced towards the wall of pure light that marked the boundary into the realm of the Ancestors without a pause. It hit the barrier, exploding into a trillion particles of coloured light, before fading away as it was absorbed to become one with the universe.

Flo's parting gift had left something very real and very permanent in its wake. Instead of returning to the Source, her Flow had stayed on Earth, its frequency altered slightly to carry a message. A message that had imprinted on the neural pathways of seven and a half billion human minds.

Hope.

Hope that after thousands of years, the gears of war would grind to a weary, bloodied halt and the sounds of gunfire would finally cease as weapons were laid down on the field of battle and causes given up in the name of peace.

That borders would be torn down, countries rebuilt, populations rehomed, peoples reunited.

That almost overnight, violence would become a rare and surprising addition to the day's news, rather than a constant, saddening reminder of the state of the world.

That political ideals would evolve and filter through societies around the globe, greed and selfishness vanishing beneath a new avalanche of compassion as the concepts of fairness and sharing were relearned.

That humanity would unite over the abuse it had inflicted on its home for centuries and band together to provide clean energy, ending the pollution that threatened to choke the planet and its future generations.

That people would *listen* to one another again... no longer merely to wait for the break in conversation that would allow *their* voice to be heard, but to hear, value and truly understand the thoughts of another being.

In that instant of pure hopefulness, the world felt lifted, as though a high wind had blown away the fog that had obscured its potential for beauty and light.

Inevitably, there would be those left unaffected by Flo's self-sacrifice, but with luck, their presence would remain unfelt as they faded into the shadows of a new world.

She had set humanity on its first, faltering steps to spiritual healing with love. Pure, hopeful, restoring love.

On any journey, the first step is often the hardest.

Sometimes, you just needed a little push.

Epilogue - The New Alternative

The dimly-lit control room was hushed as technicians monitored the facility intently.

The silence was suddenly shattered by a warning alarm and several people left their stations and rushed excitedly over to a particular terminal. The technician manning it lifted a phone and spoke into it briefly before returning his attention to the screen.

The small group returned to their posts at the approach of the woman from the glass-walled office that overlooked the control room and she joined the technician, who pointed to the reading that had prompted the alarm.

"Well? Did we contain it?"

"I'm sorry ma'am, no, parts of the facility are down for scheduled maintenance. Extraction and Storage are offline."

"How *very* disappointing."

"Yes ma'am... but also extremely fortuitous. It was so powerful, if the system had been online at the moment this happened, the whole site would have been destroyed."

"Wasting twelve years of research, eighteen billion in capital and most annoyingly, my time." The woman leant forwards to view the data, the screen reflecting in her emotionless eyes. "Lucky me, then," she stated dryly.

"The sensors *were* still going through a sweep test though," the technician went on, "and because of the strength and clarity of the pulse, they recorded telemetry *way* more detailed than anything we've witnessed so far."

"What does that mean for the project?"

"Well, now we have the precise frequency and a potential peak level to work with, we can calibrate to maximize extraction and modulate what we extract to a level the storage cells can process. Bar a little more testing, we're ready."

The woman straightened.

"Level of yield?"

The technician gestured to the room around them and the facility beyond.

"I know all of this is only a prototype and you planned more sites, but my initial feeling from the data is that you won't need them. I can't believe I'm even going to say this… the UK National Grid is just the beginning. With enough investment in new infrastructure, other energy suppliers will be a thing of the past. Fossil fuel… nuclear power… alternative energy… all extinct overnight. You *are* the new alternative. We'll have to sink hundreds of extra coils and the purity of the coil alloy will need refinement, but you're going to be able to extract the energy needs of the *entire planet* from about three acres of Salisbury Plain."

Gracy Fadette, the multi-billionaire head of Fadette Industries, tilted her head back and closed her eyes briefly as she savoured this unprecedented moment of success, completely indifferent to the woes of a now redundant industry. Not that anyone dare tell her, but for a second she looked extraordinarily like a reptile swallowing its prey.

She walked to a bank of specially shielded windows and hit a control. As the daylight outside flooded in, the shutters whirred quietly open to reveal the view beyond the control room; rolling green fields spotted with burial mounds and the huge, dark green industrial domes of the ley line bore holes, dotted at regular intervals in a circle surrounding where she stood.

From the domes, enormous coils, armoured with overlapping plates that resembled the scales of a snake's skin, arched outward and disappeared from view beneath the control room.

Fadette looked down through the reinforced glass and steel mesh of the control room floor to where the coils terminated.

Into the fertile earth of the Wiltshire landscape, they had been driven deep underground into the bases of each one of Stonehenge's outer sarsen stones.

"Begin testing immediately… then reactivate the L.E.E.C.H."

38979415R00195

Printed in Poland
by Amazon Fulfillment
Poland Sp. z o.o., Wrocław